1/99

To Josefina S.
Trujillo,

Read this book
& remember your
Past and
share it
with your
little "legacies"
that you call
Grandchildren.
With love,
Diana

Latina

WOMEN'S VOICES FROM THE BORDERLANDS

Edited by

Lillian Castillo-Speed

A TOUCHSTONE BOOK
PUBLISHED BY SIMON & SCHUSTER
New York London Toronto Sydney Tokyo Singapore

TOUCHSTONE
Rockefeller Center
1230 Avenue of the Americas
New York, NY 10020

TOUCHSTONE and colophon are registered trademarks
of Simon & Schuster Inc.

Designed by Irving Perkins Associates

Manufactured in the United States of America

1 3 5 7 9 10 8 6 4 2

1 3 5 7 9 10 8 6 4 2 (PBK)

Library of Congress Cataloging-in-Publication Data
Latina: women's voices from the borderlands/edited by Lillian Castillo-Speed.
p.   cm.
"A Touchstone book."
1. American literature—Hispanic American authors.
2. Hispanic American women—Literary collections.
3. American literature—Women authors.
4. Hispanic American women. I. Castillo-Speed, Lillian.
PS508.H57L38 1995   95-10397
810.8'09287'08968—dc20   CIP

ISBN 0-684-80381-X
0-684-80240-6 (PBK)

Acknowledgments

F irst of all, this is my chance to thank Kathryn Blackmer Reyes for her invaluable assistance at every stage of compiling and submitting these writings and for taking care of all the details. Kathy, it wouldn't have happened without you.

Many others guided me and provided know-how and information at critical times:

Carolyn Soto was the first person I consulted for "approval" to take on this project. From our old days working together in the Chicano Studies Library Publications Unit she knows what I can and can't do. As always, thank you for your good advice, freely given but as honest as I can handle.

Norma Alarcón listened to my first thoughts about the shape of the book, suggested authors, and offered support if I needed it.

Jim Opiat was generous with his time and knew what he was talking about.

Richard Chabrán has gotten me into more impossible projects than anyone else. This was one of them.

Margarita Melville hates to be called boss but is the best

one I ever had. She understands what it means to accept more work when the work we already have is never-ending.

Marisol Zapater-Ferrá from the Chicano Studies Library staff had numerous lunches with me at the Berkeley Thai House and listened to my progress reports.

Julia Curry Rodriguez helped me with an early format for the book and made me realize it wouldn't work.

Myrtha Chabrán opened her address book for me.

Ricky Rodriguez took a look at the draft and gave me smiling approval (you have to see Ricky's smile).

Betsy Amster and Angela Miller enlisted me and made it all happen in L.A. and New York.

Becky Cabaza at Simon & Schuster started calling it "our book," at which point I realized it really was a book.

Dick and Nathan were the ones I finally came home to.

To my sisters Patty and Berty

Contents

13

PART II
OUR LAND, OUR LIVES

PART III
NUESTRA POLITICA

Contents 15

Introduction

L atina literature is not new. It has been published by university presses, small presses, and Latina authors themselves. Poems, short stories, and critical essays have appeared in literary journals, slick avant-garde magazines, popular magazines, and student journals, some photocopied, stapled, and distributed free. Recently Latina prose has been widely anthologized, and several novels by Latina authors have been published by major publishing houses. Obviously there is keen interest in the writings of Chicanas, Cuban American women, Puerto Rican women, and women refugees from Central American countries. Readers are intrigued by a literature that can claim antecedents in the Spanish-language Latin American literary tradition, the English-language literature of immigrants to America, feminist literature, and the literature of the emerging voices of America's ethnic minorities.

It is a literature that to English-language readers appears to have been newly translated from Spanish, when in fact new Latina writers have taken the English language and have made it their own. It is more than just a combination of English and Spanish: it reflects the reality of women who live in two worlds. Latinas are American and yet not American at the same time.

The stories and essays in this book are arranged into sections that reflect three aspects of our lives as Latinas.

The first section, "The Past We Bring with Us," presents writings that attempt to come to terms with where we came from—and we all have a story about where we came from. We all know our grandmother's world, even though it is seen across a distance of time or geography or social status. Her story is in our ears and hearts as it continually reminds us of the girl or woman we might have been in that world.

Ana Castillo's "My Mother's Mexico" retells the family history she was told by her mother, Raquel, and her aunt Flora of how they ended up migrating to the United States. These events, which occurred long before she was born, spared Raquel's daughter from an impoverished life on the streets of Mexico City. In her family history, Ana is known as *la hija de Raquel*, the one who lives in America.

Sometimes the story is triggered by the memory of a familiar sight from home, such as "the *flamboyán* and banana and . . . No, not even the individual trees and bushes but the mass of them, the overwhelming profusion of green life that was the home of her comfort and nest of her dreams," which Aurora Levins Morales recalls in her essay "Puertoricanness."

Sometimes the story is symbolized by a ghost, as in Cristina García's "Lourdes Puente," in which a recent Cuban immigrant is visited by her dead father. He forces her to remember her past although she swears that "she wants no part of Cuba, no part of its wretched carnival floats creaking with lies, no part of Cuba at all, which Lourdes claims never possessed her." And yet our past does possess us, whether it is the past of a physical place or of a previous generation, whether told by our mothers, our aunts, our fathers, our uncles or handed down from grandmother to granddaughter.

• • •

At some point Latinas decide, despite evidence to the contrary in the questioning glances of "American" Americans, that we belong right here in the United States. Citizenship, whether we are born with it or pluck it from the tree of opportunity, is a prize or a burden, but in any case it's what we have. We grow up, torture our youthful questions into identities, and look for love, just like everybody else.

The stories in the section "Our Land, Our Lives" are written from the point of view of here and now, our own personal America. Judith Ortiz Cofer's "Twist and Shout" describes the whirlwind of adolescent yearning and the rush to sexuality, all within the time it takes for one song to play on the record player. Sandra Cisneros writes about her father's expectations of an only daughter and how she finally won his approval of her life as a writer. Julia Alvarez writes of a young immigrant girl from the Dominican Republic who is terrified by her first experience with snow. Some of the stories lead us into lives that trouble us with the premature corruption of innocence, as in the excerpt from Reid Gómez's *A Name for Cebolla* and Helena María Viramontes's "Miss Clairol."

Other stories are reminders that Latina literature is not humorless. "Grand Slam" by Denise Chávez is a nonstop, one-sided telephone conversation between Omega Harkins and her friend Mozetta that tells how Omega's long-lost boyfriend Acton Allnut comes back into her life through his appearance on the *$50,000 Grand Slam*. "Personality Fabulosa" by lesbian comic writer Monica Palacios takes us on Ramona's sardonic quest for the perfect roommate, the beautiful Alicia, the woman who can forgive her Taco Bell Spanish.

Often the personal becomes the political for Latinas. Cherríe Moraga and Gloria Anzaldúa are the foremost Latina literary political writers. They are represented in this collection by works that stretch the definition of "Latina" and "American" beyond the boundaries of the United States and even of Latin America. In "Art in América con Acento," Moraga wants to come to terms with political blame in the face of the end of the Nicaraguan revolution: "I am Latina, born and raised in the United States. I am a writer. What is my responsibility in this?" With the same directness and uncompromising criticism, Gloria Anzaldúa, in two excerpts from her landmark work *Borderlands/La Frontera: The New Mestiza*, talks about language as a weapon used against us by others and by ourselves. Graciela Limón shares Moraga's and Anzaldúa's concern with human rights beyond political boundaries. The excerpt from her book *In Search of Bernabé* gives us a glimpse into the painful trans-border journey of a Salvadoran woman who follows the ephemeral trail of her "disappeared" son.

It should become obvious from the writings in this section that Latinas do not necessarily share the same political allegiances. Cuban American women, for instance, may differ with other Latinas on the politics of Fidel Castro's Cuba. Margarita Engle's excerpt from *Singing to Cuba* is a lament for the Cuba she might have known if there had been no revolution. Latinas may also differ on the degree of radicalness they think is just right for their own brand of feminism. In "Enedina's Story," Inés Hernández-Avila gives us a running commentary on sex roles, political commitment, and community adhesiveness, all while two women are cooking chicken mole and potato salad for a political fund-raiser.

In a less overtly political account, a childhood of proper expectations is contrasted with an aversion to boredom in Lucha Corpi's "Epiphany: The Third Gift," an autobiographical story of a writer's struggle with parental convention. The final story in this collection presents a transcendent vision of conciliation and acceptance: Alma Luz Villanueva's "Place of the Dead" takes place in a country that could be anywhere, a time that could be any time, and a war that has no right or wrong side. From the horror of murdered corpses washed onto the beach, a young girl scavenges a pink seashell that she childishly believes is a gift from her mother, one of the dead.

Latinas are daughters of a motherland and daughters of a mother tongue. We are Raquel's daughters, the ones who live in America.

· · · · · · · · · · · · · · · ·

The Past
We Bring
with Us

*A*na Castillo *is the author of* So Far from God *(1993),* Sapogonia *(1990), and* The Mixquiahuala Letters *(1986), which received the American Book Award in 1987.* Massacre of the Dreamers: Essays on Xicanisma *(1994) is her latest book. Her poetry collections include* The Invitation *(1979),* Women Are Not Roses *(1984), and* My Father Was a Toltec *(1988), which will be republished with additional poems in 1995. Her work has been widely anthologized both here and abroad. A native of Chicago, she now lives in Gainesville, Florida. This is her mother's story.*

MY MOTHER'S MEXICO

Ana Castillo

My mother's Mexico was the brutal urban reality of Luis Buñuel's *Los Olvidados*. Children scamming and hustling: fire-eaters, hubcap stealers, Chiclet sellers, miniature accordion players with small, dirty hands stretched out before passersby for a coin, a piece of bread—"Please, señor, for my mother who is very sick." This was the Mexico City of my family. This was the Mexico my mother spared me.

In that Mexico City in the 1930s, Mami was a street urchin, not an orphan—not yet—with one ragged dress. Because of an unnamed skin disease that covered her whole tiny body with scabs, her head was shaved. At seven years old or maybe eight, she scurried, quick and invisible as a Mayan messenger, through the throngs of that ancient metropolis in the area known as La Villita, where the goddess Tonantzin/ Guadalupe had made Her divine appearances four times and ordered el indio Juan Diego four times to tell the Catholic officials to build Her a church. "Yes!" and off he went, surefooted and trembling. Mami, who was not Mami but little then, bustled on her own mission toward the corner where her stepfather sold used paperbacks on the curb. At midday he ordered his main meal from a nearby restaurant and ate it out of stainless steel carryout containers without leaving his "place of business." The little girl would take the leftovers and dash them off to her mother, who was lying on a petate—in the one room the whole family shared in a vecindad overflowing with families like their own with all manner of maladies that accompany destitution. Her mother was dying.

Maria de los Angeles Rocha de Castro spent her days and nights in the dark, windowless room reading novels—used paperbacks provided by her new husband from Veracruz—seconds like the food he shared with her. She copied favorite passages and verses into a notebook that I have inherited, not through the pages of a will but by my mother's will: she carried the notebook, preserved in its faded newsprint cover, over decades of migration and, one day not that long ago, handed it over to me, the daughter who also liked to read, to write, to save things.

Maria de los Angeles named her second daughter after a fictional character, Florinda, but my mother was the eldest daughter. She was not named for romance like my tia Flora—aromatic and evocative—but from the Old Testament. Raquel, a name as impenetrable as the rock in her parents' shared Guanajuatan family name, Rocha: Raquel Rocha Rocha. And quite a rock my mother has been all the days of her life, Moses and Mount Sinai and God striking lightning all over the place. Raquel the Rock.

One day, Maria de los Angeles—the maternal grandmother whom I never knew but am so much like, I'm told—asked her eldest daughter to purchase a harmonica for her. Of course it would be a cheap one that could be obtained from a street vendor not unlike her bookselling husband. This the child did and brought it to her mother's deathbed, a straw mat on a stone floor. And when the mother felt well enough, she produced music out of the little instrument in the dark of that one room in Mexico City, the city where she had gone with her parents and two eldest children with the hope of getting good medical care that could rarely be found in those days outside the capital.

Instead, Maria stood in line outside a dispensary. Dispensaries were medical clinic substitutes, equipped to offer little more than drugs, certain common injections, and lightweight medical advice. In a rosary chain of women like herself—black rebozos, babies at their breast—she waited for hours in the sun or rain, on the ground, so many lives, and that woman at the end there, yes, that one, my mother's young mother, waited, dying.

In the 1970s, while I was living alone in Mexico City, I had a medical student friend who took me to such a dispensary, where he worked most evenings. The place, located in a poor colonia, consisted of two dark rooms—one for the receptionist and the other for consultation. The dispensary was crammed to the ceiling with boxes of drugs, mostly from the United States, which were administered freely to patients. I knew almost nothing about medication, but I knew that in the United States we did not have a once-a-month birth control pill and that belladonna could not be taken without a doctor's prescription. And yet drugs such as these were abundant in the dispensary, and my young friend, not only not a doctor but in fact failing medical school, was permitted to prescribe at his own discretion.

Maria de los Angeles was newly widowed during her dispensary days, and why she married again so soon (the bookseller) I cannot say, except that she was so sick with two children that shelter and leftovers may have been reason enough. She bore two children quickly from this second marriage so unlike the first; in the earlier marriage, among other differences, it took seven years before the couple had their first child, a son born in Kansas and, two years later, a daughter, my mother, born in Nebraska.

My grandfather, my mother has often told me, worked on the railroads as a signalman. This is what brought the Guanajuatan couple to the United States. From this period—the

1920s—I can construct a biography of the couple myself, because Maria de los Angeles was very fond of being photographed. She wore fine silks and chiffons and wide-brimmed hats. Her handlebar-mustached husband with the heavy lidded eyes telling of his Indian ancestry sported a gold pocket watch. They drove a Studebaker.

After the 1929 stock market crash, Mexican workers in the United States, suddenly jobless, were quickly returned to the other side of the border. My grandparents returned, not with severance pay, not with silk dresses or wool suits, not with the Studebaker—but with tuberculosis. My grandfather died soon after.

When Maria de los Angeles died (not surprisingly, she was not saved by the rudimentary medical treatment she received at dispensaries), her children—two sons, two daughters—were sent out to work to earn their own keep. Where the sons went I don't know. But I know about the daughters—Raquel and her younger sister, Flora—because when they grew up and became women they told me, in kitchens, over meals, into late evenings, that by the time they were about ten years old they were live-in domestics.

My mother was a little servant (and that is why she now keeps a neat home). My tia Flora was sent to the kitchen of an Arab family. And although her house now is always crowded crazy chaos, she became the best Mexican cook on both sides of the border. (That is why it's a Tenochtitlan feast at tia Flora's table in her humble casita at the outpost of Mesoamerica—that is to say, the mero corazón of the Mexican barrio of Chicago: spices and sauces of cumin and sesame seeds, chocolate, ground peanuts, and all varieties of chiles; cuisines far from shy or hesitant, but bold and audacious, of fish, fowl, and meats; feasts fit for a queen.)

When my mother was about seventeen, her guardian grandparents decided to take their U.S.-born grandchildren closer to the border. The strategy of the migrating abuelos was that the U.S.-born grandchildren could get better work or, perhaps, at least better pay on the U.S. side. They settled in Nuevo Laredo. One year later my mother was either raped or, at least, clearly taken advantage of by the owner of the restaurant on the U.S. side of the border where she found work as a waitress. She has never said which it was. He was married with a family and considerably older than the teenager who bore his son. The best my great-grandfather could do at that point on behalf of my mother's honor was to get the man to provide for her. So he paid the rent on a little one-room wooden house, which of course gave him further claims on my mother. Two years later, a daughter was born.

Three years more and Mami's Mexico ended as a daily construction of her reality when, with machete in hand, she went out to make her own path. She left her five-year-old son with her sister, Flora, who was newly wed and soon to be widowed, and with her three-year-old girl followed some cousins who had ventured even further north to find work. Six months later she returned for her son, and when the three went up north this time, she would move to Chicago alone with her children. Mami remembers all this as the longest year of her life.

My mother went to work in factories, where she got some benefits and bonuses on assembly lines and varicose veins and a paralyzed thumb one day when a punch press went through it. Dona Jovita, the curandera who took care of Mami's two children, convinced Mami to marry her teenage son. The next summer I was born. Mami stayed in factories until the last one closed up and went off to Southeast Asia, leaving its union workers without work, without pay, and some without pension, and sending Mami into early retirement.

My Mami, a dark mestiza, inherited the complexes and fears of the colonized and the strange sense of national pride that permeates the new society of the conquered. To this day Mami speaks only Spanish, although she has lived in Chicago for over forty years. She throws out English words—zas, zas, zas, like stray bullets—at gringos, at grandchildren, at her African American Avon manager, like a misfiring pistol.

When I was twelve I saw Mami's Mexico City for the first time. My mother and I traveled from Chicago to Nuevo Laredo by car. It was possibly the hottest place on earth in the month of July. But Mami didn't have much choice about when to travel, since the first two weeks of July were when the factory where she worked closed down and workers were given vacation time. Mami paid a young Mexican who was looking for riders to take us. The car broke down; we slept in it at night; we were refused service at gas stations and in restaurants here and there in the South—in Texas, I remember—and finally we got to my great-grandmother's two-room wooden house with an outhouse and a shower outside. Two years before, when we visited my great-grandmother, I had made friends with the little girl next door. At that time we climbed trees and fed the chickens and took sides with each other against her older brother. That's how and why I learned to write Spanish—I wanted to write to Rosita. (My mother, after long days at the factory, would come home to make dinner, and after the dishes and just before bed, she, with her sixth-grade education, would sit me down at the kitchen table and teach me how to write to Rosita in Spanish, phonetically, with soft vowels, with humor, with a pencil and no book.) But this time Rosita was fourteen. She had crossed over to that place of no return—breasts and boys. And not long after that, Rosita ran away.

In Nuevo Laredo we were met by my tia Flora, who had also traveled from Chicago—with her five children ranging from ages fourteen to four. The husbands of these two sisters did not come along on this pilgrimage, because there are men who, despite having families, are not family men. They passed up their traditional right to accompany their wives and children on this adventure.

There were too many children to sleep in the house, so we were sent up to the flat roof to sleep under the stars. My mother had not known that she needed permission from my father to take me into Mexico, so with my cousin's birth certificate to pass me off as Mexican-born, we all got on a train one day, and I illegally entered Mami's Mexico City.

Our life in Chicago was not suburban backyards with swings and grassy lawn. It was not ample living rooms and your own bedroom. It was not what I saw on TV. And yet it was not the degree of poverty in which we all found ourselves immersed overnight, through inheritance, birth, the luck (or bad luck, rather) of destiny. It was the destiny that my mother and her sister dodged by doing as their mother, Maria de los Angeles, had decades before—for a period of her life at least—by getting the hell out of Mexico however they could. It was the destiny in Mexico that my mother's little brother Leonel refused to reject because of his hatred for capitalism, which he felt was fully embodied by the United States.

So Leonel, dark and handsome in his youth, with thin lips that curled up giving him the permanent smiling expression of a cynic, came to get us at the little hotel in Mexico City where my mother's stepfather, who was still selling books on a street corner, had installed us the night before. He met us at the train station, feeding us all bowls of atole for our late meal at the restaurant where his credit was good.

My cousin Sandra and I opened the door for tio Leonel. We didn't know who he was. We told him our mothers had gone on an errand, taking the younger children with them. My tio Leonel did not step all the way into the room. We were young females alone, and for him to do so would have been improper. He looked me up and down with black eyes, as black as my mother's, as black as mine, and knitted eyebrows as serious as Mami's and as serious as mine have become. "You are Raquel's daughter?" he asked. I nodded. And then he left.

He returned for us later, Mami and me and my tia Flora and her five children, eight of us altogether, plus big suitcases, and took us to his home. Home for tio Leonel was a single dark room in a vecindad. Vecindades are communal living quarters. Families stay in single rooms. They share toilet and water facilities. The women have a tiny closet for a kitchen just outside their family's room, and they cook on a griddle on the floor. I don't remember my uncle's common-law wife's name. I am almost certain that it was Maria, but that could be a lucky guess. I remember my cousins, who were all younger than me, and their crazy chilango accents. But I don't remember their names or how many there were then. There were nearly ten—but not ten yet—because that was the total number my uncle and his woman would eventually have. Still, it felt like ten. So now there were four adults and at least thirteen children, age fourteen and under, staying in one room.

We didn't have to worry about crowding the bathroom, because the toilets were already shared by the entire vecindad. There were no lights and no plumbing. At night sometimes my uncle cleverly brought in an electrical line from outside and connected a bulb. This was not always possible or safe. The sinks, used for every kind of washing, were unsanitary. Sandra and I went to wash our hands and faces one morning and both stepped back at the sight of a very ugly black fish that had burst out of the drainpipe and was swimming around in the large plugged-up basin.

For entertainment we played bolero with our cousins, who were experts—bolero, the handheld toy, not Ravel's music. The object of the game was to flip a wooden ball onto a peg. My little cousins could not afford a real bolero, of course, and therefore made their own, using cans, old string, and stones or cork.

A neighbor in the vecindad who owned the local candy stand had a black-and-white TV. At a certain hour every evening, she charged the children who wanted to, or rather, who could afford it, to sit in the store to watch their favorite cartoon show.

I was twelve, Sandra (my cousin and also my best friend) thirteen, and her brother Eloy fourteen. We were beyond cartoon shows and taking bolero contests seriously, and we were talking our early teen talk to one another in English. It was 1965, and the Rolling Stones were singing "Can't get no satisfaction" in English over Spanish radio on my cousin's made-in-Japan transistor, and we insolent U.S.-born adolescents wanted no part of Mexico—not the Mexico of the amusement park, La Montaña Rusa, where we went one day and had great fun on the roller-coaster; not the Mexico of sleeping under the stars on the roof of my tio Aurelio's home in Nuevo Laredo; not the Mexico of the splendid gardens of Chapultepec Park, of the cadet heroes Los Niños Héroes, who valiantly but fatally fought off the invasion of U.S. troops. But a Mexico where we all slept on the mattress our mothers had purchased for us on the first night in my tio Leonel's home. It was laid out in the middle of the room, and six children and two grown women slept on it crossways, lined up neatly like Chinese soldiers in the front line at night in the trenches. My tio and his wife and children slept all around us on piles of rags.

We had, with one train ride, stepped right into our mothers' Mexico City, unchanged in the nearly two decades since their departure.

Then in 1976, when I was living on my own in California, I met my family at the appointed meeting place—my tio Aurelio's in Nuevo Laredo—and traveled south by van with everybody to Mexico City. My tia Flora, this time without any of her children, came along too. The great-grandmother, Apolinar, had died, and we had only recently received word of it. The grand-uncle and border official, tio Aurelio, had a heart condition, and we would not see him again after this visit. My tia Flora's veracruzano bookselling father had also died that year. We had only the little brother Leonel to visit. The young anti-capitalist—once so proud of his sole possession (a new bicycle that eventually was stolen), devoted to his family in his own way (although the older children had gone off on their own, while the youngest sold Chiclets on the streets)—was on his deathbed at forty.

He was dying of corroded liver, cirrhosis ridden. By then his lot had improved, so he had two rooms, a real bed, and electricity, but not much more. We stood around his bed and visited awhile so he could meet his brother-in-law and some other members of my mother's family whom he had never known before.

We went to visit his oldest daughter, around my age, at the house where she worked as a live-in domestic. She could not receive company, of course, but was allowed to visit with us outside for a bit.

We went to visit her older brother, too. He had an honest-to-goodness apartment—three whole rooms and its own kitchen. He worked in a factory and had a young family of his own.

One evening my tia Flora and I ran into Leonel on the street, not far from where the cousin with the apartment lived. He was now a yellowish wire of a man and appeared quite drunk. His pants were held up by a rope. He glanced at me and then asked my tia Flora, "Is this Raquel's daughter?" My tia, in her usual happy-sounding way, said, "Yes, yes, of course she is the hija of Raquel." And then Tia, who is more veracruzana than chilanga—that is, more palm than granite—laughed a summer rainstorm laugh.

Of course I was and am the daughter of Raquel. But I was the one born so far north that not only my tio but all my relatives in Mexico found it hard to think me real. The United States was Atlantis, and there was no Atlantis; and therefore, having been born there, I could not exist. Tio Leonel nodded at my aunt, who was real, but not at me, who was a hologram, and went on his way. "My poor brother, he looks like Cantin-flas," my tia said, comparing him to the renowned Mexican comedian famous for his derelict appearance and street ways. That was the last we saw of him, and by end of summer he had died.

If the double rock in Mami's name and the castle at the end through marriage had dubbed her the stoic sister, the flower in Flora's name perfumed her urban life and warded off the sadness of trying times. And those had been many in my tia's life, multiplied with the years as her children grew up far from Mexico in Chicago's poverty.

So it was that night that my tia and I, riding a city bus, jumped off suddenly in a plaza where trios and duos of musicians gathered for hire, and we brought a late-night serenade to Mami and family at our hotel. That was when my tia Flora and I bonded as big-time dreamers, and it was that night, after the serenade and after Dad (who came on this trip) had brought out a bottle of mezcal and we had all shared a drink with the musicians, that Mami told me some of the stories I tell you now.

By migrating Mami saved me from the life of a live-in domestic and perhaps from inescapable poverty in Mexico City. But it was the perseverance of Raquel the Rock and the irrepressible sensuality of Flora the thick-stemmed calla lily that save me, too. "Ana del Aire," my mother calls me. Woman of the air, not earthbound, rooted to one place—not to Mexico, where Mami's mother died, not to Chicago, where I was born, not to New Mexico, where I've made a home for my son, but to everywhere at once.

And when the world so big becomes a small windowless room, I draw from the vision of Maria de los Angeles. I read and write poems. I listen to music, I sing—with the voice of my ancestors from Guanajuato who had birds in their throats. I paint with my heart, with acrylics on linen and cotton. I talk to my son, to my lover, and with my comadres on the telephone. I tell a story. I make a sound and leave a mark—as palatable as a prickly pear, more solid than stone.

A licia Gaspar de Alba grew up in El Paso, Texas. She has taught freshman composition and English as a second language at the University of Massachusetts in Boston and has transcribed children's books into Braille. Her work has appeared in Three Times a Woman: Chicana Poetry (1989). She currently lives in California, where she is working on a novel and a second collection of poetry. "Facing the Mariachis" appeared in her first book of short fiction, The Mystery of Survival and Other Stories (1993), which won the 1994 Anaya Premio Aztlán.

FACING THE MARIACHIS

Alicia Gaspar de Alba

Mercedes woke up screaming again. Her husband sat up in the bed and reached for his glasses and his cigarette case. He struck a match, held it in front of her face for a moment, then lit a cigarette.

"Is this one of your customs?" he asked in his gringo-like Spanish.

Mercedes buried her face in her hands. She was afraid, not just because of the dream, but because she knew he was getting tired of all this nonsense and mystery. They had been on their honeymoon for only a week, and she had already made the same scandal three times.

"Talk to me, Mercedes," he said. "Tell me what the problem is. Let me help you."

Mercedes shook her head and would not look at him. "I hope the man in the office didn't hear me *this* time," she said, staring down at the sheet.

"Who cares about that?" he said. "The important thing is that you tell me what's wrong. This didn't happen before we were married. Are you unhappy?"

"*¡Ay, José!*" she said, "how many times do I have to tell you that I'm happy? It has nothing to do with you or with us."

"What is it, then?"

The thick smoke of American tobacco hung over the bed like a mosquito net.

"I have to go to confession tomorrow," she said. "There's something in my soul that doesn't let me sleep in peace."

"Do you know what it is?"

Mercedes covered her mouth with her hand and shook her head again.

"Then how are you going to confess it, Mercedes?"

She shrugged. "Sins come out in the confessional," she said. He tried to hold her, but she pulled away.

The next morning, while José ate breakfast in the court-yard of the hotel, Mercedes hurried to the Basilica of the Virgin of Solitude, *La Soledad*, the miraculous patroness of Oaxaca. At the entrance to the cathedral, Mercedes got on her hands and knees and crawled up to the altar beside an Indian woman whose knees bled.

"Help me, Señora," she muttered once she knelt at the communion banister below the Virgin's shrine. "I'm so afraid he'll divorce me when he finds out. But I have to tell him the truth. Guide me, *Virgencita, por favor!* Give me courage."

The slanted eyes of *La Soledad* looked down at Mercedes, and Mercedes took her rosary from her purse and prayed a *Padre Nuestro* and the first decade of Hail Marys. *Go to the Man of the Thunderbolt*, she heard the Virgin say, *it is his help you need, not mine.*

Still on her knees, Mercedes crept to the room in the basilica where a black Christ, known to the people as *El Señor del Rayo*, hung on a black cross, his shrine crammed with *mila-gros* and daisies and lilies of the valley. Mercedes made the sign of the cross.

"Señor," she whispered, "give me the light and the strength of the thunderbolt. If you help me to tell him the truth, and if you help him to understand it, I promise I will return in one year to baptize this child here in your shrine.

"*Padre Nuestro que estás en el cielo* . . . ," she prayed, watching the caretaker of the church replace the expired candles at the foot of the crucifix. She felt the beads passing under her fingers as she mumbled the rest of the rosary, the smell of the melted wax guiding her back to the adobe room in La Subida where her deepest secret had been conceived.

Estrella González handed her a cup of tea that was so bitter it numbed Mercedes's tongue and made the rest of her body languid as a sponge. *La Vieja* told her to undress and to lie down on the straw mat with her knees bent. The tea gave her a strange kind of fever; her eyes burned and her ears felt like ovens. She could barely discern what Estrella González was doing through the burning film over her eyes and the glare of all those candles. She had seen a large, black egg on *La Vieja*'s altar, and now Estrella González was holding the egg over Mercedes's face, speaking in a language that Mercedes did not recognize. She laid the egg between Mercedes's breasts.

" *'Ek'etik!*" called *La Vieja* to the dark air. "*Tsek! Kurus'ek!*"

Mercedes watched *La Vieja* approach her altar, take a scorpion from an earthen bowl, and place the scorpion under her tongue. Mercedes had heard the rumors about *La Vieja*'s immunity to the scorpion poison; it was said that, in fact, her powers came from that poison and that was what made Estrella González the most potent *bruja-curandera* in all of México; but Mercedes had never imagined that she would witness such a thing. She watched as the poison shocked the old woman's body into a convulsive dance. Her eyes became red flames. Her skin shone as though wires of lightning ran in her veins. She spit the carcass of the scorpion on the floor, and she shrieked. Mercedes felt a sudden nausea welling up, a mixture of fear and the bitter tea boiling in her stomach.

She closed her eyes, and when she reopened them, Estrella González was bending over her, taking the black egg apart in two perfect halves. She threw the top half aside; a gray-blue substance that smelled of starch steamed in the bottom half. The *bruja* put a drop of this thick, hot liquid on Mercedes's tongue; Mercedes felt her nipples harden, her genitals grow moist.

"*Yo soy el recuerdo y el destino*," Estrella González uttered in Spanish. "I am the memory and the destiny. *El huevo y la culebra*. The egg and the snake."

She placed another drop of the substance on each of Mercedes's nipples. Mercedes felt her hips moving as if José were on top of her. Her belly undulated to the rhythm of *La Vieja*'s chant:

"*Tu vientre será la piñata. La piñata cargará el recuerdo. Cuando se quiebre la piñata, el recuerdo será el destino de la que viene.*"

Now, Estrella González tipped the egg over Mercedes's belly and let a fat drop of the substance fill her navel. Mercedes felt rays of fire radiate through her womb, melting her genitals. Even her lungs burned. Her tongue was like a live coal. The *bruja* cupped the claw of her hand over Mercedes's navel, digging her cracked nails into the flesh, and repeated the chant:

"Your womb shall be the piñata. The piñata shall carry the memory. When the piñata breaks, the memory will be the destiny of she who comes."

The fire had spread down into her legs and feet. Mercedes raised her knees parallel to her ribs. She needed air. She needed air to stream through all the holes in her body and cool the hot contractions in her womb.

Estrella González poured what was left in the egg into her own mouth. She lowered her head between Mercedes's thighs, pressed her lips below the nest of black hair, and spit the starchy substance into Mercedes. Mercedes shuddered as she had never shuddered with José.

When Mercedes awoke from the ritual the fever was gone. She had a headache and a dull pain around her navel, but she could sit up on the *petate* and get herself dressed. She noticed they were in the main room of the hut now, instead of the adobe room where the ritual had taken place. Estrella González was clapping tortillas into shape, and the room was filled with the aroma of *nixtamal*.

"She will be born on the year that begins on the flower day, the day called *Xochitl*," the old woman said, placing a raw tortilla on the griddle.

Mercedes buttoned up her blouse. She was hungry and embarrassed at having climaxed in *La Vieja*'s mouth during the ritual.

"Do you know what name you are going to give her?" Estrella González asked. She laid another tortilla on the *comal*.

"*No, mi vieja*. I haven't thought about it." Deep inside her, Mercedes did not really believe that *La Vieja*'s magic had impregnated her.

"I have just told you the name," said *La Vieja*.

Mercedes replayed what the old woman had said. "You mean *Xochitl?*" she asked.

"Only by seeding the new world with the old names will the memories come back," said Estrella González.

"I'm sorry, *mi vieja*. I don't understand you."

La Vieja turned the tortillas to let them cook on the other side. Mercedes felt saliva gathering under her tongue. She braided her hair as *La Vieja* spoke.

"Five hundred years ago, the name Mercedes and the religious order from whence that name comes did not exist in our language or our culture. Then, *they* came. Took our gods and our land away. Changed our language and our ways. But the memories stayed, even though you do not remember them, and even after five hundred years of silence, the memories are still alive."

She took the tortillas off the *comal* and wrapped them in a flour sack.

"The one inside you will be a voice in the new generation, Mercedes. If she does not have an old name, the new world will devour her. She will never bloom if the memories are buried. With a name like *Xochitl*, she will find it more difficult to forget. Now come. It is time to eat."

Mercedes found José waiting for her on a bench in the *zócalo*, shading a bunch of gardenias under his Panama hat. Mercedes swallowed back her fear and smiled at him as she took the fragrant flowers.

"*¿Ya estás mejor?*" he asked after kissing her lightly on the mouth.

She nodded and touched the gardenias to her nose.

"You won't have any more nightmares?"

"José," she said so softly it sounded like her shadow had spoken. "I have to tell you something. I've prayed, and the Man of the Thunderbolt has answered me. I couldn't ask for your forgiveness beforehand, but the *Señor del Rayo* said you would understand. He said Chicanos are different from Mexicans; your minds are more open than ours, he said."

José stood up, took her hand, and led her to one of the open-air cafés that bordered the plaza. When the waitress appeared, he ordered two mezcal margaritas for himself. Mercedes asked for black coffee. She waved away the little vendor girls who passed with Chiclets and *canastas* and the boys who wanted to shine their shoes. She began her confession after the waitress had set their order on the table.

"For three nights," she started, looking down at the coffee, "I've dreamt that I'm standing before a firing squad, my head covered up in a black sack."

José finished the first margarita in one swallow.

"In the dream, perhaps in real life, I know I deserve to be shot for what I've done, but still, I want to plead for my life, or for another form of death, at least, but I have a gag on my mouth and cannot speak. Then I hear a voice shout *¡Fuego!* The bullets explode, and my belly bursts into flames. That's when I wake up screaming."

José drank his second margarita. "What have you done?" he asked.

"You're not going to like this," she said.

"I'm a man," he said and held up two fingers to the waitress. Again, Mercedes waited for the waitress to bring his margaritas. She sipped her coffee and watched her husband's face. He traced the crust of salt on one of the glasses.

"I fought in Viet Nam, Mercedes. Nothing you could say could be worse than what I lived in that war."

Mercedes was beginning to feel dizzy. She had neglected to eat breakfast, and now her blood was craving sugar. She dipped half her spoon into the sugar bowl and stirred it into the tepid coffee.

"When I was fourteen our *curandero*'s assistant, Apolonio . . . raped me in my father's cornfield," she confessed. "I was too afraid and too ashamed to tell anybody, so I kept it a secret and in that way gave him license to do it to me again. Seeing that no punishment came to him, he did it several times, and he started the rumor that I made eyes at him, and that I appeared to him in his dreams in the form of a cow begging him to take my milk. When I became pregnant, my mother forced me to tell her who the father was, but she didn't believe that Apolonio had raped me. She, too, had heard the rumors that I flirted with Apolonio, and as punishment, she made me marry him."

She drank the sweetened coffee, grimacing at the taste, at the memory of Apolonio.

"He was so disgusting, chasing after me all the time, too sick with his lust to understand that it was wrong to have relations with a pregnant girl. I was only fourteen years old. My body hadn't even finished forming yet."

Mercedes's voice trembled. José stroked her hand.

"Apolonio came from a cursed family. Each generation bred a new sickness into the blood. His parents were brother and sister, and his family had been doing that for a long time. With my diabetes and Apolonio's bad blood, never mind his brutality, I didn't expect the baby to be normal. But I *never* suspected the monster that came out of my body."

Mercedes squeezed her eyes shut and saw again the watermelon-shaped head, the rheumy eyes on either side of it. Heard again that horrible catlike howl that filled the village like the music of death.

"Even Apolonio could see that there was something terribly wrong with the child, that he was an aberration, a thing of the devil. The priest stopped by to bless the child and ended up excommunicating us instead, saying that God had punished us for practicing our heathen beliefs. The whole village turned against us, except my father. It was my father who suggested that I seek the help of Estrella González, the wise woman of La Subida. He said that she would be able to advise me better than anybody and perhaps even help me release the boy's soul from that tortured little body."

Mercedes looked up at José. "If you had seen him, José. Those eyes of his caked with that yellow mucus that hardened around his eyelids and made him scratch so hard he drew blood and howled even louder than he normally did. If you had seen the way he beat his head on the floor giving himself bruises and bumps that only deformed his face even more than it already was. And the way he convulsed when Apolonio kicked him in the stomach to make him stop howling. I was going crazy. I knew I had to listen to my father.

"I walked all the way to La Subida. It took me four days to get there and another day just to find the wise woman's house in that labyrinth of prickly pears. She didn't want to help me at first. Said she was a *curandera*, not an *hechicera*, that she had the power to heal, not to hurt. When I told her that she would be healing the boy's soul by releasing him from that cursed body, she told me to go back home and bring the boy to her, but I think she had already decided to help me because when I returned, she had the poison ready."

"She poisoned him?" José said.

Mercedes shook her head. "I did," she answered.

José lit a cigarette and watched a mariachi band that was walking across the *zócalo*.

"Is that all?" José said, keeping his gaze on the mariachis.

"I had another problem," Mercedes went on. "As soon as Apolonio recuperated from the shock of that monster, or forgot how it had come into being, he started chasing after me again. It didn't scare him at all when I threatened him with the machete. In fact, that made his lust grow, and he would take it out and rub himself in front of me and let it squirt on the floor. I went back to Estrella González, and she gave me some powders to make him impotent. But you see, I was just fifteen and already had a dead son. I could see a whole family of monsters coming out of my womb. I didn't trust those powders. I begged Estrella González to give me something stronger, an extract like the one she'd made for the boy."

The Americans at the table beside them had flagged down the mariachis, and Mercedes did not feel like raising her voice over *"Cielito lindo."* José asked for another margarita; Mercedes ordered orange juice. She could see that José was getting nervous. His eyebrows had started to twitch.

The Americans listened politely to *"Cielito lindo"* and *"De colores."* Then they clapped, paid the musicians, and went back to talking in English. The mariachis wandered down to the far end of the café.

Mercedes swallowed some juice and prepared herself for the worst part of the confession, imploring the Man of the Thunderbolt to help her finish what she had started. "I know this will be hard . . ."

José held up both his hands. "Wait!" he said. "If you're going to tell me that you poisoned that animal you had to marry, if that's the sin you had to confess, we don't have a problem, *mi amor*. Protecting yourself isn't a sin. And it would have been more cruel to let that boy live. In the United States we call that kind of death euthanasia."

"I didn't know there was a word for it," Mercedes said, her eyes starting to sting.

"Well, there is, and it is *not* a sin. So stop punishing yourself. I love you, Mercedes. I can't blame you for what you had to do." He stroked her face with the back of his hand and her tears spilled over his fingers.

"José," she murmured, "are you sure?" The words felt like thorns in her throat.

"*¡Música!*" José yelled to the mariachis, waving his hat to get their attention. Mercedes held her breath. She could not tell him now that poisoning Apolonio and the boy was just the background to her real secret. She could not tell him that, as payment for the wise woman's potions, she had agreed to let Estrella González plant a child inside her with her magic. A child she had not believed would take root. A child that now fed herself on Mercedes's blood.

On the day that the stranger who will be your second husband proposes to you, the old woman had said fifteen years ago as Mercedes walked out of her hut with Apolonio's poison, *I will come to you in Mitla and bring you some herbs to prepare your body.*

Prepare my body for what, mi vieja?

For you to repay me for my infusions. Todo se paga en la vida, Mercedes. *Everything must be paid for in life.*

"What song do you want to hear?" José asked her once the mariachis were gathered before them.

Mercedes could not speak. She was dizzy again. The orange juice and the coffee bubbled like acid in her stomach. The thorns in her throat had become nails. José asked for the "*Corrido de Gregorio Cortez,*" but the mariachis didn't know it.

"That's a *corrido* from the north, *¿qué no?* From Texas, isn't it?" said the man on the *guitarrón.*

"Our specialty is '*El niño perdido,*' " said one of the trumpeters. "Would you like to hear it?"

"*Bueno, pues,*" said José, throwing his legs up on an empty chair and his arm around Mercedes. He gestured to the waitress to bring another round.

The two trumpeters walked to the back of the arcade while the guitars, the violins, and the *guitarrón* started to play.

There were no words to the music; the melody itself formed the story of a lost boy crying to be found. The strings were the voices that called out to him; the keening of the distant trumpets was the lost boy's response.

Mercedes did not want to hear this counterpoint. Each time the horns blew, a dog in the plaza howled, and in that howling, Mercedes heard the wails of her dead son, a sound that was buried in the marrow of her bones. She realized then that she was reliving the dream. Lined up before her in their black suits the mariachis were her executioners and the bullets were the wailing notes of the trumpet, growing louder as the lost boy drew closer, blasting her with the memory of her son.

He had been quiet for fifteen years, and now that another body was forming inside her, his spirit was trying to scream its way back into her womb. "The memories are still alive," Estrella González had said. "*Todo se paga en la vida.*" Mercedes felt her eyes blow open like balloons. She knew there was no way to poison a spirit. Or a memory.

"*¿Les gustó?*" the *guitarrón* man asked them when the piece was finished.

"*¡Fantástico!*" said José, and he promised to buy them each a shot of mezcal if they would play "*El niño perdido*" one more time.

"*Claro que sí, con mucho gusto,*" said the trumpeter.

"We dedicate it to the señora," said one of the others.

S andra Benítez is the daughter of an American-born father and a Puerto Rican mother. The bilingual Benítez spent her youth in Mexico, El Salvador, Puerto Rico, and in rural Missouri. In addition to writing fiction, she is a creative-writing teacher. Benítez has received a Loft-McKnight Award of Distinction for fiction, a Jerome Foundation Travel and Study Grant, as well as a 1992 Minnesota State Arts Board Fellowship. She was the Hispanic Mentor for the Loft Inroads Program from 1989 to 1992. Her fiction and essays have appeared in the Chariton Review and A View from the Loft. She currently lives in Edina, Minnesota. The following is a chapter from her first novel, A Place Where the Sea Remembers (1993).

FROM *A PLACE WHERE THE SEA REMEMBERS*

Sandra Benítez

The next day, after work, Marta Rodríguez was in Remedios's hut. It was her first time here. The hut was simply furnished. There was a cot, a dresser in one corner, a table and chairs in another. Grasses and herbs hung in bunches from the ceiling. A second table was near a window but Marta did not allow her eyes to rest too long on it. There were lighted candles on the table, some white, some black. There was incense burning and it threw up a spiral of smoke and an acrid stench. There were objects on the table, the sight of which was unsettling. Marta followed *la curandera* to the empty table. The healer was old. She had a face like the bark of some ancient tree. Tall and big boned, her body appeared more youthful than her face. A long skinny braid was draped like an inverted question mark down her back. When Remedios pulled one of the chairs out from under the table, a striped cat napping on the seat gave a sharp meow and jumped off. Marta stepped back. Cats frightened her. In the *mesón* she'd heard tell of a cat smothering a baby while it slept in its hammock. Another cat, a black one, awakened perhaps by the yowl of the first, crept out from under the table. Both cats leaped through one of the hut's opened windows.

Remedios seemed not to notice the cats or Marta's uneasiness. She motioned for Marta to sit. "So Luz Gamboa is a friend of yours," Remedios said.

Marta nodded.

When they were both seated, Remedios said, "Let's not waste each other's time. *Dame las manos.*"

Marta laid her hands in Remedios's and the old one closed her eyes. Her hands were very hot and she clasped Marta's gently, swaying a little as she did. Soon a deep vibrating hum came from somewhere deep within her, and after a moment Remedios opened her eyes. "This condition of yours," she said, jutting her chin in the direction of Marta's belly. "It happened against your will."

"*Es cierto,*" Marta said, feeling tears welling up. In all this time hardly anyone had believed her. She had spoken the truth to her family. She had told them about the beach, about the sting the sea grass had made against her thighs and buttocks. She had told them about Roberto's suffocating weight, about his hand pressed hard over her mouth. She said all this and more, but her family had not believed the way it truly happened. She could tell it in their eyes, in the fact that her story had not raised their indignation.

Marta did not withdraw her hands from the warmth of Remedios's grasp. "I need your help," Marta said, then she went on, allowing all her story to spill out.

"I see," Remedios said after Marta had grown silent.

"Can you make Cande change his mind? Can you use one of your potions to make him do it? I can pay. I work at the hotel, so I can pay."

"Child, this is not a question of money or of potions."

"What do you mean?" If not these things, what then?

"I will say this as gently as I can." The healer's large hooded eyes softened in the way a person's do when preparing another for bad news. Marta pulled her hands away from the healer's and dropped them into her lap.

"A girl like you," Remedios said, "a girl like you should not go across the border."

Remedios's pronouncement was a blow. "But you don't understand . . ."

"*Un momento,*" Remedios said, holding up a hand. "*El norte* is a place where girls like you are lost. It is a place that hardens and ruins girls like you."

"I am ruined already," Marta Rodríguez said, passing a hand over her belly. She felt her heart hardening against this old woman who talked as if she knew her.

"You are not ruined. True, you've had your share of troubles, but going north would only give you more."

Marta pushed back her chair and stood. "I came because I want you to make Cande change his mind. Will you do it or not?"

"I can do it, but I will not." Remedios pushed back her own chair, but she did not rise. "You must listen to me when I tell you that I see things about you that you do not know about yourself."

For some moments Marta was silent, the dream of her getaway swirling like a wild wind inside her. "And so you won't help me," she said at length.

"I will not help you if it means helping you reach *el norte.*"

"With your help or not, I'm going there."

"Very well," Remedios said, standing now and heading for the door. "There is nothing more to say."

"No, there is nothing more to say."

Marta left the hut as the orange ball of sun slipped below the tops of the trees in Remedios's yard. In the distance, the sea was a dark pane of glass and Marta thought that her life seemed as bleak as this sea. El Paso, she said to herself. I *will* go to El Paso. She repeated the words in a cadence that propelled her down the hill and along the road that led into Santiago. With each step she felt more determined and sure of herself. She did not need Remedios and her silly potions. Marta herself would go to Cande. She would explain the problem and Cande would listen. In the end, because they were family, Cande would change his mind.

It was Candelario himself who opened the door. He and Chayo were eating, and Chayo jumped up from the table when Marta came in. "Tita," Chayo said, rushing over. "Yesterday you left so quickly."

"Here I am," Marta said.

"Come and eat," Chayo said, hurrying back to the table. She pushed a plate in her sister's direction.

"I'm not hungry." Marta dropped into a chair. Candelario had gone back to eating, his head inclined over his plate.

Chayo moved a fork through the mound of beans on her plate. "Yesterday, after you left, I thought you were too angry to come back."

"I'm not angry. I'm happy about your baby. I didn't say it yesterday, but I am." She touched Candelario's shoulder. "I'm happy for you too, Cande."

Candelario looked up and smiled at her and then continued eating.

Candelario's smile was like a signal to Marta. "Do you think when my baby comes, you and Chayo can still take it? I know you told Chayo that you couldn't, but do you think you could change your mind? I am going to El Paso. I'll have work there. If it's money you need, I'll send you everything I make."

Candelario put his fork down. "I didn't tell Chayo we couldn't take your baby. I promised to take it, and once I give my word, that is that."

"But Chayo said . . ."

"It's your sister who does not want it now. It's Chayo who changed her mind."

Marta gasped. She turned to look at Chayo, who was coming around the table.

"It's not what you think," Chayo said. "It's just that when my baby comes, I want it to be only Cande and the baby and me." She dropped down beside Marta's chair as if she were asking for a blessing. "This is my first baby, Tita. I have waited a long time for it."

Marta's chair scraped across the floor. "You lied to me," she said. "My only sister lied to me." She turned and, for the second time in as many days, fled from her sister's house.

Outside it was growing dark. Marta went down the arroyo until she was in town. She walked aimlessly down one street and then another, her mind numb to the presence of others and to the shadows that had begun to fill the doorways of the houses along the way. Soon she came to the highway at the edge of town. She stopped and looked across it. *El brujo*'s house stood there, and Marta nodded as if to acknowledge the way fate had placed her here. She crossed the highway and walked into the yard.

El brujo, don Picho Lara, emerged from a wide ravine that started a few meters from the back of his house. A large black dog was at his side and it spotted Marta first. The dog barked and rushed up to Marta, who held herself rigid and tried to look fearless. "Don Picho," she cried, "call the dog back."

El brujo clapped sharply. "*¡Diablo!*" he yelled, and the dog trotted back to him.

An eye out for the dog, Marta went toward the sorcerer, who was short and thick and powerful in appearance. He wore loose-fitting trousers and a blousy shirt. Serpents and jaguars were embroidered on the shirt. "*¿Quién sos?*" he asked.

"Marta Rodríguez."

"*¿A qué venís?*"

Why had she come? Because she had a sister who would not honor a family member's right to ask a favor of another. "It's my sister. She is very selfish."

El brujo pointed to a pair of chairs sitting under a span of corrugated tin jutting from the roof. The two went over and sat down. The dog sprawled between them. "So, tell me more."

Marta Rodríguez plunged into her story, and the sorcerer studied her while she spoke, his fingers stroking the goatee sprouting from his chin. "Do you think you can do something?" Marta asked when she was finished.

El brujo gave a devilish smile. "Oh, there's plenty I can do."

"There is?" she said, wondering to herself why this surprised her.

"There is."

Marta rearranged herself in the chair. "And the cost?"

El brujo fingered what looked like a rabbit's foot hanging from a cord draped around his neck. *"Todo depende,"* he said.

"I need a price," she said, emboldened by the thought of the coil of bills concealed in the jar under her bed.

He waved his hand as though in irritation. "Very well, the price is ten thousand pesos."

"And what will you do for the money?"

It had grown much darker. *El brujo's* face was now in shadow, and the serpents and jaguars on his shirt were indistinguishable from one another. "I will cause the child to no longer be a burden."

Marta gave a jump. When she had first learned of her pregnancy, she'd been determined to see a certain doctor who could wipe clean the slate of her encumbered life. But now . . .

El brujo went on, "I will need something that has been close to the child. Some object of clothing that is worn over the belly. When you bring me this, I can begin."

"But it's too late for me," Marta Rodríguez said. "In four months my baby will come."

At this statement, *el brujo* threw back his head and he laughed so raucously that the dog stood up and looked around. *El brujo* leaned forward so that his rabbit's foot swung away from his neck and dangled in midair. "Girl," he said, "it's not your baby I'm speaking of. It's your sister's. It's her child I'll work my magic on."

Marta felt the blood rush from her face. She pictured *el*

brujo's magic wresting the baby from her sister's womb, but then she pictured her own child taking its place in Chayo's arms.

"What will it be?" the sorcerer asked. "Yes or no?"

Marta Rodríguez's cheeks were hot, and her mouth was so dry that she felt unable to speak, but she did.

"*Sí*," she said, surprised only by how right her answer sounded.

*C*ristina García *was born in Havana, Cuba, and grew up in New York City. She has worked as a correspondent for* Time *magazine in San Francisco, Miami, and Los Angeles, where she currently lives. This excerpt is the story of one of the main characters of her first novel,* Dreaming in Cuban *(1992). García is working on a second novel.*

LOURDES PUENTE

Cristina García

"Lourdes, I'm back," Jorge del Pino greets his daughter forty days after she buried him with his Panama hat, his cigars, and a bouquet of violets in a cemetery on the border of Brooklyn and Queens.

His words are warm and close as a breath. Lourdes turns, expecting to find her father at her shoulder, but she sees only the dusk settling on the tops of the oak trees, the pink tinge of sliding darkness.

"Don't be afraid, *mi hija*. Just keep walking and I'll explain," Jorge del Pino tells his daughter.

The sunset flares behind a row of brownstones, linking them as if by a flaming ribbon. Lourdes massages her eyes and begins walking with legs that feel held by splints.

"I'm glad to see you, Lourdes. Thank you for everything, *hija*, the hat, the cigars. You buried me like an Egyptian king, with all my valuables!" Jorge del Pino laughs.

Lourdes perceives the faint scent of her father's cigar. She has taken to smoking the same brand herself late at night when she totals the day's receipts at the kitchen table.

"Where are you, Papi?"

The street is vacant, as if a force has absorbed all living things. Even the trees seem more shadow than substance.

"Nearby," her father says, serious now.

"Can you return?"

"From time to time."

"How will I know?"

"Listen for me at twilight."

Lourdes arrives home with a presentiment of disaster. Is her mind betraying her, cultivating delusion like a hothouse orchid? Lourdes opens the refrigerator, finds nothing to her liking. Everything tastes the same to her these days.

Outside, the spring rains resume ill-temperedly. The drops enter through the kitchen window at impossible angles. A church bell rings, shaking down the leaves of the maple tree. What if she has exhausted reality? Lourdes abhors ambiguity.

She pulls on the shipyard bell that rings in Rufino's workshop. Her husband will assure her, Lourdes thinks. He operates on a material plane. His projects conduct electricity, engage motion with toothed wheels, react in concert with universal laws of physics.

Rufino appears, dusted with blue chalk. His fingernails, too, are blue, an indigo blue.

"He's back," Lourdes whispers hoarsely, peering under the love seats. "He spoke to me tonight when I was walking home from the bakery. I heard Papi's voice. I smelled his cigar. The street was empty, I swear it." Lourdes stops. Her chest rises and falls with every breath. Then she leans toward her husband, narrowing her eyes. "Things are wrong, Rufino, very wrong."

Her husband stares back at her, blinking rapidly as if he'd just awakened. "You're tired, *mi cielo*," Rufino says evenly, coaxing Lourdes to the sofa. He rubs her insteps with a cool lotion called Pretty Feet. She feels the rolling pressure of his thumbs against her arches, the soothing grip of his hands on her swollen ankles.

The next day, Lourdes works extraconscientiously, determined to prove to herself that her business acumen, at least, is intact. She sails back and forth behind the bakery counter, explaining the ingredients in her cakes and pies to her clients. "We use only real butter," she says in her accented English. "Not margarine, like the place down the block."

After her customers make their selections, Lourdes leans toward them. "Any special occasions coming up?" she whispers, as if she were selling hot watches from a raincoat. If they answer yes—and it's always a musical yes to Lourdes's ears—she launches into her advance-order sales pitch.

By two o'clock, when the trainee reports for work, Lourdes has cash deposits on seven birthday cakes (including one peanut butter-and-banana-flavored layer cake topped with a marzipan Elvis); a sixty-serving sheet cake for the closing recital of the Bishop Lowney High School marching band; a two-tiered fiftieth-anniversary cake "For Tillie and Ira, Two Golden Oldies"; and a double-chocolate butter cream decorated with a wide high heel for the retirement of Frankie Zaccaglini of Frankie's EEE Shoe Company.

Lourdes's self-confidence is restored.

"See this," she announces to her new employee, Maribel Navarro, riffling her orders like a blackjack dealer. "This is what I want from you." Then she hands Maribel a bottle of Windex and a roll of paper towels and orders her to clean every last inch of the counter.

Lourdes spends the afternoon training Maribel, a pretty Puerto Rican woman in her late twenties with a pixie cut and stylishly long nails. "You're going to have to trim those if you want to work here," Lourdes snaps. "Unsanitary. The health department will give us a citation."

Maribel is pleasant with the customers and gives the correct change, but she doesn't show much initiative.

"Don't let them get away so easily," Lourdes coaches her. "You can always sell them something else. Some dinner rolls, a coffee ring for tomorrow's breakfast."

Nobody works like an owner, Lourdes thinks, as she places fresh doilies under the chiffon pies. She pulls out a tray of Florentine cookies and shows Maribel how to arrange them on overlapping strips of wax paper so they look more appealing.

"The Florentines are seven ninety-five a pound, two dollars more than the other cookies, so weigh them separately." Lourdes pulls a sheet of tissue paper from a metal dispenser and places it on the scale with a cookie. "See. This Florentine alone weighs forty-three cents. I can't afford to throw that kind of money away."

Business picks up after five o'clock with the after-work crowd stopping by for desserts. Maribel works efficiently, tying the boxes of pastries firmly with string just as she was taught. This pleases Lourdes. By now, she has almost dispelled the effect of her father's visitation yesterday. Could she have imagined the entire incident?

Suddenly Lourdes's wandering eye, like a wary spy, fixes on the quarters sliding across the counter to Maribel. It observes Maribel packing the two cinnamon crullers in a white paper bag, folding the top over neatly, and thanking the customer. It watches as she turns to the register and rings up fifty cents. Then, just as the eye is about to relax its scrutiny, it spots Maribel slipping the coins into her pocket.

Lourdes continues waiting on her customer, an elderly woman sizing up a mocha petit four. When she's done, Lourdes strides to the register, pulls out nine singles and a roll of pennies for the afternoon's work, and hands it to Maribel.

"Get out," Lourdes says.

Maribel removes her apron, folds it into a compact square on the counter, and leaves without saying a word.

· · ·

An hour later, Lourdes walks home from the bakery as if picking her way through a minefield. The Navarro woman has shattered Lourdes's fragile peace of mind. Breezes from the sluggish river seem to inscribe her skin with metal tips. She crawls to an edge inside herself, longs to be insensate, a slab of brick. Lourdes thinks she detects the scent of her father's cigar, but when she turns there's only a businessman hailing a taxi, his hand waving a cigarette. Behind him, a linden tree drops a cluster of seeds.

When Lourdes was a child in Cuba, she used to wait anxiously for her father to return from his trips selling small fans and electric brooms in distant provinces. He would call her every evening from Camagüey or Sagua la Grande and she would cry, "When are you coming home, Papi? When are you coming home?" Lourdes would welcome her father in her party dress and search his suitcase for rag dolls and oranges.

On Sunday afternoons, after high mass, they went to baseball games and ate roasted peanuts from brown paper cones. The sun darkened Lourdes's skin to the shade of the villagers on the bleachers, and the mix of her father's cologne and the warm, acrid smells of the ballpark made her giddy. These are her happiest memories.

Years later, when her father was in New York, baseball became their obsession. During the Mets' championship season, Lourdes and her father discussed each game like generals plotting a battle, assessing the merits of Tom Seaver, Ed Kranepool, and Jerry Koosman. They glued transistors to their ears all summer, even during Jorge del Pino's brief hospital stays, and cheered when the Mets caught fire and the Cubs finally folded.

On October 16, 1969, Lourdes, her father, doctors, nurses, orderlies, patients, nuns, and a priest who arrived to administer last rites to a dying man crowded the television room of the Sisters of Charity hospital for the fifth game of the World Series. When Cleon Jones camped under the final fly ball against the Orioles, all hell broke loose. Patients, bare-assed in their hospital gowns, streaked down the corridors chanting, "WE'RE NUMBER ONE!" Someone popped a bottle of champagne and tears streamed down the faces of the nuns, who'd prayed fervently for such a miracle.

At Shea Stadium, the crowd tore onto the field, ripping up home plate, pulling up fat clods of turf and raising them high over their heads. They set off orange flares and fire-crackers and chalked the outfield fence with victory slogans. Across the river in Manhattan, on Wall Street and Park Avenue, Delancey Street and Broadway, people danced under showers of computer cards and ticker tape. Lourdes and her father laughed and embraced for a long, long time.

When she had first left Cuba, Lourdes hadn't known how long they'd be away. She was to meet Rufino in Miami, where the rest of his family had fled. In her confusion, she packed riding crops and her wedding veil, a watercolor landscape, and a paper sack of birdseed.

Pilar ran away in the Miami airport, her crinoline dress swinging like a tiny bell through the crowd. Lourdes heard her daughter's name announced over the loudspeaker. She couldn't speak when she found Pilar, sitting on the lap of a pilot and licking a lime lollipop. She couldn't find the words to thank the uniformed American who escorted them to their gate.

After several days, they left Miami in a secondhand Chevrolet. Lourdes couldn't stand Rufino's family, the endless brooding over their lost wealth, the competition for dishwasher jobs.

"I want to go where it's cold," Lourdes told her husband. They began to drive. "Colder," she said as they passed the low salt marshes of Georgia, as if the word were a whip driving them north. "Colder," she said through the withered fields of a Carolina winter. "Colder," she said again in Washington, D.C., despite the cherry-blossom promises, despite the white stone monuments hoarding winter light. "This is cold enough," she finally said when they reached New York.

Only two months earlier, Lourdes had been pregnant with her second child back in Cuba. She'd been galloping through a field of dry grasses when her horse reared suddenly, throwing her to the ground. The horse fled, leaving her alone. Lourdes felt a density between her breasts harden to a sharp, round pain. The blood bleached from her fingernails.

A large rodent appeared from behind an aroma tree and began nibbling the toes of her boots. Lourdes threw a rock at it, killing it instantly. She stumbled for nearly an hour until she reached their dairy farm. A worker lent her his horse and she rode at a breakneck pace back to the villa.

Two young soldiers were pointing their rifles at Rufino. His hands circled nervously in the air. She jumped from her horse and stood like a shield before her husband.

"Get the hell out of here!" she shouted with such ferocity that the soldiers lowered their guns and backed toward their Jeep.

Lourdes felt the clot dislodge and liquefy beneath her breasts, float through her belly, and slide down her thighs. There was a pool of dark blood at her feet.

Rufino was in Havana ordering a cow-milking machine when the soldiers returned. They handed Lourdes an official sheet of paper declaring the Puentes' estate the property of the revolutionary government. She tore the deed in half and angrily dismissed the soldiers, but one of them grabbed her by the arm.

"You're not going to start that again, are you, *compañera?*" the tall one said.

Lourdes heard the accent of Oriente province and turned

to look at him. His hair, tamed with brilliantine, grew dense and low on his forehead.

"Get out of my house!" Lourdes yelled at the men, more fiercely than she had the week before.

But instead of leaving, the tall one increased the pressure on her arm just above the elbow.

Lourdes felt his callused palm, the metal of his ring clapping her temple. She twisted free from his grip and charged him so abruptly that he fell back against the vestibule wall. Lourdes tried to run past him but the other soldier blocked her way. Her head reverberated with the clapping palm.

"So the woman of the house is a fighter?" the tall soldier taunted. He pressed his face close to Lourdes's, pinning her arms behind her back.

Lourdes did not close her eyes but looked directly into his. They were unremarkable except for the whites, which were tinged with the filmy blue of the blind. His lips were too full for a man. As he tried to press them to Lourdes's mouth she snapped her head back and spat in his face.

He smiled slowly and Lourdes saw a stained band along his front teeth, like the watermarks on a pier. His gums were a soft pink, delicate as the petals of a rose.

The other soldier held Lourdes down as his partner took a knife from his holster. Carefully, he sliced Lourdes's riding pants off to her knees and tied them over her mouth. He cut through her blouse without dislodging a single button and slit her bra and panties in two. Then he placed the knife flat across her belly and raped her.

Lourdes could not see but she smelled vividly as if her senses had concentrated on this alone.

She smelled the soldier's coarse soap, the salt of his perspiring back. She smelled his milky clots and the decay of his teeth and the citrus brilliantine in his hair, as if a grove of lemons lay hidden there. She smelled his face on his wedding day, his tears when his son drowned at the park. She smelled his rotting leg in Africa, where it would be blown off his body on a moonless savanna night. She smelled him when he was old and unbathed and the flies blackened his eyes.

When he finished, the soldier lifted the knife and began to scratch at Lourdes's belly with great concentration. A primeval scraping. Crimson hieroglyphics.

The pain brought a flood of color back to Lourdes's eyes. She saw the blood seep from her skin like rainwater from a sodden earth.

Not until later, after the tall soldier had battered her with his rifle and left with his lumpy, quiet friend, after she had scoured her skin and hair with detergents meant for the walls and the tile floors, after stanching the blood with cotton and gauze and wiping the steam from the bathroom mirror, did Lourdes try to read what he had carved. But it was illegible.

Seven days after her father's visitation, Lourdes looks out her bakery window. The twilight falls in broad violet sheets. In the corner store, the butcher closes out his register. Bare fluorescent tubes and a rack of ribs hang from the ceiling, obscuring his profile. The florist rattles shut his gate next door, securing it with a fist-sized lock. Across the street, the liquor store is open, a magnet to the wiry man in the sagging tan suit cajoling people for spare change.

Lourdes recognizes a passerby, a heavyset woman with a veiled pillbox hat who praised her Boston cream pies. She is dragging by the hand a little boy in short pants and knee socks. His feet barely touch the ground.

On her way home, Lourdes passes a row of Arab shops, recent additions to the neighborhood. Baskets of figs and pistachios and coarse yellow grains are displayed under their awnings. Lourdes buys a round box of sticky dates and considers the centuries of fratricide converging on this street corner in Brooklyn. She ponders the transmigrations from the southern latitudes, the millions moving north. What happens to their languages? The warm burial grounds they leave behind? What of their passions lying stiff and untranslated in their breasts?

Lourdes considers herself lucky. Immigration has redefined her, and she is grateful. Unlike her husband, she welcomes her adopted language, its possibilities for reinvention. Lourdes relishes winter most of all—the cold scraping sounds on sidewalks and windshields, the ritual of scarves and gloves, hats and zip-in coat linings. Its layers protect her. She wants no part of Cuba, no part of its wretched carnival floats creaking with lies, no part of Cuba at all, which Lourdes claims never possessed her.

Four blocks from her home, Lourdes smells her father's cigar behind a catalpa tree.

"*Mi hija*, have you forgotten me?" Jorge del Pino chides gently.

Lourdes feels her legs as if from a distance. She pictures them slipping from their sockets and moving before her in a steady gait, still wearing their rubber-soled shoes, their white-ribbed stockings. Cautiously, she follows them.

"You didn't expect to hear from me again?"

"I wasn't even sure I heard you the first time," Lourdes says tentatively.

"You thought you'd imagined it?"

"I thought I heard your voice because I wanted to, because I missed you. When I was little I used to think I heard you opening the front door late at night. I'd run out but you were never there."

"I'm here now, Lourdes."

There's a ship leaving the harbor, its whistle resigned as an abbot in prayer, fracturing the dusk.

Lourdes recalls the plane ride to Miami last month to pick up Pilar. The airport was congested and they circled the city for nearly an hour before landing. Lourdes could smell the air before she breathed it, the air of her mother's ocean nearby. She imagined herself alone and shriveled in her mother's womb, envisioned the first days in her mother's unyielding arms. Her mother's fingers were stiff and splayed as spoons, her milk a tasteless gray. Her mother stared at her with eyes collapsed of expectation. If it's true that babies learn love from their mothers' voices, then this is what Lourdes heard: "I will not remember her name."

"Papi, I don't know what to do anymore." Lourdes begins to cry. "No matter what I do, Pilar hates me."

"Pilar doesn't hate you, *hija*. She just hasn't learned to love you yet."

Aurora Levins Morales is the daughter of an American Jewish father and a Puerto Rican mother. She currently resides in Berkeley, California. "Puertoricanness" appeared in the book she and her mother, Rosario Morales, coauthored, Getting Home Alive *(1986). It captures her realization that no matter where she lives she is "all Puerto Rican, every bit of her."*

PUERTORICANNESS

Aurora Levins Morales

It was Puerto Rico waking up inside her. Puerto Rico waking her up at 6:00 A.M., remembering the rooster that used to crow over on 59th Street and the neighbors all cursed "that damn rooster," but she loved him, waited to hear his harsh voice carving up the Oakland sky and eating it like chopped corn, so obliviously sure of himself, crowing all alone with miles of houses around him. She was like that rooster.

Often she could hear them in her dreams. Not the lone rooster of 59th Street (or some street nearby . . . she had never found the exact yard though she had tried), but the wild careening hysterical roosters of 3:00 A.M. in Bartolo, screaming at the night and screaming again at the day.

It was Puerto Rico waking up inside her, uncurling and shoving open the door she had kept nearly shut for years and years. Maybe since the first time she was an immigrant, when she refused to speak Spanish in nursery school. Certainly since the last time, when at thirteen she found herself between languages, between countries, with no land feeling at all solid under her feet. The mulberry trees of Chicago, that first summer, had looked so utterly pitiful beside her memory of *flamboyán*

70

and banana and . . . No, not even the individual trees and bushes but the mass of them, the overwhelming profusion of green life that was the home of her comfort and nest of her dreams.

The door was opening. She could no longer keep her accent under lock and key. It seeped out, masquerading as dyslexia, stuttering, halting, unable to speak the word which will surely come out in the wrong language, wearing the wrong clothes. Doesn't that girl know how to dress? Doesn't she know how to date, what to say to a professor, how to behave at a dinner table laid with silver and crystal and too many forks?

Yesterday she answered her husband's request that she listen to the whole of his thoughts before commenting by screaming, "This is how we talk. I will not wait sedately for you to finish. Interrupt me back!" She drank pineapple juice three or four times a day. Not Lotus, just Co-op brand, but it was *piña*, and it was sweet and yellow. And she was letting the clock slip away from her into a world of morning and afternoon and night, instead of "five-forty-one-and-twenty-seconds—beep."

There were things she noticed about herself, the Puertoricanness of which she had kept hidden all these years, but which had persisted as habits, as idiosyncrasies of her nature. The way she left a pot of food on the stove all day, eating out of it whenever hunger struck her, liking to have something ready. The way she had lacked food to offer Elena in the old days and had stamped on the desire to do so because it *was* Puerto Rican: *Come, mija . . . ¿quieres café?* The way she was embarrassed and irritated by Ana's unannounced visits, just dropping by, keeping the country habits after a generation of city life. So unlike the cluttered date books of all her friends, making appointments to speak to each other on the phone days in advance. Now she yearned for that clocklessness, for the perpetual food pots of her childhood. Even in the poorest houses a plate of white rice and brown beans with *calabaza* or green bananas and oil.

She had told Sally that Puerto Ricans lived as if they were

all in a small town still, a small town of six million spread out over tens of thousands of square miles, and that the small town that was her country needed to include Manila Avenue in Oakland now, because she was moving back into it. She would not fight the waking early anymore, or the eating all day, or the desire to let time slip between her fingers and allow her work to shape it. Work, eating, sleep, lovemaking, play—to let them shape the day instead of letting the day shape them. Since she could not right now, in the endless bartering of a woman with two countries, bring herself to trade in one-half of her heart for the other, exchange this loneliness for another perhaps harsher one, she would live as a Puerto Rican lives *en la isla*, right here in north Oakland, plant the *bananales* and *cafetales* of her heart around her bedroom door, sleep under the shadow of their bloom and the carving hoarseness of the roosters, wake to blue-rimmed white enamel cups of *jugo de piña* and plates of *guineo verde*, and heat pots of rice with bits of meat in them on the stove all day.

There was a woman in her who had never had the chance to move through this house the way she wanted to, a woman raised to be like those women of her childhood, hardworking and humorous and clear. That woman was yawning up out of sleep and into this cluttered daily routine of a Northern California writer living at the edges of Berkeley. She was taking over, putting doilies on the word processor, not bothering to make appointments, talking to the neighbors, riding miles on the bus to buy *bacalao*, making her presence felt . . . and she was all Puerto Rican, every bit of her.

P *at Mora, a native of El Paso, Texas, is a Chicana educator, poet, mother, and lecturer. She writes poetry, essays, and children's books. Her published poetry collections are* Chants *(1984),* Borders *(1986), and* Communion *(1991). Her writings have also appeared in several journals and anthologies. Currently she lives in Cincinnati, Ohio. The following remembrance of her aunt Lobo is one of her favorite readings. It appeared in* Nepantla *(1993), her first collection of essays.*

REMEMBERING LOBO

Pat Mora

We called her *Lobo*. The word means "wolf" in Spanish, an odd name for a generous and loving aunt. Like all names it became synonymous with her, and to this day returns me to my childself. Although the name seemed perfectly natural to us and to our friends, it did cause frowns from strangers throughout the years. I particularly remember one hot afternoon when on a crowded streetcar between the border cities of El Paso and Juarez, I momentarily lost sight of her. "Lobo! Lobo!" I cried in panic. Annoyed faces peered at me, disappointed at such disrespect to a white-haired woman.

Actually the fault was hers. She lived with us for years, and when she arrived home from work in the evening, she'd knock on our front door and ask, "*¿Dónde están mis lobitos?*" "Where are my little wolves?"

Gradually she became our *lobo*, a spinster aunt who gathered the four of us around her, tying us to her for life by giving us all she had. Sometimes to tease her we would call her by her real name. "*¿Dónde está Ignacia?*" we would ask. Lobo would laugh and say, "She is a ghost."

74

To all of us in nuclear families today, the notion of an extended family under one roof seems archaic, complicated. We treasure our private space. I will always marvel at the generosity of my parents, who opened their door to both my grandmother and Lobo. No doubt I am drawn to the elderly because I grew up with two entirely different white-haired women who worried about me, tucked me in at night, made me tomato soup or hot *hierbabuena* (mint tea) when I was ill.

Lobo grew up in Mexico, the daughter of a circuit judge, my grandfather. She was a wonderful storyteller and over and over told us about the night her father, a widower, brought his grown daughters on a flatbed truck across the Rio Grande at the time of the Mexican Revolution. All their possessions were left in Mexico. Lobo had not been wealthy, but she had probably never expected to have to find a job and learn English.

When she lived with us, she worked in the linens section of a local department store. Her area was called "piece goods and bedding." Lobo never sewed, but she would talk about materials she sold, using words I never completely understood, such as *pique* and *broadcloth*. Sometimes I still whisper such words just to remind myself of her. I'll always savor the way she would order "sweet milk" at restaurants. The precision of a speaker new to the language.

Lobo saved her money to take us out to dinner and a movie, to take us to Los Angeles in the summer, to buy us shiny black shoes for Christmas. Though she never married and never bore children, Lobo taught me much about one of our greatest challenges as human beings: loving well. I don't think she ever discussed the subject with me, but through the years she lived her love, and I was privileged to watch.

She died at ninety-four. She was no sweet, docile Mexican woman dying with perfect resignation. Some of her last words before drifting into semiconsciousness were loud words of annoyance at the incompetence of nurses and doctors.

"No sirven." "They're worthless," she'd say to me in Spanish. "They don't know what they're doing. My throat is hurt-

ing and they're taking X rays. Tell them to take care of my throat first."

I was busy striving for my cherished middle-class politeness. "Shh, shh," I'd say. "They're doing the best they can."

"Well, it's not good enough," she'd say, sitting up in anger.

Lobo was a woman of fierce feelings, of strong opinions. She was a woman who literally whistled while she worked. The best way to cheer her when she'd visit my young children was to ask for her help. Ask her to make a bed, fold laundry, set the table or dry dishes, and the whistling would begin as she moved about her task. Like all of us, she loved being needed. Understandable, then, that she muttered in annoyance when her body began to fail her. She was a woman who found self-definition and joy in visibly showing her family her love for us by bringing us hot *té de canela* (cinnamon tea) in the middle of the night to ease a cough, by bringing us comics and candy whenever she returned home. A life of giving.

One of my last memories of her is a visit I made to her on November 2, *El Día de los Muertos*, or All Souls' Day. She was sitting in her rocking chair, smiling wistfully. The source of the smile may seem a bit bizarre to a U.S. audience. She was fondly remembering past visits to the local cemetery on this religious feast day.

"What a silly old woman I have become," she said. "Here I sit in my rocking chair all day on All Souls' Day, sitting when I should be out there. At the cemetery. Taking good care of *mis muertos*, my dead ones.

"What a time I used to have. I'd wake while it was still dark outside. I'd hear the first morning birds, and my fingers would almost itch to begin. By six I'd be having a hot bath, dressing carefully in black, wanting *mis muertos* to be proud of me, proud to have me looking respectable and proud to have their graves taken care of. I'd have my black coffee and plenty of toast. You know the way I like it. Well browned and well buttered. I wanted to be ready to work hard.

"The bus ride to the other side of town was a long one,

but I'd say a rosary and plan my day. I'd hope that my perfume wasn't too strong and yet would remind others that I was a lady.

"The air at the cemetery gates was full of chrysanthemums: that strong, sharp, fall smell. I'd buy tin cans full of the gold and wine flowers. How I liked seeing aunts and uncles who were also there to care for the graves of their loved ones. We'd hug. Happy together.

"Then it was time to begin. The smell of chrysanthemums was like a whiff of pure energy. I'd pull the heavy hose and wash the gravestones over and over, listening to the water pelting away the desert sand. I always brought newspaper. I'd kneel on the few patches of grass, and I'd scrub and scrub, shining the gray stones, leaning back on my knees to rest for a bit and then scrubbing again. Finally a relative from nearby would say, '*Ya, ya, Nacha,*' and laugh. Enough. I'd stop, blink my eyes to return from my trance. Slightly dazed, I'd stand slowly, place a can of chrysanthemums before each grave.

"Sometimes I would just stand there in the desert sun and listen. I'd hear the quiet crying of people visiting new graves; I'd hear families exchanging gossip while they worked.

"One time I heard my aunt scolding her dead husband. She'd sweep his gravestone and say, '*¿Porqué?* Why did you do this, you thoughtless man? Why did you go and leave me like this? You know I don't like to be alone. Why did you stop living?' Such a sight to see my aunt with her proper black hat and her fine dress and her carefully polished shoes muttering away for all to hear.

"To stifle my laughter, I had to cover my mouth with my hands."

*P*atricia Preciado Martin is a native of Arizona and a lifelong Tucsonan. She has been active in many facets of the Mexican American community of Tucson and for ten years has devoted her time to writing, collecting oral history, and developing the Mexican Heritage Project at the Arizona Historical Society. She is the author of The Legend of the Bellringer of San Augustin *(1980)*, a bilingual children's book. Her works also include collections of oral histories: Images and Conversations: Mexican Americans Recall a Southwestern Past *(1983) and* Songs My Mother Sang to Me: An Oral History of Mexican American Women *(1992)*. She has also written two books of short stories, El Milagro and Other Stories *(1995) and* Days of Plenty, Days of Want *(1988)*. "Tierra a Tierra" tells the story of the adobe house Doña Otilia's father built and its cycle from earth to earth.

78

TIERRA A TIERRA

Patricia Preciado Martin

PART I: 1910

This is the way you make adobes: You lie in bed sleepless, staring into the darkness of the ceiling shadows made mysterious by the moon, waiting for Mamá to call you to get up. The cock has not even crowed, but you know that Mamá has been a long time in the kitchen preparing the *canasta* of food for the day at the river. Through a crack in the door you can see the faint glow of the kerosene lamps. You can hear Mamá's determined footsteps, the faint rustle of her petticoats, and the snap of the mesquite *leña* in the wood-burning stove. You can smell the aroma of all the *bocaditos* she has prepared for the *día de campo*. She has made flour tortillas and wrapped them in an embroidered cloth. She has made fried chicken and *salsa de chile verde* and *frijoles con queso* which will stay warm in a blue enameled pot. There will be *sandía*, too, and *empanadas de camote*, and *limonada* in an earthenware crock.

You lie impatient and expectant, but obedient. You know that if you get up too soon, Mamá will scold you for being an *encimosa* and getting underfoot.

Papá is in the corral hitching up the reluctant mare to the wagon. You can hear the stubborn mare snorting and stamping, and your father's soft clucking admonishments. At last you hear the creak of the wagon wheels, the clink of the bridle, and the mare's rhythmic plodding in the fine dust of the *callejón*. Papá will hitch the mare to the ancient *álamo* by the gate and come into the house and begin loading the buckboard with provisions. He will not forget the guitar.

The glow under the door begins to fade as the bedroom fills with soft morning light. My twin bothers, *flojos* that they are, lie sprawled in their cot, snoring in unison, their arms interwoven like two rag dolls, as inseparable in their dreams as in their waking hours. The baby sleeps peacefully in her cradle, her cherubic face glowing in the dawn like a miniature replica of the moon that has now dropped below the western horizon.

(I remember well the evening Papá began hewing the cradle from rough-sawn pine boards. He worked rapidly, wordless, concentrating, his brow furrowed, the aromatic pine chips piling up at his feet. I knew that it would not be long before there was another López mouth to feed. I remember, particularly, his large veined hands with the long delicate fingers, the nails bruised from hammers that had missed their mark. His varnish-stained palms were flecked by the innumerable slivers of all the wood he tried to bend to his artistic will while he plied his carpenter's trade. He was, with all those slivers, half tree, half man, strong and tall and straight and silent—a forest of a man, who provided *sombra* for all. And when he finished the cradle, Papá gave me a penknife and I carved a clumsy flower on the headboard, praying all the while secretly that the new baby would be a girl. My wish came true, and they named her Margarita, like the flower I had carved that day. And all of my life, because of that flower, I have felt blessed.)

The door opens. Mamá calls in a whisper: "*¡Otilia! ¡Levántate ya!*" I spring from my bed, fully awake, being careful not to disturb my mischievous older brothers, jealous of my grown-up responsibilities and my time alone with Mamá and

Papá. I dress hurriedly. Today I will wear faded dungarees and a shirt of homespun, and *botas*. Mamá will braid my hair with rags. No silly ironed curls with ribbons. No frilly starched dress or stiff patent shoes that pinch. No lacy anklets that leave itchy little ridges in my skin. No reminders to: *¡Bájate; cuídate; siéntate; cálmate; no te ensucies!* Today, Mamá, relaxed with her *novela* beneath the canopy of the cottonwood by the lulling river, a contented baby crooning at her side, will furl her banner and call a truce in her war against dirt and impropriety. And I will run free on the riverbanks, my *trenzas* unraveling, my boots abandoned and solitary in the crook of the tree. And I will catch frogs and June beetles and sail leaf boats and build castles of river mud and sticks.

Papá and the *cuates* will dig an earthen pit close to the river's edge. They will turn the clay-filled earth over and over with spades, mixing it with river water and straw. When I tire of play, I will roll up my dungarees to my knees and help, sorting out the large pebbles and then working the muddy mixture with my feet until it oozes between my toes. When the earth and straw and water are of the right consistency, Papá and the twins will hoist the laden buckets out of the pit and fill the rectangular wooden frames that form the adobes. I help tamp the mixture into the forms, smoothing the cool wet clay to the corners with my hands. I survey my handiwork and sign each one that I have made with the print of my bare foot. The frames are then set out into the sun to dry. In time, the cache of adobes, like giant terra-cotta dominos, will grow until there is enough to make a wall. And then another wall. And then a room. And then another room. (Papá does not notice my footprints until the day he begins to lay the sun-dried bricks along the outline of the house marked with string. He laughs and lifts me high in the air with his sunburned arms. "These," he declares, "are for Otilia's house.")

When the day is done, I help load the wagon with the empty baskets and the pillows and blankets. While I wait for the others, I make a hiding place among the pungent straw and blankets. I inhale the sunset in great rosy breaths and try to pluck the evening star for my finger. Glad for the solitude, glad for the dove's lament, glad for the *grillo*, glad for the shining river, glad for the earth's turning and turning—the generous spinning earth that will yield up to us willingly, block by adobe block, room by adobe room, a new home on a barren lot on Anita Street.

• •

The Federal Housing Act of 1961 strengthened the concept of Urban Renewal . . . Under the Urban Renewal Act, public acquisition of land would be necessary. Consequently, when the area is ready for redevelopment, and following two acquisition appraisals, the city proceeds acquiring the land at "its present fair value for present owners." Such an endeavor is accomplished by negotiation, and if that fails, then eminent domain is exercised. Land acquired is then sold to private developers for its fair value after it has had two re-use appraisals . . . Usually the return from the sale to private developers fails to offset the acquisition, planning, clearance and off-site improvement costs. One important reason is that the land is purchased with structures which must be removed.

• •

PART II: 1973

The unexpected knock at the door causes Doña Otilia López, *viuda de Martínez*, to suspend her knitting needles in midair. Poised like that, the needles look ferocious, difficult to associate with the confectionary of bonnets, booties, and baby sweaters that materialized out of their metallic clicking. Doña Otilia sighs and places her latest project—yellow booties shaped like ducks—into the sewing basket at her feet. For grandchild number fifteen. Or was it fourteen? She always lost count. She glances at the electric Westclock she keeps centered on a crocheted doily on the radio-phonograph console. The console, which her husband Rosendo had bought after the war, had not worked for years, but she had kept it anyway, it being, in her opinion, her most elegant and practical possession. She stowed sweets for her grandchildren in the turntable, yarn and thread in the record cabinet. The top of the console served as the resting place, not only of the clock, but of four generations of family photographs—antique sepias in ornate metal frames, black-and-white snapshots, Technicolor wedding poses, blurred Polaroid images.

(In a large hand-carved frame of walnut, bedecked with two faded black ribbons, grinned the innocent and eager faces of the *cuates* dressed in jaunty sailor whites. They had enlisted together despite the pleas of Mamá. Twelve months later they would both be dead—propelled by a torpedo from the iron bunk they shared in the stern of the submarine. In step. Embracing in death as in life. When the telegram arrived, Papá planted two pine trees in their memory in the backyard. Two salt tamaracks grew there instead, from all the tears he shed that day. He did not speak for a year. And when he spoke, he said, "The house belongs to Otilia." And then, it seemed, the tree in him died. He grew frail and withdrawn, his trunk withered before its time, the leaves of his canopy dried and scattered by the winds of his grief.)

The trusty little Westclock hummed eleven. An unlikely hour for callers. Too early for lunch. Too late for *café*. Probably salesmen. Or Jehovahs. The Jehovahs are persistent in spite of the fact that Doña Otilia's home altar, with its perpetually lit candles, was visible from the doorway, the array of saints, virgins, martyrs, and *Santo Niño*s glazing sternly at any interlopers bearing unorthodox propaganda. The altar itself was not only a heavenly, but an earthly shrine as well. Mementos of the rites of passage of Doña Otilia's family . . . funeral mass holy cards, baptismal and confirmation certificates, dried remnants from *quinceañera* and wedding bouquets, anniversary souvenirs—all were arranged lovingly among the *santos* and the plastic flowers from the Five and Dime.

Doña Otilia crosses the room, her *chanclas* slapping on the threadbare carpet. Her eldest son, José, who had gone to night school and had done well for himself, had insisted, against her protests, on that carpet. He was *muy de moda*, up on things, and said it made the house more modern. Besides, it was for her own good. Throw rugs were dangerous. She might catch her foot and slip and break her hip, and that would be that. As she makes her way to the door, Doña Otilia notices that the old wooden floor of pine planks that her father had so painstakingly laid so many years ago was once more beginning to show through the worn fibers of the cheap carpet. *"Todo a su tiempo,"* she thought to herself, satisfied. She had noticed too, lately, the sagging roof, flaking paint, and cracked plaster that exposed the adobe walls of her house. She liked it that way, she mused, even though José was always worrying himself with painting, plastering, and repairs. But to Doña Otilia it was as if the house were trying to reveal itself, throwing off its superfluous garments, like an aging queen removing her makeup. Doña Otilia smiles.

Doña Otilia opened the front door. Through the latched screen she could make out the blurred faces of two men. Both wear dark suits and ties. *(¡Qué simples! ¡En este calor!)* Both are perspiring profusely and mopping their brows with white monogrammed handkerchiefs. They shift from foot to foot, uncomfortable with the heat and with their unfamiliar surroundings. They are not salesmen or Jehovahs. There are no wares or pamphlets. They carry, instead, black briefcases that bode something official. The scruffy little mongrel of Doña Amelia next door barks ferociously from behind the broken slats in the picket fence. The curtain at the window moves slightly as Doña Amelia positions herself to get the best view and to hopefully be within earshot. There will be much speculation and discussion of the strangers over afternoon coffee.

Doña Otilia chuckles to herself because for once she will have the upper hand of the conversation.

The shorter of the two men speaks first, in halting high school Spanish.

—*¿Es Usted Señora. Otilia López Martínez?*

—*Sí, Señor.*

—*¿Es Usted la dueña de esta casa?*

Proudly. *"Sí, Señor."*

He raises his black briefcase and snaps it open, revealing the contents: official forms in triplicate. The tall man then waves a business card in his chubby fingers. Doña Otilia marvels at the pinkness of his skin—the same color as the bonnet for her grandchild number nine. Or was it number ten? She squints at the card through the screen, having left her reading glasses behind with her knitting. The card is embellished with the blue and gold seal of the city. It reads:

Donald K. Murphy   City of Tucson
Urban Renewal Project Relocation Counselor
Bilingual

• •

When the Old Pueblo's Urban Renewal Office was first established, interviews were conducted with residents of the area to be demolished. Preliminary work on relocation problems was mapped out. Thereafter, a marketability study and re-use appraisal of the neighborhood were completed. An eighty-two-member citizen's advisory redevelopment committee, which had been appointed by the mayor, held its first meeting in October, 1969. At this time subcommittees were formed to deal with planning, financing, relocation, legislation and public information. In April, 1971, the city's advisory committee adopted the subcommittee's report and recommendations for planning for the Old Pueblo District. The plan included a Community Center with a Music Hall, Theatre, and Concert Arena. Later stages of the plan called for an office plaza, condominiums, and a Mexican style village with restaurants and shops that would be a tourist attraction. Upon approval by the mayor and council, the financing of the plan was presented to the voters of Tucson who approved it by an overwhelming majority.

• •

PART III: 1976

Sam Morgan worked a toothpick in the gap between his front teeth to get at the piece of bacon rind that had been stuck there since breakfast. After he had dislodged the fragment of pork, he continued to chew on the toothpick, moving it dexterously from one side of his mouth to the other. He did this habitually, hence his nickname, Woody. To his coworkers at Johnson Demolition and Salvage Company, the toothpick had become an integral part of his personality, like the Dallas Cowboy cap he invariably wore to protect his ruddy face from the sun. In spite of the cap, the sensitive skin on his nose was always peeling from exposure.

Morgan's back felt stiff that morning, and he kept shifting his position in the metal seat of the bulldozer, adjusting a cushion against the small of his back. He used his right hand to operate the shift lever and his left to steer the bulldozer into position, lining it up with the gaping doorway of the old adobe house he was about to raze—number 57 in his plot map. The doors and windows of the house, and anything else salvageable and salable like bathroom and kitchen fixtures and usable lumber, had already been removed, and the walls and the roof of the humble structure had begun to sag in acceptance and resignation. This one's gonna be a cinch, Morgan thought matter-of-factly to himself. Maybe he and the crew could take an early lunch.

It was only 9:00, and although he had had his usual big breakfast—four eggs, pancakes, bacon, orange juice, and coffee—Morgan was already thinking about lunch. His wife had packed him his favorite—bologna sandwiches slathered with mayonnaise, and Hostess Twinkie cupcakes to wash down with Kool-Aid. He was looking forward not only to his meal, but to the camaraderie of the noon hour. He and the rest of the crew could always find a shady spot under a big old tree on the Mexican side of town. They would sit in a semi-circle, leaning against the rough bark, and boast about women and fishing and argue football. He had already picked out today's lunch site—two brooding tamaracks that towered in the empty lot behind house number 57.

Morgan was feeling lucky. Work had been steady since old man Johnson and his son had gotten a big contract with the city. Rumor had it that they had contributed generously to the mayor's reelection campaign, and rumor had it also that there were a lot of fat-cat bankers and contractors who were very happy. But Morgan had no interest in the wheeling and dealing of politics or high finance. The relevant thing to him was that there were over three hundred houses in thirty-four square blocks of city-owned land to be demolished. It would take at least a year and it paid union wages and overtime. Which was a darn sight better than working as a security man at the salvage yard out on the old Nogales Highway when there was no contract work. He disliked the tedium of the job, but what he disliked most was showing effete interior designers around, while they scoured the place for "antiques" and exclaimed over what Morgan dismissed as junk. That was woman's work. But operating the dozer took skill and being job foreman gave him status in his coworkers' eyes.

With the dump trucks and front loaders idling by, García, the flagman, signaled Morgan forward, keeping a wary eye all the while on neighborhood truants who might venture too close to falling debris. Morgan whistled the theme from "M*A*S*H" between the gap in his teeth and stepped on the accelerator. The bulldozer clanked and sputtered and spewed thick diesel smoke into the clear morning air. Morgan made a mental note to himself to spend a day overhauling it in the shop the next time they got rained out. With Morgan guiding it carefully, the dozer jolted forward slowly and at last met the wall of the old adobe with a resounding thud. The house shuddered but held. Morgan shifted into reverse and with García guiding him, backed up a hundred feet to gain momentum. He lurched forward and rammed again. There was a loud crashing sound and then what seemed to be a suspension of all sound— an ear-piercing muting of men, children, engines, birds, dogs, and idle conversation.

Then the old adobe house trembled, sighed, splintered, cracked, and collapsed in on itself with a small explosion, enveloped in a shroud of dust that mercifully hid its final hour from view.

Then the dusty veil rose like fine powder into the golden morning air, carried aloft by a sudden westerly breeze from the river valley. The dusty cloud, catching the sunlight, gained momentum and floated over City Hall and the County Buildings and La Ramada Condominiums and the Federal Building and the Hilton Resort Hotel—until it settled, mote by golden mote, footprint by tiny footprint, on the parched and abandoned bed of the river.

*P*atricia Blanco was born in Phoenix, Arizona. She currently
lives in San Francisco, California, where she teaches expository
writing at the University of San Francisco. She is working on a book
of poems, Night of Pink Stones. *The following story, written in the
style of an oral history, has the immediacy of listening to one's grandmother in her kitchen.*

ROSARIO MAGDALENO
Patricia Blanco

I

So when I came to Phoenix in 1945, I stayed with my cousins on Maricopa Street and shared a bed with my cousin Kika. The son, Chepe, had TB and I took one look at him and knew he was going to die. And you know they were terrible cooks. All they ever ate was beans and tortillas for breakfast and *avena* and coffee. And then the same thing for lunch. Then for supper maybe a little meat or *sopa*. So one day I said, "Why don't we make a salad?" and my Aunt Ricarda said, "Oh I don't like salads," and I said, "Well maybe Chepe would." And so she asked him and he said, "Yes, I would." So after that I started making things. I made salads and pot roasts and mole and enchiladas. And then I would make pies. My mother and father used to make pies out of dried fruit because at that time it was cheaper than fresh. I told Kika, "I think I'll make some pies," and she said, "Out of what?" So I made so many pies—apricot and apple and others. And I made fudge and *jamoncillo*. Oh, Chepe loved my fudge. He would tell Kika, "Why don't you ask Chayo to make some fudge," and so I'd make some for him.

It was such a hot summer and fall. He'd sit out on the screened porch with his cane—just sit and look out all day long, come in to eat, and go back out again. Sometimes my aunt would sit there and talk to him.

I always did love to bake since I was a little girl. On Sundays I would bake them muffins or this *pan batido* that Nana used to make. Then one night my Aunt came into the bedroom and said, *"Está muriendo Chepe."* My cousin Mary and I ran down to the church and knocked and knocked. Finally the priest came to the door and we told him and he said, *"Sí, ahorita voy."* That was the first time I'd noticed the nights were getting cooler. It was such a beautiful night. I remember there was a harvest moon. Then we ran back to the house and by the time we got there he had died. His brother was already loading the truck with his cane and clothes and mattress. He took them out to the dump that night and burned them.

II

You know, my cousin Mary was so spoiled. She never did any work around the house and she was always complaining about something, always wanting something that the other girls had. I used to tell her, "Go to school. You can't do anything without a high school education." So she finally decided to go. One Saturday we took the streetcar down to the Salvation Army and we bought an old Smith-Corona typewriter for her for fifteen dollars—one of those big, heavy black steel kind. She wrote a letter on it to her brother who was stationed in Germany just after the war. He wrote her back saying he was so proud of her that she was in school. I remember he told her, "I'll help you. I'll send you money."

But she wasn't serious. She didn't even last the month.

• • •

III

Once when my father was walking home from work, he found a dime on the sidewalk. So he went to Don Pedro's store and bought a loaf of bread and that night we ate those slices of bread as if they were cake. They tasted so good to us. We never had bread, only the corn tortillas my mother made. And at school it was considered a sign of prosperity to have bread to make sandwiches. At school we were ashamed of our burritos and we would try to hide them in our hands as we ate our lunch.

But you know there were times when we had more to eat during the Depression than we did before or afterwards because the government gave us surplus food. The welfare department set up an office in Miami and all the unemployed miners put in for welfare. At first they wouldn't give anything to people from Mexico and if you said anything they would tell you, "Go back to Mexico; we'll give you $250 to go back." Finally, one of the better-educated *mexicanos*, Mr. Baroldy, spoke to the higher-ups in Phoenix, and they said they could not deny aid to *mexicanos* since their children were born here. So they gave us half-rations. And later on after more interventions, they gave us full rations.

Oh, it was so nice when our order would come through. They would give us one quarter gunnysackful of carrots, turnips, beets; one pound each of meat and one pound of butter. It was years before I could eat beets after that. I ate so many during the Depression.

But before then, before those programs, sometimes we just didn't have enough. I remember one afternoon my sister and I were so hungry and my mother had just made some tortillas, but there were only enough for dinner. I wanted one so bad, so Carmen and I each took one. We went outside and played on the tire swing my father had made for us. It was a very cold day and there we were swinging and laughing, eating those tortillas still warm and I was so hungry. My dad happened to come home just then, and he asked us what we were eating. We told him we were eating the tortillas my mother had made for dinner. He only looked at us with a very serious face and said, "Why are you doing that? Don't you know that if you eat those now we won't have enough for everyone?" Oh, he had tears in his eyes he felt so bad. He hated saying that to us because he knew we were hungry. I'll never forget how he asked us that question. And I didn't know what to answer.

IV

My father used to say, "There's no more excess baggage than an orphan. They'll always point to you and tell you, 'You're too lazy. You eat too much.' "

Well you know, his father died when he was two and his mother when he was thirteen. At first, after he was orphaned, he went to live with his brother Lucio, but I guess he was never very happy there. He had so much pride; if someone would ask him, "Are you hungry?" he'd say no. "I'd just tighten my belt one more notch," he used to tell us. He never wanted to beg. I remember him saying to my mother, *"Cómo pasé hambres." Pobrecito. Sufrió mucho.* Later, his brother Nicolás took him in. And his sister-in-law never begrudged him. They were good to him. His brother told him, "I want you to finish school," so Nicolás sent him to school and he finished the sixth grade, which for Mexico at that time was an accomplishment. He was always grateful for that.

In Miami, on cloudy days, he would go to bed—just go to bed and stay there for hours, because they reminded him of the day his mother died.

. . .

V

Mijita, now that you've asked me how my father died, I'm going to tell you once and then I don't want you to ever ask me again. He died in the Claypool mines, in a mining accident. I was a junior in high school and someone came to our classroom with a message. When my teacher looked straight at me and motioned me into the hall, I just prayed, "Please don't let it be my mother." I knew it was one of them and I knew it would be better if we didn't lose my mother, with all those little children to take care of. Can you imagine—ten children and some still in diapers, without a mother?

Oh, that was a black day. So terribly sad. And the house that night—all of us crying and crying. Our dog, Otelo, howled all night. He knew, somehow. Every evening he used to listen for my father's footsteps coming up the *cañón*. He could recognize them from far away. When he'd hear my father coming, he'd cock up one ear and then run to the top of the hill and watch to see him coming. Then he'd run down to meet him and he'd be so happy. For months after my father died, he'd still wait at the top of the hill in the afternoons, watching for him to come walking home.

VI

Sometimes I'll ask Joe or Carmen about something from our childhood in Grover's Canyon, and they won't remember. Even though they're older than me and they lived there longer, they don't remember things the way I do. Like one time I was asking my brother Joe, "Remember that family that lived on the other side of the *cañón*, what was their name?" "I don't remember." "Of course you do; they had two boys that were friends with you." "No, I don't remember them."

But I remember that family so well. They had this little girl, Lydia, and we were friends. Oh, we used to play by the hour, jumping rope, sewing clothes for our dolls—we had dolls then, before the Depression. And Lydia gave me this metal box with a lid on it, a real cute little box, to keep my doll clothes in. One day my father saw it and said, "Oh, that would make a good box to keep my tools in." So I gave it to him; I was glad to give him something that he needed. And then when he died, my brother Cuco took the box and the tools and I told him one day, "That box should be mine. I gave it to my father because he wanted it, but it was mine; my friend Lydia gave it to me." But he never did give it back.

I have so many memories, things I remember seeing that are as clear as if they were right here before me. There was this *cañón* next to ours called Warrior Canyon and the *mexicanos* lived on the top half and the gringos lived on the bottom. There was this old woman that lived up at the top. You know in those days all old women wore black and she looked so old. Every day she would take a walk along the top of the *cañón*. That is one of my first memories—seeing her walking up there talking to herself, gesturing. She was a little retarded, actually. Or maybe she was crazy; I don't know. But she wasn't all there. There she would be on the top of the hill holding conversations with herself, shaking her finger. Sometimes we would wave and she would wave back. And sometimes her grandchildren would be looking for her and start calling to her. Something must have happened to her, to make her go crazy. But we were used to things like that. And we never asked why.

*K*athleen Ann González lives in San Jose, California, and teaches English at Santa Teresa High School. She was the recipient of a 1994 Summer Seminar grant through the National Endowment for the Humanities. In the following story the boyhood world of fathers and uncles is told through the words of a daughter and niece. "That Was Living" received a San Jose State University Phelan Award in 1989.

THAT WAS LIVING

Kathleen Ann González

My father used to tell stories of his childhood that absolutely fascinated me. He grew up in the Depression, and kids back then had to think of free ways to have fun, things that didn't require toys or special equipment or admission costs. Modern kids like me didn't know how to have real fun because we needed money to have it. We needed other things to entertain us. Not so my Dad.

Picture San Jose when Stevens Creek Boulevard was still a blacktopped road. Orchards didn't just dot the landscape, they dominated it. The miles of rich, black Santa Clara Valley soil outnumbered the few miles of concrete and asphalt, and everyone's backyard gardens flourished gloriously under the clear, unblemished sky. Little Santa Clara was still a sleepy town—unless you were little Gilbert and his brother and cousins striving to wake up the streets.

The kids all called Gilbert Four Eyes. Because he wore glasses? No. Because Gilbert's pants had holes in the knees that looked like eyes looking back. Or if you counted the holes in his seat, you would have to call him Six Eyes. Everyone had a nickname in those days. Cousin Joaquin was *Chapolín*—the grasshopper—because he couldn't walk anywhere, he had to skip. And Angelo was known as Ninnybottle because by age five you could still see him playing in the streets with the big rubber nipple of his baby bottle between his lips. They all called cousin Arthur Ol' Batatabloomers like a sweet potato because he had the baggiest drawers of the bunch. Nor were the girls exempt from such verbal shenanigans. Cousin Teresa went by Pinocchio since she had the bad habit of pulling on the end of her nose. Poor Maria Louisa caught the derision of her cousins by gossiping too often. *Moscamuerta*—the Dead Fly—was her curse.

Yet the saddest fate must have belonged to little moon-faced Carlos. He had the darkest complexion of the cousins and the sweetest disposition of all. One day Angelo, equipped with ninnybottle, was playing in the yard when the Devil jumped on his shoulder and tickled his ear. Looking over at Carlos, Angelo couldn't help shouting, "Chocolate bar! Chocolate bar!" For Carlos, this was devastation. He froze, and huge, glistening tears wept from his black eyes as he looked at his cousin. The other kids gathered round to join in the chant. "Chocolate bar!" "Carlos is a chocolate bar!" How heartless kids can be. But it was later, after World War II when Carlos was dying of cancer, that Angelo stood steadfastly by his side and would not leave him. Carlos would not utter a single epithet throughout his painful dying; Angelo always said, "That's the mark of a true gentleman."

Of course, adults were not exempt from this nickname game. Tio Pepe, better known as *Pies de Tablas* or Flatfoot, had worked for years in the boiler room of the Pratt-Low Cannery to earn his name. Even Gilbert's papa had a nickname—*Pintaíscho* or the Painted One, because his run-in with smallpox left scars like paint marks all over his face. We've come so far since then. Nowadays, kids only have to worry about acne. Gilbert knew better than to call his papa anything but "Sir." Some of the cousins, however, were not so respectful (or maybe they just ran faster). Uncle Frank, or tio Paco, who smoked that bitter Tuxedo-brand tobacco, was taunted with the epithet *Paco Retaco*. Maybe he wasn't really "shaped like a taco," but his broken leg from his Pratt-Low days kept him from catching up with his abusers.

But is it abuse or fun? In fun, the kids could be so irreverent, too. My dad tells of a humid summer evening when he and Joaquin were wandering around downtown Santa Clara and got themselves into mischief. Santa Clara evenings are so beautiful—the earth keeps its warmth from soaking up the daylight sunshine, and it is a delight to feel the toasty dirt under one's feet. A little breeze wafts down off the Almaden foothills and ruffles the leaves on the big walnut trees. This is how I recall summer as a child, when it's so tempting to stroll along the streets of the neighborhood, so I can picture Gilbert and Joaquin wandering down Franklin Street by Santa Clara University just looking for something to do.

That night there happened to be a congregation of evangelists meeting to hear the stump speaker. They had gathered in a dusty brown tent in the dirt lot downtown by the post office on the corner of Monroe and Franklin. The piano clanged and the preacher bellowed. The followers rolled on the swept dirt floor in the ecstasy of their faith. As Gilbert and he shuffled along kicking their shoes in the earth, Joaquin spotted a shininess in the weeds of the empty lot and stooped to pick up the broken knife. Mischief gleamed in his childish eye. He and Gilbert stealthily crept closer to the Holy Rollers' tent, keeping their footsteps to a silent patter, until they reached its side. Fwack, Fwack. The ropes snapped apart, the tent collapsing in a heap over its inhabitants. "Praises be!" cried the folks from the floor. The piano continued to bang as two guilty cousins ran all the way home to Lewis Street.

Gilbert and Joaquin could always forget their misdeeds by committing more the next day. They might play at "the Pit." They might make rubber guns. Or they might have weed wars with the Portuguese kids on the next street.

"Mama, Fred and I are going to play at the Pit," Gilbert

would cry as the two of them slid out the back door hiding the mischievous grins on their faces.

"All right, boys. Alfredo, you watch after your little brother."

Out at the Pit, the boys would have a field day scurrying through the wreckage looking for broken wheels and skates, ball bearings, inner tubes, bottle tops, and anything else fanciful or useful for their wild imaginations. The rats scurried through the wreckage, too, but with the different plan of hiding from young boys with good aim.

The Pit. Needless to say, Mama didn't know that the Pit was the secret code name for the city dump. When Papa came home from work and asked where the boys were, he didn't expect to hear the Pit either, but he could decipher the inexpert code name and know Fred and Gilbert's secret. Off he marched to drag the boys home.

Papa made another famous march one time at the old swimming hole. Little Gilbert and Fred wheeled out their one rickety bike, Fred pumping Gilbert on the handlebars. It was much harder to pedal on those dirt lanes and blacktops, but I suppose there was less traffic for the bikers to fear. They traveled down Trimble Road. Back then, Trimble was one lonely lane that led to the next sleepy town called Milpitas. You wouldn't recognize Trimble now as Montague Expressway. The boys had wheedled a package of weenies from Mama—it was their turn to bring them—and the Portuguese boys brought summer squash and horse beans from their backyard gardens. Once at the creek bed, they made a bonfire, wet the food, and buried it in the ashes to fix themselves a true tramp-style meal while they swam in the water hole.

Now, as I've said, this was the Depression. Only rich kids had money for swimming trunks, and Mama better not catch her kids cutting the legs off their trousers, even if there were holes in the knees. What else could Gilbert and Fred do but join the others skinny-dipping?

Just picture the bright sun sifting cozily down through

the trees, creating shadow patterns on the creek bed. The boys recline around the burning logs, accidentally dropping weenies in the fire from time to time, digging squash from the ashes to then toss from palm to palm while it cooled. A near pastoral perfection.

Suddenly, silence broken by a piercing whistle. I can even hear that whistle in my head because my father used it to call my brothers and me when we were children. Gilbert and Fred froze because they knew it meant only one thing: Papa.

There stood Papa on the bridge above them. There stood Papa viewing them in the buff. There stood Papa giving them the Look. Papa disappeared. The boys dressed as fast as they could, pulled the clothes over their still-wet bodies, and hopped on their one bike to pedal at breakneck speed down Trimble Road to home.

"Don't ever swim there again," said Papa in that even, calm voice that struck worse fear than a bellowing threat.

Gilbert always wondered why Papa never said any more to them about the water hole after that day, why they never got a thrashing. But they knew they had done wrong.

The days spent with the Portuguese kids weren't always so pastoral and peaceful, though. At other times a bitter rivalry caused war, battlefront, and artillery. Then there were rubber guns.

My dad made these simple wooden toys for me when I was a kid, and I thought them better than any of the fancy plastic popguns or space ray guns. With a rubber gun, I could be on even par with my bigger, older brothers because I was the feline, stealthy little sister who could use guerrilla tactics. But back in Dad's childhood memory, those rubber guns meant serious playing and a means of survival.

A rubber gun consisted of a chunk of wood cut in the shape of a gun—usually a handgun or rifle, a clothespin snitched from Mama's line, and cut strips of inner tubes from the Pit or the one bicycle. The inner-tube bands were stretched from the nose of the gun to the clothespin at the back, which acted as the trigger. Joaquin, one of the more ingenious cousins, had fashioned a machine gun by adding a wooden wheel to his rifle with a volley of twenty-five clothespins. He had the further advantage of confounding his enemy should his gun fall into their hands because they wouldn't know the sequence to shoot the bands in and would instead shoot themselves. Another of the boys had discovered that knotting the inner tube in the middle made his shot go further and harder, leaving a swollen scarlet welt on its target's arm.

The kids would hide behind the cars, garbage cans, or whitewashed fences and aim at their rivals. All of the families on Monroe Street were Spanish or Mexican, but if the cousins crept one block over out of their territory onto Lewis, they entered the street of the Portuguese. Gilbert's family was the only Spanish one on the block. Perhaps without understanding their own feelings, the cousins saw this one difference as reason enough for battle.

If rubber guns didn't work or if the kids couldn't find discarded inner tubes that week, they could always resort to using weed bombs. Weeds were plentiful and free and fast and easy to fashion into potent weapons. Just pull up a handful of weeds with a good-sized hunk of dirt on the bottom, soak the dirt in some gutter water to make it extra sticky and wet, add a hefty rock to be particularly nasty, pack the dirt bomb into a solid sphere, and chuck it at full speed at *el loco* across the street. The weeds make a wonderful comet tail at the back to direct your aim and accelerate the bomb.

Little Four Eyes squatted behind the walnut tree on the corner. From the corner of his eye he spied a movement across the street on Lewis Street. Four Eyes turned his head and motioned over his shoulder to Ninnybottle, "There's the enemy!" The two of them gathered forces, pulled together their stockpile of rocks and weeds, and conferred on how best to attack. The enemy hadn't realized he'd been spotted. Ninnybottle fired first, fwoosh, getting gutter water all over his hand-me-down shirt and down his arm in the process. "Rats," he muttered. But the shot had struck its mark. The enemy was hit! Up he stood, spattered mud and grass dripping down the side of his face. "Papa's gonna get you!" yelled Fred across the street to Gilbert as he wiped his cheek with his sleeve. Ninnybottle and Four Eyes just giggled as they slunk off to gloat over their victory.

Angelo and Gilbert often paired together—or were paired together by the others—because they were the two littlest of the cousins. But they were happy to stick together, even when victimized, because it was better than being a single victim. In fact, whenever the cousins played "Tarzan, King of the Jungle," Gilbert and Angelo were always duped.

In the empty lot behind the Trinity Church on Monroe and Liberty stood two ancient fig trees. Their limbs were gnarled and tangled in muscular contortions, their leaves and branches twined in and about each other to form an endless, answerless labyrinth. Most of the kids knew just how to crawl among the puzzle to find their way in and out. But there were penalties for those who were not so smart.

This was the war between the Warriors and the Peasants in the great Tarzan trees. Of course, it was also the war between the Big and the Little. Angelo and Gilbert were the Little, the Peasants. All the others were the Big. If the Big decided the Little were being mean to them—and this was a totally arbitrary decision based on whether or not they felt mean—they could sentence the Little to a stay in the hoosegow where the leaves and branches and limbs wove so tightly together as to form an inescapable deep cell from which the Little could not escape, being too short.

"That Arthur, he's so mean," grumbled Gilbert from inside their tree prison. "We've gotta go see the new Tarzan movie next Saturday and find out how he gets even."

"I just wish I could call the animals to help us," said Angelo. "Where's Cheeta when you need him?"

The only way they could escape the dungeon was to give their captors the secret password: "A gotcha boom ba oh beedy um." But do you think Gilbert could remember this?

"A gotcha." "A bootcha." "A botcha goom."

"Rats."

I wonder if that's why Angelo developed a photographic memory later in life.

So Gilbert and Angelo and Fred and all the cousins would find a way to get to the movies on Saturday so they could cheer their heroes Tarzan or the Lone Ranger. The movies were only ten cents then, but in those poor days that was a nearly impossible amount to gather. The cousins couldn't let down their heroes by not going to the movies. Where there's a will, there's a way.

The "way" was through Pepsi-Cola, an upstart company at that time. Five Pepsi bottle tops and a penny would get Gilbert into the show where he could cheer Tom Mix or Buck Rogers, laugh with Spanky or Groucho, or yell along with Tarzan. Gilbert and Fred arranged with all the local gas stations and Ma and Pa groceries to clean out their pop machines and collect all the bottle tops.

Of course, since Pepsi-Cola was just a baby, not many people bought that soda at that time. This left the boys with bags of extra bottle tops after they had collected all the Pepsi ones. What to do? Well, why not pave the backyard walkway! Just what I would have thought of. The walkway became a steady chore for the boys. From the back stoop, past the walnut tree, by the toolshed, to the vegetable garden, Gilbert and Fred would smack the bottle tops into the soft soil. Turn one over, heft the wooden mallet, and tap, tap. Take another, tap, tap. The job never ended because once the first layer settled deeper in the dirt, another layer had to be added. Wooden mallet, tap, tap.

Even with all the hard work and poverty, I envy the children of my dad's generation because they had opportunities I will never have. That's a switch—people usually think that my generation has more opportunities since we have computers and TV and pavement. But I disagree. I look back at little Gilbert and Fred and wish I could have swum in the creeks when they still consisted of water instead of rocks. I wish I could have looked forward for months to the traveling Ringling Brothers instead of being bored by having too many entertainments to choose from. And, most of all, I wish I could have pulled mounds of dripping vermillion watermelon in my little red wagon back from the pickling plant to my Santa Clara home. That's why I envy Gilbert most.

Watermelon quenches that summer thirst in the dry heat of Santa Clara. The Santa Clara Pickling and Preserve Factory stood downtown beside the Santa Clara Mortuary and behind the Casa Grande Theater. On Washington between Franklin and Liberty, it was only a few blocks from Gilbert's home. Those few blocks were a long journey for Four Eyes's little legs, but it would be worth every mouthwatering bite. The pickling factory wanted only the rinds, so they threw their unwanted red hearts in the bin out back. What a field day for *los niños*! Fred used to say that someday when he was rich he would buy himself a whole watermelon. But with the melon hearts practically in his backyard, Fred could live like a king in the middle of the Depression. The king of hearts!

The kids would often tramp down as a group to the pickling factory and then load up their wagons and tubs and sacks with all the watermelon they could carry. They would play the child Saint Nick and deliver the fruit to the relatives that lived all along Monroe Street. Gilbert's tia Rosario, Nino Martin, and Nina Lola, Piez de Tablas, and Paco Retaco. It was important that the cousins be nice to Nino Martin because his was the home where the recalcitrant cousins were sent for "reeducation."

Despite the bottle-top hunts or the watermelon trips, Gilbert and the others never knew they were poor. The Depression raged, work was scarce, and they often had to do without; yet their basic needs were always met. Somehow Mama found a way to make the beans stretch a little further, and Papa was a wizard at finding a use for every last nail, scrap of wood, or ounce of human energy. Wasting was simply not considered.

It wasn't until the cousins went to Fremont Elementary that they realized they were different from other kids. Many of the little girls had starched new frocks and Shirley Temple curls. Or the boys would not be wearing hand-me-downs from previous generations of cousins. Gilbert realized his own poverty one day when it was time for milk and graham crackers during recess. Gilbert had no nickel but he still got his snack. Someone (his teacher?) was watching out for him.

It's funny for me to think of all the cousins as children running around the streets of Santa Clara. To me, Monroe was the old part of town where my great Aunt Rose and Uncle Dort lived. It was the area of my rival high school, first called Santa Clara High and then Buchser Junior High. I can hardly picture that the house where I grew up in Mariposa Gardens was a prune orchard on the outskirts of town when my father was growing up.

I know the cousins as middle-aged people with children my own age and older. I picture them gathered together at the funeral of Maria Louisa or at the wedding of Joaquin's son, where I have seen them laughing and reliving the days of their youth, the stories I have just recounted. I imagine them with their nicknames. I wonder if I will ever have the chance to relive my own childhood with my youthful friends in this city of Santa Clara that so swiftly grows and changes and dissipates out to the hills.

*A*rlene Mestas is from Manassa in the San Luis Valley of southern Colorado and is a member of a prominent ranching family. She has been a high school English teacher and administrator in northern New Mexico schools. The humor in this story of her father's funeral undercuts the somberness of the occasion.

HOW PANCHO WAS NEARLY LATE TO HIS OWN FUNERAL

Arlene Mestas

P ancho, my dad, was always late. He would not and could not be hurried. His tardiness was legendary. On Sundays, he would look after his animals, talk to God about the weather, and then he showered at the hour Mass began.

Midway through the sermon we would enter church. Late to Mass, late to meetings. And even late when he took my brother to the S.A.T., which began promptly at 8:00 A.M. He probably thought it was similar to a social, but my brother was not allowed to take the test, as much as my dad argued with the test director. Even the local butcher told stories on my dad. He said that they often watched my dad drive up with a steer to be butchered just as they were closing up for the night. Apparently, he had done it often enough that they too knew my dad could not be hurried. He took me to my wedding about half an hour late. My husband-to-be's family was pacing outside the church, probably thinking that their son was about to marry an unreliable woman. But I felt my dad was trying to hang on to me as long as possible. The summer sky looked like *View of*

Toledo that evening when my dad refused to rush me to the church in Pojoaque.

"You will be late to your own funeral," my mother would rail at him. She often started the car to warm it up before driving to Mass. She sat in the car ten to fifteen minutes before my dad finished showering. He'd walk out, grinning, his green eyes twinkling, and wearing his Stetson—his rancher's trademark.

I was getting ready for a camping trip and Fourth of July family reunion in El Rito Canyon. My daughters had already gone ahead with other family members, who had come in from as far away as Los Angeles. I had just spent the weekend with my mom and dad in Alamosa and had returned to Española to get ready. My dad had been hospitalized Thursday, June 28, because he was not feeling well. When he was released, he'd been given medication to speed the blood flow. He felt young again and full of energy, he said. But after trying to close a barn gate, he'd gotten very tired and impatient with himself.

"My cowboy days are over," he said to me Friday evening as we sat on the sofa. "I get tired too fast."

"But, Dad, you're just out of the hospital—really, you shouldn't even be out there. You know I can feed the calves." I glanced around looking for a second from my mother. But her anxiety kept her in the kitchen. She knew my dad was dying, something none of us would admit. She had told us that she was afraid of being left alone with Dad. I think all of us knew he was close to death, but none of us would give voice to this horrible thought, except my mom.

A few weeks before, when my sister left for Spain, I heard a voice warning me. I hugged my sister good-bye while a sole thought came to me loudly—"Do you want us to call you if Dad dies?" This gloomy thought came from nowhere and hung over me as I waved good-bye.

Later she told us, "He looked at me as if he were looking at me for the last time, and I just had to come back to give him one last hug."

My brother Kiko, who was in California on vacation, had postponed his trip several times because he had misgivings about leaving Dad alone at the ranch. While I had been there over the weekend, my brother called to check on everything. I had wanted to yell at him to get home because Dad was sick. But, of course, I couldn't say that—we were all gathered around the phone to make small talk. My dad sat there listening to me and my mother, monitoring the conspiracy of silence regarding his condition.

And so I left Saturday afternoon to get ready for the reunion. My mom and dad were on their way to an old and dear friend's fiftieth wedding anniversary. I think Dad had probably sweet-talked the doctor into letting him out just so that he could go dancing one last time. A dance with Doña Sebastiana, *la huesuda*, who had come to waltz off with him. Pancho was just trying to pack in as much living as possible before he left us.

Early on Tuesday morning, July 3, my mom called to tell me Dad was back in the hospital and really was very sick; I should hurry if I wanted to see him alive. I thought it was just nerves on my mother's part, as she frightened easily. I had just seen him two days ago and he was fine. Then my younger sister, Esther, called to say that Dad had had a very mild heart attack; but he was feeling well—almost good enough to go to the reunion.

Just as at a birthing, the calls from Vince, my brother-in-law, came faster and faster. "Your dad is really sick." The second one, "You'd better hurry." And then, "There's no hurry now." My phone bill recorded the three collect calls that brought the painful news.

And so my dad died with my mom, Esther, and his younger son, Johnny, in attendance. Judi was in Spain and Kiko was who-knew-where in California. We had told him not to call every night since everything was all right. I put the bag of pretzels down and began packing another type of bag of clothing for myself and family.

I arrived in Alamosa early in the evening, after having

gone to El Rito to pick up my daughters and to inform family members of my dad's death. Family members sat around and talked about my dad while waiting for other family members to arrive. My sister-in-law Vicki walked in in tears. "Go see Johnny," she told me. "He needs you." He and I were the youngest and the oldest—the bookends. My brother, who had been with my dad when he died, now refused to accept that my dad was gone. As he and his wife had driven up he had pointed to the light in the corrals and said—"Dad's waiting for me. I've got to go help him." He refused to come into the house and wanted to go into the corrals, where Dad waited for him. I took Johnny by the arm and coaxed him to come in. He continued to want to go to the corrals but didn't make a move to go out. Johnny was given a sedative and put to bed. The next day he remembered not wanting to come into the house. There are many people who have witnessed a loved one taking his leave. It is possible that Johnny did see Dad in the corrals. Now I wish that I had gone to the corrals with him.

Earlier that evening we had called the tour that Judi was with in Spain, and they told us that she had gone to Morocco and would be back in three days. She called the following night about two in the morning. "Please don't bury him until I get home. I have to see him." So we agreed to wait to bury him.

In the meantime, Kiko and his family moseyed home and stopped at an aunt's in Farmington before hearing of Dad. We were at the mortuary the evening of the fourth to view the body when Kiko arrived, having driven at *mata caballo* speed. His wife, Patsy, was white from the terrifying drive and their children were crying.

Judi was having a terrible time making connections from Spain.

The Hermanos prayed a rosary for my dad in Manassa while we continued to wait for the last family member to arrive. She sat in a plane in Madrid five hours waiting for the fog to lift and missed a connecting flight from New York to Saint Louis.

We had another rosary in Alamosa on Friday. Most members of the very large extended Mestas family had arrived for this rosary.

In Saint Louis, Judi missed a connecting flight to Albuquerque and had to spend the night there.

On Saturday morning we attended the Requiem Mass. It was followed by a dinner in Manassa. There seemed to be hundreds of us, all closely connected to Pancho. He was taken back to Alamosa to spend the weekend at the mortuary. I picked Judi up on Saturday night in Albuquerque; we were crying and embracing each other as we remembered our last moments with Dad.

Finally, my dad was laid to rest on Monday. Had it not been my dad, we would have laughed at the *difunto* that rolled around like an *alverjón maduro* from one rosary to another.

"May the angels of the Lord come to meet you," sang my cousins as my dad was lowered into the ground.

. . . .

PART II

Our Land, Our Lives

*J*udith Ortiz Cofer is the author of the novel The Line of the
Sun *(1989).* Terms of Survival *(1987) is a collection of her
poetry.* The Latin Deli *(1993) and* Silent Dancing *(1990) are
compilations of poetry, prose, and personal essays. A native of Puerto
Rico, she is associate professor of English at the University of Georgia.
"Twist and Shout" appeared in* The Latin Deli.

TWIST AND SHOUT

Judith Ortiz Cofer

I t's 1967, summer, and I'm as restless as all of America. The Beatles are inundating the airwaves in our apartment building, drowning out our parents' salsas. My mother has left me alone to keep an eye on the red kidney beans boiling for dinner, while she goes to the bodega for *orégano* or some other ingredient she needs. She had tried in vain to make me understand what it is, but I have resisted her Spanish. As soon as she has gone down one flight of stairs, I run up two, to 5-B, where the music has been playing loud enough for me to hear from my room. The door is unlocked and I burst in on Manny dancing with his sister, Amelia, who is fifteen and wants to be called Amy. Amy's best friend Cecilia (Ceci) is stretched out on the sofa like Elizabeth Taylor in *Cleopatra*. They are all singing along with the Beatles' "Twist and Shout." Manny and Amy are dancing too close for brother and sister. They are grinding their bodies together, chest to chest and hip to hip.

I have a crush on Manny, who is Puerto Rican like me but

has blue eyes and curly blond hair. His father was an American. Amy is dark like me: different fathers.

Manny suddenly grabs me from where I have flattened myself against the door to watch them dance. He's much taller than I am and too old to be in the eighth grade—fourteen. Their mother moves them from place to place in the city a lot, so they've both been held back a couple of grades. All the Puerto Rican girls are crazy about Manny. He's a great dancer, and there's a rumor—not a virgin. Manny pushes Amy away and wraps himself around me. I feel my heart pounding against my rib cage like when I jump double-Dutch rope in the school playground. I'm using my arms and elbows against him, to try to get a little air between us. I want to get close to Manny but not so close that I can't breathe. I'm a little scared at the way his body is moving and his hot mouth is pressing on my head. He is singing along with John Lennon, and I feel every word on my skin, since his wet lips are traveling down my neck. I manage to twist my face away just as Lennon hits the high note; over his shoulder I see Amy and Ceci making out on the sofa. *They are kissing on the mouth.* Their faces are contorted into what looks like pain but what I have learned to recognize, from the Spanish TV soap operas my mother and I watch at night, as passion.

Manny has me pinned to the wall and is grinding his hips into mine. It hurts a little, since I'm skinny and my pelvic bones stick out, but it feels good too. I think this is what I came up to 5-B for, but too much all at once. Suddenly I remember my mother's red kidney beans. I have a vision of them boiling down into a sticky, sour paste. That's what can happen if you don't watch them. The thought of what my mother would do gives me the strength I need to pry myself out of Manny's iron grasp. He springs away from me and into a spin like one of the Temptations—what a good dancer he is. He could be on TV. I watch him land on the tangle of arms and legs that are Amy and Ceci on the sofa. Like an octopus having a snack, they pull him down and engulf him.

I hear them laughing above the music and the group's throat-scraping final shout.

As I enter our kitchen, I smell the beans: almost done. Their shells will be tender but still intact. I add a little water—just to be on the safe side. Then, still feeling a little weak in the knees, I sit down at the table to watch them.

*H*elena *María Viramontes teaches at Cornell University. She has been coordinator of the Los Angeles Latino Writers Association and literary editor of* Xhismearte *magazine, and she has received the University of California, Irvine, Chicano Literary Award.* The Moths and Other Stories *(1985) is her collection of short stories. Her work has appeared in several anthologies. She has a novel entitled* Under the Feet of Jesus *(1995). In "Miss Clairol," ten-year-old Ofelia (known as Champ) helps her mother Arlene prepare for a date.*

MISS CLAIROL

Helena María Viramontes

Arlene and Champ walk to Kmart. The store is full of bins mounted with bargain buys from T-shirts to rubber sandals. They go to aisle 23, Cosmetics. Arlene, wearing bell-bottom jeans two sizes too small, can't bend down to the Miss Clairol boxes, asks Champ.

—Which one, *amá?* —asks Champ, chewing her thumb nail.

—Shit, *mija,** I dunno. —Arlene smacks her gum, contemplating the decision. —Maybe I need a change, *tú sabes.* What do you think? —She holds up a few blond strands with black roots. Arlene has burned the softness of her hair with peroxide; her hair is stiff, breaks at the ends, and she needs plenty of Aqua Net hairspray to tease and tame her ratted hair, then folds it back into a high lump behind her head. For the last few months she has been a platinum "Light Ash" blonde, before that a Miss Clairol "Flame" redhead, before that Champ couldn't even identify the color—somewhere between

---

* An abbreviation of *mi hija*, or *my daughter*, this is a term of endearment used by women when addressing friends or younger women.

orange and brown, a "Sun Bronze." The only way Champ knows her mother's true hair color is by her roots, which, like death, inevitably rise to the truth.

—I hate it, *tú sabes*, when I can't decide. —Arlene is wearing a pink, strapless tube top. Her stomach spills over the hip-hugger jeans. Spits the gum onto the floor. —Fuck it. —And Champ follows her to the rows of nail polish, next to the Maybelline rack of makeup, across the false eyelashes that look like insects on display in clear, plastic boxes. Arlene pulls out a particular color of nail polish, looks at the bottom of the bottle for the price, puts it back, gets another. She has a tattoo of purple XXX's on her left finger like a ring. She finally settles for a purple-blackish color, Ripe Plum, that Champ thinks looks like the color of Frankenstein's nails. She looks at her own stubby nails, chewed and gnawed.

Walking over to the eye shadows, Arlene slowly slinks out another stick of gum from her back pocket, unwraps and crumbles the wrapper into a little ball, lets it drop on the floor. Smacks the gum.

—Grandpa Ham used to make chains with these gum wrappers —she says, toeing the wrapper on the floor with her rubber sandals, her toes dotted with old nail polish. —He started one, *tú sabes*, that went from room to room. That was before he went nuts —she says, looking at the price of magenta eye shadow. —*¿Sabes qué?* What do you think? —lifting the eye shadow to Champ.

—I dunno know —responds Champ, shrugging her shoulders the way she always does when she is listening to something else, her own heartbeat, what Gregorio said on the phone yesterday, shrugs her shoulders when Miss Smith says, OFELIA, answer my question. She is too busy thinking of things people otherwise dismiss like parentheses, but stick to her like gum, like a hole on a shirt, like a tattoo, and sometimes she wishes she weren't born with such adhesiveness. The chain went from room to room, round and round like a web, she remembers. That was before he went nuts.

—Champ. You listening? Or in la-la land again? —Arlene
has her arms akimbo on a fold of flesh, pissed.

—I said, I dunno know —Champ whines back, still looking at the wrapper on the floor.

—Well you better learn, *tú sabes*, and fast too. Now think,
will this color go good with Pancha's blue dress? —Pancha is
Arlene's *comadre*. Since Arlene has a special date tonight, she
lent Arlene her royal blue dress that she keeps in a plastic bag
at the end of her closet. The dress is made of chiffon, with
satinlike material underlining, so that when Arlene first tried it
on and strutted about, it crinkled sounds of elegance. The
dress fits too tight. Her plump arms squeeze through, her hips
breathe in and hold their breath, the seams do all they can to
keep the body contained. But Arlene doesn't care as long as it
sounds right.

—I think it will —Champ says, and Arlene is very
pleased.

—Think so? So do I, *mija*.

They walk out the double doors and Champ never remembers her mother paying.

It is four in the afternoon, but already Arlene is preparing for
the date. She scrubs the tub, Art Labo on the radio, drops crystals of Jean Naté into the running water, lemon scent rises with
the steam. The bathroom door ajar, she removes her top and
her breasts flop and sag, pushes her jeans down with some dif-
ficulty, kicks them off, and steps in the tub.

—*Mija. MIJA* —she yells. —*Mija*, give me a few bobby
pins. —She is worried about her hair frizzing and so wants to
pin it up.

Her mother's voice is faint because Champ is in the
closet. There are piles of clothes on the floor, hangers thrown
askew and tangled, shoes all piled up or thrown on the top
shelf. Champ is looking for her mother's special dress. Pancha
says every girl has one at the end of her closet.

—Goddamn it, Champ.

Amidst the dirty laundry, the black hole of the closet, she finds nothing.

—NOW.

—Alright, ALRIGHT. Cheeze *amá*, stop yelling —says Champ, and goes in the steamy bathroom, checks the drawers, hairbrushes jump out, rollers, strands of hair, rummages through bars of soap, combs, eye shadows, finds nothing; pulls open another drawer, powder, empty bottles of oil, manicure scissors, Kotex, dye instructions crinkled and botched, finally, a few bobby pins.

After Arlene pins up her hair, she asks Champ, —*¿Sabes qué?* Should I wear my hair up? Do I look good with it up? — Champ is sitting on the toilet.

—Yea, *amá*, you look real pretty.

—Thanks, *mija* —says Arlene. —*¿Sabes qué?* When you get older I'll show you how you can look just as pretty —and she puts her head back, relaxes, like the Calgon commercials.

Champ lies on her stomach, TV on to some variety show with pogo-stick dancers dressed in outfits of stretchy material and glitter. She is wearing one of Gregorio's white T-shirts, the ones he washes and bleaches himself so that the whiteness is impeccable. It drapes over her deflated ten-year-old body like a dress. She is busy cutting out Miss Breck models from the stacks of old magazines Pancha found in the back of her mother's garage. Champ collects the array of honey-colored-haired women, puts them in a shoe box with all her other special things.

Arlene is in the bathroom, wrapped in a towel. She has painted her eyebrows so that the two are arched and even, penciled thin and high. The magenta shades her eyelids. The towel slips, reveals one nipple blind from a cigarette burn, a date to forget. She rewraps the towel, likes her reflection, turns to her profile for additional inspection. She feels good, turns up the radio to . . . your love. For your loveeeee, I will do anything, I will do anything, forrr your love. For your kiss . . .

Champ looks on. From the open bathroom door, she can see Arlene, anticipation burning like a cigarette from her lips, sliding her shoulders to the ahhhh ahhhhh, and pouting her lips until the song ends. And Champ likes her mother that way.

Arlene carefully stretches black eyeliner, like a fallen question mark, outlines each eye. The work is delicate, her hand trembles cautiously, stops the process to review the face with each line. Arlene the mirror is not Arlene the face who has worn too many relationships, gotten too little sleep. The last touch is the chalky, beige lipstick.

By the time she is finished, her ashtray is full of cigarette butts, Champ's variety show is over, and Jackie Gleason's dancing girls come on to make kaleidoscope patterns with their long legs and arms. Gregorio is still not home, and Champ goes over to the window, checks the houses, the streets, corners, roams the sky with her eyes.

Arlene sits on the toilet, stretches up her nylons, clips them to her girdle. She feels good thinking about the way he will unsnap her nylons, and she will unroll them slowly, point her toes when she does.

Champ opens a can of Campbell soup, finds a perfect pot in the middle of a stack of dishes, pulls it out to the threatening rumbling of the tower. She washes it out, pours the contents of the red can, turns the knob. After it boils, she puts the pan on the sink for it to cool down. She searches for a spoon.

Arlene is romantic. When Champ begins her period, she will tell her things that only women can know. She will tell her about the first time she made love with a boy, her awkwardness and shyness forcing them to go under the house, where the cool, refined soil made a soft mattress. How she closed her eyes and wondered what to expect, or how the penis was the softest skin she had ever felt against her, how it tickled her, searched for a place to connect. She was eleven and his name was Harry. She will not tell Champ that her first fuck was a guy named Puppet who ejaculated prematurely, at the sight of her apricot vagina, so plump and fuzzy. —*Pendejo* —she said —you got it all over me. —She rubbed the gooey substance off her legs, her belly, in disgust. Ran home to tell Rat and Pancha, her mouth open with laughter.

Arlene powder-puffs under her arms, between her breasts, tilts a bottle of Love Cries perfume and dabs behind her ears, neck and breasts for those tight caressing songs which permit them to grind their bodies together until she can feel a bulge in his pants and she knows she's in for the night.

Jackie Gleason is a bartender in a saloon. He wears a black bow tie, a white apron, and is polishing a glass. Champ is watching him, sitting in the radius of the gray light, eating her soup from the pot.

Arlene is a romantic. She will dance until Pancha's dress turns a different color, dance until her hair becomes undone, her hips jiggering and quaking beneath a new pair of hosiery, her mascara shadowing under her eyes from the perspiration of the ritual dance, spinning herself into Miss Clairol, and stopping only when it is time to return to the sewing factory, time to wait out the next date, time to change hair color. Time to remember or to forget.

Champ sees Arlene from the window. She can almost hear Arlene's nylons rubbing against one another, hear the crinkling sound of satin when she gets in the blue and white shark-finned Dodge. Champ yells goodbye. It all sounds so right to Arlene, who is too busy cranking up the window to hear her daughter.

*J*ulia Alvarez was born in the Dominican Republic and came to the United States when she was ten years old. Homecoming, her first book of poetry, was published in 1986 and will be republished with new poems in 1995. Her latest book is a novel, In the Time of the Butterflies (1994). Julia has taught poetry in several schools. In this short excerpt from her acclaimed novel How the Garcia Girls Lost Their Accents (1991), she captures perfectly the fear and the wonder of a young immigrant girl from the Dominican Republic who has never seen snow before.

SNOW

Julia Alvarez

YOLANDA

Our first year in New York we rented a small apartment with a Catholic school nearby, taught by the Sisters of Charity, hefty women in long black gowns and bonnets that made them look peculiar, like dolls in mourning. I liked them a lot, especially my grandmotherly fourth-grade teacher, Sister Zoe. I had a lovely name, she said, and she had me teach the whole class how to pronounce it. *Yo-lan-da.* As the only immigrant in my class, I was put in a special seat in the first row by the window, apart from the other children so that Sister Zoe could tutor me without disturbing them. Slowly, she enunciated the new words I was to repeat: *laundromat, cornflakes, subway, snow.*

Soon I picked up enough English to understand holocaust was in the air. Sister Zoe explained to a wide-eyed classroom what was happening in Cuba. Russian missiles were being assembled, trained supposedly on New York City. President Kennedy, looking worried too, was on the television at home, explaining we might have to go to war against the Communists. At school, we had air-raid drills: an ominous bell would go off and we'd file into the hall, fall to the floor, cover our heads with our coats, and imagine our hair falling out, the bones in our arms going soft. At home, Mami and my sisters and I said a rosary for world peace. I heard new vocabulary: *nuclear bomb, radioactive fallout, bomb shelter.* Sister Zoe explained how it would happen. She drew a picture of a mushroom on the blackboard and dotted a flurry of chalk marks for the dusty fallout that would kill us all.

The months grew cold, November, December. It was dark when I got up in the morning, frosty when I followed my breath to school. One morning as I sat at my desk daydreaming out the window, I saw dots in the air like the ones Sister Zoe had drawn—random at first, then lots and lots. I shrieked, "Bomb! Bomb!" Sister Zoe jerked around, her full black skirt ballooning as she hurried to my side. A few girls began to cry.

But then Sister Zoe's shocked look faded. "Why, Yolanda dear, that's snow!" She laughed. "Snow."

"Snow," I repeated. I looked out the window warily. All my life I had heard about the white crystals that fell out of American skies in the winter. From my desk I watched the fine powder dust the sidewalk and parked cars below. Each flake was different, Sister Zoe had said, like a person, irreplaceable and beautiful.

*R*eid Gómez is a San Francisco–raised Navajo Chicana. She currently lives in El Cerrito, California. A Name for Cebolla, *her unpublished manuscript, has been written with Crayons (a writer's group), Cherríe Moraga, and the strength of her mother.*

FROM *A NAME FOR CEBOLLA*

Reid Gómez

Sometimes the sun goes down grey, and Grandma prays for fire. There's a few moments when no one can find her. When the TV comes on and no one's home but me and I am trying to cook the frozen chicken Mommi bought in a box at the Safeway. It's during that time, when Grandma disappears before her plaster Mary and Jesus, that I get afraid of dark time and storytelling, that I get afraid of the Bible where it got all the pictures of arrowheads and purple robes, and the house is quiet for three minutes of eternity. It's the time I'm most afraid of Grandma's prayers and Jesus. It's the time I see through everything.

When I go to church on Sunday, I know he's watching me. Grandma sits in the third pew, close enough so people know she's a good woman. Grandma kneels the whole Mass, with her back bent and her head down, like she and God is having some special talk. While all this time I'm watching him, and he looks straight back at me.

He hangs there on the cross, in his underwear, and I

know he must be feeling real bad. I don't know why people come and stare at him and don't ever give him a blanket to cover himself. He can't get one himself, 'cause he's busy there bleeding dry blood. Once I saw him twitch his left leg, to let me know he's watching me.

Every Sunday I get real quiet and I can hear Grandma mumbling like running water about Grandpa and Mommi. And every Sunday I sneak up to the first pew, to see if he'll bleed some of his dry blood on me, and I get real quiet to see if I can hear him mumbling like Grandma. But he don't ever pray nothing I can hear, and his lips, well I never seen them move. Yet.

Our church has a dome in the front and a wooden Jesus with tomato-colored blood. The church is dark and damp, and all the pews squeak just from your breathing.

Father Dennis asked us how we wanted it fixed; he thought it was too smelly and dirty for praying. I liked it. It was like being inside *la Virgen*'s womb with its little orange lighted hole.

But Father Dennis, he decided the mural needed painting. He decided it needed painting beige, unbrown, unearth, almost the color of his own sucked-on and chewed-up fingernails.

Father Dennis decided that every last picture would be covered, all the stories cleaned out and painted over with three thick coats.

The church has the apostles for stained-glass windows. And when Father Dennis reads the Gospel, the lips of Matthew start moving. Even though it is the father's voice, I know that it's really Matthew telling the stories about Jesus and his long curly hair.

When they painted over the mural, they also got rid of the wooden Jesus. He was mahogany. The Jesus they got now is beige plaster, just like the ceiling. This Jesus is shiny and he's got fire-engine red blood and a big hole in his side.

Francis, the boy next door, said the new Jesus is hollow. He saw a big hole in his back when they were nailing him up there after the new paint had dried.

I think he's right, 'cause this Jesus don't twitch his leg at me. He just hangs there shiny and matching the walls.

Grandma prayed the rosary every day at three o'clock.

She said bloody knees were a sign of God's love and sleeping on the cold floor would get you to heaven.

She would pray with her eyes closed, kneeling there fondling her chain of beads. She'd roll the one she was working on between her thumb, fore-, and middle fingers. She'd rub it slow, like it was going to save her from Grandpa and the bedsprings she refused to hear.

And she would pray it three times while Mommi made the tortillas, cooked the beans, and waited for her whipping.

Grandma died on Friday morning, and on Saturday we knew.

Mommi and I had to clean her house. We started Saturday, and it was dark and damp and holding secrets.

Grandma shared her room with Mary and Jesus on the wall above her bed. They saw her in the afternoon at three P.M. start her looking. She'd look hard with her eyes shut, afraid of mirrors, afraid of Jesus' green eyes and afraid of smelling. 'Cause Grandpa smelled; he smelled like wine and pee.

So Grandma didn't drink and she didn't pee. All day every day she would pray and twist the white caps off of brown plastic. *Tick-tick-tick, push down and twist*, it was her ritual. Like saying ten Hail Marys and you get to say one Our Father. *Tick-tick-tick, push down and twist* and she would open up, look down, and find small little beads just like the ones on her rosary. Darvon, Valium, Demoral. I think Valium was her favorite, 'cause we found bottles of that in every room, hiding. I don't know why she kept them there, all empty and waiting to tell on her. 'Cause when she would pray, we only knew that she was good at counting beads.

*D*enise Chávez *is a native of New Mexico. She is the author of numerous plays, works for children, and stories that have won several important literary awards. The title story of her collection* The Last of the Menu Girls *(1986) won the Puerto del Sol fiction award for 1985. Denise has recently published a novel,* Face of an Angel *(1994).*

Her home base is Las Cruces, New Mexico. This is the voice of Omega Harkins . . .

GRAND SLAM

Denise Chávez

M ozetta, are you there? What's the matter with your phone? Yes, it's me, Omega Harkins. As I was saying before I was so rudely interrupted, I have to tell you what happened to me this morning. Well, it all started a few days ago when my niece, Norlee, called me. Acton had called her from California. Acton, Acton Allnutt. Acton was my first boyfriend, the "first one," if you know what I mean, Mozetta, the *absolute* first, but not by any means the best, if you know what I mean. The best. Do you have a party line, Mozetta? Oh, okay. Well, it seems as if Acton called Norlee, she's down there at the State University majoring in Forestry. I don't know any woman, for crissakes, would want to go into *that* line of work, analyzing reindeer shit and whatever else you do in forests, but anyway, Mozetta, get this, Acton called. He always did like all of us, even Mother, even after she told him to leave me alone. What could I say? Poor Acton. So Acton called, get this, to tell us all, especially me, well, and maybe Mother, because she never did believe he'd amount to much, that he was going to appear on a game show, that new one, on Channel 4, *$50,000 Grand Slam*, on the General Category, and that we should all

watch him, especially me. Acton? He got married about five
years ago to an Italian. He was going to die in Viet Nam when
we broke up, but he got sent to Italy instead where he got some
architecture student pregnant and they moved to California
and had a kid. What? It was a girl. Acton? He's down there at
some big California university near the beach majoring in
Dairy. Damn, Acton, I wrote this in my last Xmas card, why
the hell are you out there majoring in Dairy? I wrote him an
Xmas card that his wife never saw, it seems that he always collects the mail, but then again, it must be something European.
I thought so too, Mozetta. I think you're right about that. Rock
doesn't give a damn about the mail, but then again, I guess he
does if it's his paycheck, only he doesn't get his paycheck in the
mail, so it wouldn't matter anyway. What was I saying? Well, I
ought to write Acton a letter, send him an Xmas card this year.
It was about this time, around that time we met. I mean me and
Rock. Xmas. I had a fever and met Rock at a rock concert. It all
fell into place, if you know what I mean. Acton's action wasn't
anything like Rock's, where was I? Oh, okay. Norlee didn't
know who the hell Acton was, but then she remembered. I'd
told her all about him late one night when we were in bed at
Mother's and we couldn't sleep. You know, for a freshman in
Forestry, Norlee is pretty advanced, if you know what I mean.
You do? Okay, so Acton called to tell us to call all his friends.
Porky Hartzo . . . Corney Hawkins . . . Little Dickie . . . to
call them all and tell them that he, Acton Allnutt, was going to
be on a game show in Los Angeles, California, in the General
Category, with a special emphasis in Dairy and the New Testament. This was a few days ago, Mozetta. Well, Norlee finally
got a hold of me at work. I was stamping a new price on the Le
Sueur's. They've gone up. Can you believe it? What is this
world coming to? It's a good thing I don't eat Le Sueur's. Me, I
just buy the Town House variety. They're just as good. There's
something suspicious about the baby size of those peas, they
don't seem real. Give me a mouthful of pea, I say, not a—you
like that joke about the pea soup . . . hold that chicken and

make it pea? Huh, Mozetta? Well, Pres came up to me as I was sixty-fouring those Le Sueur's and told me that I had a long-distance call from my niece, Norlee, she's a freshman at State. I couldn't believe it! So I ran down the aisle and into the office. Wences was in there eating his lunch and I said, will you excuse me, I have a long-distance call from my niece, Norlee, she's a freshman at State majoring in Forestry, maybe someday you'd like to meet her. I said all that you know, to make it seem like a very important call. No, I wasn't going to introduce, what for? Him? But he wouldn't move out and I said, come on, Wences, you can eat your lunch in the back just like everyone else. The plucky kid likes to eat in Mr. Hedvale's office. Old Bunny is his great-uncle or something like that. Can you imagine having a name like Wences Hedvale, for crissakes? I mean, it's out of season. That Wences, he's a pain! I can never get him to take out anything, all he does is hang out near the magazine rack and breathe on the *Oui*s and the *Cavalier*s. I mean, I don't believe this kid's fixation. Well, he's about sixteen, blond with frizzy tangled hair. A real pimply kid from the nose down, the rest of his face as smooth as a baby's rear. Wences, do you mind, I said, this is long-distance. Privately long-distance. It's my niece from State. It's an emergency. Okay, he said, I'm gonna tell my uncle about this, you know what you can do with that phone. I said, I'm gonna tell Mr. Hedvale on *you*, Wences, I've been an employee of the Stop and Save for going on six years, to which he said, Tell Bunny to . . . by this time I could hear Norlee saying, he called you, he called all the way from Los Angeles, California, to tell you about his great appearance on the *Grand Slam*. The program will be on this next week, meaning this week, he lost the twenty thousand, she said. He did, he did, but how? How, I said, that Acton's sharp as A and even more, what happened? He won a car but he doesn't like it, so he's going to sell it, Norlee said. He lost? He lost? How? How? He couldn't remember the name of Napoleon's dog. For crissakes, I said over the phone, he lost for *that*? What was the category? Famous dogs of history, she said. For crissakes, what kind of car was it? He didn't say, she said. Where is it now? When did he call? How did he sound? He asked about you, Omega, and I told him you were fine. I told him you were "engaged." Engaged? Hell! Now what'd you want to say that for? Me and Rock have an understanding, that's all. Did Acton say anything else? Tell me, Norlee, what did he say? The program is on this week, I gotta go now, Omega, I have practice. Practice for what, Norlee? I almost yelled, the kid had built up my excitement and now she was leaving me to the Le Sueur's and that aisle staring me in the face, #15, Canned Vegetables, and to Wences, to that plucky kid. I could tell he was outside the door listening. What practice, Norlee? I'm a Caperette, she says. What's a Caperette? Omega, she exclaimed, it's only the top-ranked girls' sword drill team in the West! Give it up, Norlee, I said, it's a radical organization. I don't believe in swords. Don't be silly, she said, and hung up. I was crushed but I went back to the pea pile, past Wences, and sat down on my little stool, my stamper all inky all over my hands, my head full of thoughts and my heart full of lost feelings for Acton. Where did we go wrong? Why didn't he die and end our mutual misery? Now he was alive and well and driving a Vega or Camaro in Los Angeles. Acton, I sighed. Acton, where did we go wrong?

Mozetta, there I was sitting next to Rock and he was sliding on his pants, yawning himself awake, half of him in the daylight and half of him in the night, it was the craziest thing. I turned on the TV, and Rock says, what are you doing now? And I told him a friend of mine, stressing the *friend*, was going to be on the *Grand Slam*. Rock, I said, we gotta watch this. Who is this dude, he says? He's a *friend* of mine, we're just *friends*, that's all, we grew up together, I said to him aloud, but to myself: Acton, Acton, where did we go wrong?

He's going to be on the *Grand Slam*, Rock, we have to watch this. Then the TV flashed several faces in front of the bed, that's where we were, on the bed. I had on my bathrobe, the fuzzy one that Mother gave me, and Rock was there next to

me. I saw Acton's face all of a sudden. Mozetta, I couldn't believe it, he looked like his daddy! I was so shaken up. Rock kept
saying: Is that him, is that him? Where did you meet him, who
is he, stuff like that. I met him in a play, I said, in high school,
kinda whispering, he was my alcoholic husband, it was a melo-
drama. Sure, Rock says, you the actress, uh huh. You're fulla it,
and we watched Acton play, and he won! He won $15,000 to-
day, this was this morning, I'm talking about, Mozetta, and the
questions were real hard. Like who is the Beatles' manager and
about Dolley Madison. But anyway, the thing about all this is
that I simply could not believe how much Acton looked like his
daddy, and I've met the man. He's tall and fat and has a bald
head with some swirly hair. He looks like a crayfish. And he has
beautiful blue eyes, just like Acton, and Mozetta, to tell you the
truth, I felt sick, nauseated almost. Another thing, here it was
today, and yet it was last week and tomorrow. By today I mean
today, and by last week I mean last week when it was filmed,
and Acton won and lost and by tomorrow I mean . . . I don't
know what I mean. It was simply weird and nauseating and I
thought I would die to see Acton in a suit, smiling and sighing
in that funny way he used to sigh. He looked so scared and
small and defenseless and fat . . . Mozetta, I fell in love again,
or maybe I fell in love for the first time. Only this time, I saw
Acton as his daddy, fat, balding, and old, and I felt sorry about
that and that made me love Acton. Like never before. I never
did like Acton too much but he hung around me all the time
and liked me so darn much, I had to pretend some. It was all a
lie, but I didn't know that until later. But at first, he was fine,
Mozetta, attentive, my first real boyfriend, if you know what I
mean. The first. I like that, a man being attentive. But to show
you the kind of person he really was, well, when we broke up,
he figured out how much he spent on me all those years, and
told me. How do you like that? Oh. About $1,500. I mean, it
wasn't too much was it, after all *I'd* given him. I mean, here he's
got $15,000 for knowing who the Beatles' manager was . . . not
to mention a new Camaro. But anyway, what does it all mean?

It means Acton was there in a suit, smiling and sighing, sighing and smiling, and I was in my living room sitting next to Rock, and him putting on his pants and me in my bathrobe. That's what it means. Then Rock said, who is this guy to you? And I said back, what do you mean, who is this guy to you, you have terrible English! And I suppose Ackburn is a Shakespeare, Rock said. Acton, I yelled, Acton! He's a friend, he's a friend, that's all!

And there I was Mozetta, there on the bed, and Acton was on the TV, and he had just won the $15,000 and I couldn't stay tuned to see what his decision would be tomorrow because that's my shift at the store, and it really didn't matter 'cause I knew he'd already lost. It seemed like such a lie to me, all of it, me in the robe, Rock there, scratching himself, and Acton, on the TV, answering questions about the Beatles. It was too strange. The part that really got me was the part about time. Here it was today and Acton's today was yesterday and mine was today's and he won and lost and tomorrow what would he decide? Well, Mozetta, I just can't stay tuned. I can't. Acton looks too much like his daddy. Afterwards, I went into the bathroom and looked at my face and felt sad. All day I felt sad. I did crazy things in the soup section. I got lost and put asparagus in the chicken noodle and when Wences came up to tell me about listening to my phone conversation, well, I just started to cry, there in the soup section. It seemed like such a lie. All of it. Oh, I . . . you have to go now . . . Tosty's back from work and wants his supper . . . oh, okay, I'll call you tomorrow. Oh, Mozetta, I tell you, it was too . . . too . . . I don't know, you know what I mean? I just can't find the words. I told Rock that we'd met in a play, that he was my alcoholic husband . . . now why'd I say *that*, I wonder? Mozetta, you there?

L ety Martínez González migrated to the United States from Mexico in 1990. She may still be on this side of the border. Her letter home to her family in Oaxaca shows her anger at her circumstances and her concern for the baby she had to leave behind.

P atricia Zárate immigrated to the United States from Mexico in 1981. In this letter she lets her family know where she is and writes: "I am not going to fail you! Of that I assure you!!"

TWO LETTERS HOME

*Lety Martínez González
and Patricia Zárate*

•••

Lety Martínez González
Los Angeles, CA
4 de Junio de 1990

Argelia González Morales
Oaxaca, Oaxaca, México

Argelia, Jaime, Nancy, Abuelita,

¿Qué tal? ¿Cómo están? Espero que todo esté bien en la casa que yo por aquí me siento muy triste. Pues nunca en mi vida llegué a pensar que tendría que pasar tantas y tantas cosas para estar aquí. Antes que nada quiero contarte que no lloré mucho cuando me despedí de ustedes pues me dí mucho valor ya que la aeromosa nos informó que volaríamos en el avión donde transportaron al papa Juan Pablo II, como verás mi avión iba bendecido y me sentí muy bien de saberlo. Después en 35 minutos llegamos a México y confirmamos el vuelo y nos esperamos a que anunciaran nuestro vuelo pero antes comimos un sandwich y un refresco. Cuando lo anunciaron nos

• •

Lety Martínez González
Los Angeles, CA
June 4, 1990

Argelia González Morales
Oaxaca, Oaxaca, Mexico

Argelia, Jaime, Nancy, Grandma,

What's up? How are you all? I hope all's well at the house because I'm feeling very sad here, since never in my life did I come to think that I'd have to go through so many, many things in order to be here. Before anything, I want to tell you that I didn't cry very much when I said goodbye to all of you; well I made myself be brave since the stewardess informed us that we would be flying in the plane that transported Pope John Paul II, as you'll see, my plane was blessed and I felt very good knowing this. Thirty-five minutes later we arrived in Mexico City and we confirmed the flight and we waited for them to announce our flight, but first we ate a sandwich and a

143

trasbordamos al avión. Me tocó en la ventanilla les diré que se siente muy bonito. A Gabi la pasaron en otro asiento pues no permiten que haya niños cerca de la ventanilla. Después nos anunciaron que nos pasarían unos audífonos para escuchar música o ver una película, al poco tiempo que nos los pasaron, nos sirvieron la comida, por cierto muy sabrosa, y nos pasaron la película, también muy divertida.

Llegamos a Tijuana. El aeropuerto está feo, tuvimos suerte para pasar sin que nos registraran maletas ni nada, saliendo compramos un tíquet para el camión que nos llevaría al motel Alaska. Cuando llegamos Gabi me dejó afuera con el niño, Tijuana está horrible, no tiene nada más que puros tugurios en la noche, pero te diré que Guilfrido llegó por el niño mientras que nosotros alquilamos un cuarto, dando las 11 de la noche nos dirijimos a una lonchería disfrazada, pues en realidad era una cantina, de ahí hablamos con la persona que me iba a pasar. Pero me dijo que me esperara para el otro día pues todo era muy precipitado en ese momento, de ahí nos regresamos a la lonchería y llegó un enanito que nos dijo que nos esperáramos, pero no nos gustó su aspecto, y que nos regresamos al hotel pasamos a cada rato por la dichosa zona roja todo está corrompido, nosotros dándonos valor, pues hay muchos hombres en la calle, y también mujeres pero tú ya sabes cuales, ¿no? Dormimos en el hotel y al otro día se comunicó el señor diciéndonos que no nos moviéramos del hotel y que llegaría a las 2 de la tarde, llegó y nos dijo que a las 9 de la noche volvería a pasar por nosotros para llevarnos a la lonchería. En ese tiempo comimos algo y dormimos a las 9 llegó el señor nos llevó y dió órdenes a sus trabajadores, estuvimos esperando hasta las 10 cuando llegaron los muchachos que nos pasarían, y nos dieron órdenes que saliéramos todos por parejas. Yo me fui con el enanito, y Gabi con otro muchacho que pasaría con nosotros. A continuación te haré un pequeño croquis del recorrido inmenso que hicimos.

1. De aquí salimos y caminamos estas 5 cuadras.
2. Pasamos el Boulevard.

soda. When they announced it we boarded the plane; I got the window and I'll tell you that feels really beautiful. They gave Gaby another seat, since they don't allow there to be children near the window. Then they announced that they would give us headphones to listen to music or watch a movie, shortly after they passed them out they served the meal, really delicious by the way, and they ran the movie, likewise very entertaining.

We arrived in Tijuana. The airport's ugly, we had the luck to pass through without them inspecting our bags or anything. On the way out we bought a ticket for the bus that would take us to the Alaska motel. When we arrived Gaby left me outside with the boy, Tijuana's horrible, it has nothing but pure slums at night, but I'll tell you that Wilfrido arrived for the boy while we were renting a room. When it struck 11 at night they directed us to a disguised diner, well in reality it was a cantina, from there we talked with the person who was going to take me across. But he told me to wait until the next day since everything was very rushed at that moment, from there we went back to the coffee shop and a dwarf arrived who told us to wait, but we didn't like his looks and so we went back to the hotel, passing all the while through the so-called *Zona Roja*, everything is corrupt, and us making ourselves be brave, well there are many men in the street and women too, but you know which ones, don't you? We slept at the hotel and the next day the man called, telling us not to move from the hotel and that he'd arrive at 2 in the afternoon, he arrived and told us that at 9 at night he'd come by for us again to take us to the diner. In that time we ate something and slept, at 9 the man arrived, he took us and gave orders to his workers, we were waiting until 10 when the guys who would cross us over arrived, and they gave us orders that we all go out in pairs. I went with the dwarf, and Gaby with another guy who would cross with us. I'll make you a sketch below of the immense trip we took.

1. We left from here and walked these 5 blocks.
2. We crossed the Boulevard.

3. Alambrado.
4. Esto recorrimos de alambrado caminando.
5. Por aquí entramos, 1 cuadra, toda esta parte del borde tiene alumbrado y faros.
6. Esto es un puente donde compramos bolsas para pasar aguas negras.
7. Esta es una zona arenosa.
8. Todo ésto es como 6 cuadras.
9. Aquí pasamos una poza de aguas negras.
10. Esta es la calle donde constantemente pasan los de la migra.
11. Esto que remarco con la pluma es una fosa donde tienes que pasar casi a gatas.
12. Y éstos como arbolitos son puros arbustos.
13. Gabi cayó en aguas negras.
14. Coche de policía.
15. Calle de tierra. Aquí tuvimos que tirarnos para que no nos agarraran. Y cuando el coche pasó nos arrancamos una carrera.
16. Esta fue toda la carrera. Ahí sí ya no aguantaba las piernas.
17. Aquí saltamos a la barranca porque ahí sí nos vio la migra y nos dijo que nos detuviéramos.
18. Cuando saltamos me caí porque una persona se agarró de mí y era un gordo panzón. Me levanté gracias a otro muchacho que me jaló.
19. Aquí salimos para entrar a este pinche país.
20. Caminamos esta boulevard. Ya estábamos supuestamente del otro lado.
21. Esto ya es E.U., un fraccionamiento.
22. Aquí nos subieron a unos coches de ellos para ir a San Diego.

Quiero aclarar que en el mapa donde puse una *Y* la recorrimos como 4 veces, pues el muchacho no sé si eran sus nervios pero no encontraba la salida, hasta que nos encontramos a otro

3. Wire Fence.
4. We traveled along the fence, walking.
5. We entered here. 1 block. This whole part of the border has lights and searchlights.
6. This is a bridge where we bought plastic bags to cross the *aguas negras.*
7. This is a sandy area.
8. All this is like 6 blocks.
9. Here we crossed a large puddle of *aguas negras.*
10. This is the street where those of the *migra* constantly pass by.
11. This that I mark over with the pen is a pit where you have to cross practically on all fours.
12. And these things like trees are pure shrubs.
13. Gaby fell in the *aguas negras.*
14. Police car.
15. Dirt road. Here we had to throw ourselves down so they wouldn't grab us. And when the car passed we were off to the races.
16. This was all running, to the point I couldn't bear my legs anymore.
17. Here we jumped into the gully because the *migra* saw us there and told us to stop.
18. When we jumped I fell because someone grabbed me and it was a fat potbellied guy. I got myself up thanks to another guy who urged me on.
19. Here we left to enter this fucking country.
20. We walked up this street. Now we were supposedly on the other side.
21. This now is the U.S., one block.
22. Here they put us into some of their cars to go to San Diego.

I want to clarify that on the map where I put a *Y* we ran back and forth like 4 times since the guy, I don't know if it was his nerves but he couldn't find the way out, until we ran into

coyote que venía atrás de nosotros, fue que le dijo, y pasamos con toda la inmensidad de plantas, tuvimos que saltar troncos, aguas negras, todo fue muy distinto a lo que yo había visto, o me habían contado. Gabi dice que yo tuve mucho valor, pues ella iba muerta de nervios, pero no te creas. Si estoy aquí es porque creo en Dios y porque en esos momentos le pedía a la virgen de Guadalupe, Juquila y la virgen de la Soledad y mi hijo sobre todo contaba mucho para mí. Pero ahora ya estoy aquí, con dolores y arañasos, moretones y para acabarle de amolar con este monstruo en mi garganta llegué. Pero estoy aquí. Ayer llegué en la madrugada como a las 5 de la mañana, ahora como anécdota cuando saltamos a la barranca el enanito fue agarrado por la migra pues cuando caímos por lo corto de sus piernas no pudo levantarse, y cuando corrimos hubiera querido abrazarlo, pues te desespera que sus piernitas no dieran abasto para correr, pues aunque no lo creas, yo nunca había corrido así de rápido, ahora me río pero en esos momentos yo no sentía mi saliva, mis golpes, nada, todo fue peor que en las películas. Yo creo que si recorrimos como 7 a 10 kilómetros, pero en fin yo no vuelvo a pasar así en serio, oye sigue las flechas que te pongo y lee lo que te digo en cada una de ellas.

Esto que sigue es para ti Arge lo anterior si leéselos.

Bueno pasando a otra cosa hoy llega Silvia espero llegue con bien. Cuéntame, ¿como ha estado mi bebé, lo llevaste ayer al doctor qué te dijo de sus pies, su peso, su estatura, o qué te dijo cómo está, dime con quién se ha estado durmiendo, si ha comido bien? Lo extraño mucho. Y mi papá, ¿cómo está, qué dijo; y Nancy cómo se sintió Nancy y mi abuelita, cómo está? Porque yo me siento como pendeja, es más me siento de la chingada, ayer fuimos al doctor porque el niño tiene vómito y está super rosado pues yo creo que ese día que se quedó con Rosa no lo atendieron bien, pero en fin Wester ya está mejor. Gabi también. A Everardo ya le dije lo que me recomendaste que le dijera y me dijo que ya habló con mi papá, Everardo ya tiene coche, grabadora, televisión, con decirte que el propio Guicho ayer compró una Caribe en 150 dólares que está super mejor

another *coyote* who came up behind us, he was the one who told him, and we passed through an immensity of bushes, we had to jump tree trunks, *aguas negras*, it was all very different from what I had seen, or what they had told me, Gaby says I was very brave, since she was going to die of nerves, well don't believe it. If I'm here it's because I believe in God and because in those moments I asked the Virgin of Guadalupe, Juguila, and the Virgin of Solitude, and above all my son counted a lot to me. But now I'm here, with pains and scratches, bruises and to finish the grind off with this monster in my throat. But I'm here. I arrived yesterday in the early morning at like 5 in the morning. Now by way of an anecdote, when we jumped into the gully the dwarf was grabbed by the *migra*, since when we fell he couldn't get up because of the shortness of his legs, and when we ran I would have liked to take him in my arms, well it drives you to despair that his little legs wouldn't give enough to run. Well though you won't believe this, I've never run so fast, now I laugh but in those moments I didn't feel my saliva, the blows, nothing, everything was worse than in the movies. I believe that we traveled like 7 to 10 kilometers, but in short I won't cross like this again, seriously, listen, follow the arrows that I put down here for you and read what I tell you in each one of them.

What follows is for you, Arge, the foregoing, yes, read it to everyone.

Anyway, moving on to another thing, today Silvia arrives, I hope she arrives well. Tell me how my baby has been, you took him to the doctor yesterday, what did he tell you about his feet, his weight, his height, or what did he tell you in general, how is he? Tell me with whom he's been sleeping, if he's eaten well. I miss him very much. And Papa, how is he, what did he say? And Nancy, how did Nancy feel? And Grandma, how is she? Because I feel like a fool, what's more I feel all fucked-up, yesterday we went to the doctor because the boy's vomiting and he's super-pink, since I think the day he stayed with Rosa they didn't look after him very well, but in short Wester is better now, Gaby too. I already told Everardo what you recom-

que la Caribe blanca del compadre. Oye, hablando de él lo que pasó, ya no hablo de eso, porque yo estoy dispuesta a aclarar todo, oye, ¿qué dirá de que me vine? ¿Quien sabe? ya ni escribí la carta para Hilda, bueno ahora sí me despido mañana empiezo mi otra carta. Contéstame pronto. Saludos a todos, yo te tendré informada.

Besos a mi bebé. Cuídenlo.

Atentamente,
Lety

mended that I tell him, and he told me that he already talked with Papa, Everardo now has a car, cassette recorder, television, not to mention the fact that yesterday Guicho himself bought a VW Caribe for 150 dollars that's way better than the white Caribe my boy's godfather has. Listen, speaking of him, what happened, I won't say any more about that, because I'm willing to clarify everything, listen, what will he say that I came? Who knows? I didn't write the letter to Hilda yet, anyway now I say goodbye, tomorrow I'll begin my other letter. Answer me soon. Greetings to all, I'll keep you informed.

Kisses for my baby. Take care of him.

Warmly,
Lety

••

Patricia Zárate
Ventura, CA
27 de Febrero de 1981

José Zárate y familia
Guadalajara, México

Hola Papá, Mamá, Hermanos,

Espero que se encuentren muy bien a pesar de todo.
Ya se habrán enterado que estoy en Estados Unidos (California), y se preguntarán que hago aquí.
Antes que nada quiero pedirles que tengan mucha confianza en mí. Me vine con el deseo de trabajar acá unos meses para juntar un poco de dinero.
Yo tengo mucha fé en que me va a ir muy bien, y eso es importante. Aquí todo es diferente a México, ¡pero les aseguro que todo lo que aprendí de ustedes no se me va a olvidar nunca!!
Los recuerdo mucho y eso va a ser decisivo en mi comportamiento. *¡No les voy a fallar! Se los aseguro!!*
Llegando a E.U. el miércoles en la mañana traía dos direcciones de personas con las que podía llegar una es la de Panchi y sus hermanas que deseché la posibilidad porque pensé que en vez de ayudarme me perjudicaría. La otra dirección es la de un matrimonio amigos míos, que fue por la que opté, y estoy segura que si los conocieran dejarían de preocuparse. Ellos son mexicanos, tienen dos hijas, chiquitas. Ellos por la mañana trabajan, a las niñas se las cuida una persona mientras estoy yo sola en la casa, hasta a las 4 P.M. que ellos regresan, y como aquí es diferente, la gente ya no sale a la calle. Yo he salido con ellos al centro y a buscar trabajo, éstas son las posibilidades que tengo:

1. Dependencia de la Universidad de California Centro de Estudios Chicanos. Trabajaría escribiendo a máquina, cosas en español. No importa si no hablo

• •

Patricia Zárate
Ventura, CA
February 27, 1981

Jose Zárate and Family
Guadalajara, Mexico

Hello Papa, Mama, brothers and sisters,

I hope this finds you very well in spite of everything.

By now you will have found out I'm in the United States (California) and you will be asking yourselves what I'm doing here.

Before anything I want to ask you to have a lot of trust in me. I came with the desire to work here a few months in order to gather a little money.

I have great faith that it's going to go very well for me, and this is important. Here everything is different from Mexico, but I assure you I'm never going to forget anything I learned from you!!

I remember you a lot and this is going to be decisive in my behavior. *I am not going to fail you! Of that I assure you!!*

When I arrived in the U.S. Wednesday morning I had two addresses of people I could head for, one is of Panchi and his sisters, but I threw out that possibility because I thought that instead of helping me it would only hurt. The other address is that of some married friends of mine, which was the one I opted for, and I'm sure that if you knew them you'd quit worrying. They're Mexican, they have two daughters, little ones. They work mornings, someone takes care of the girls. Meanwhile I'm alone in the house until 4 P.M., when they return, and since it's different here, people don't go out into the street then. I've gone with them downtown and to look for work, these are the possibilities I have:

1. Office of the University of California Center for Chicano Studies. I would work typing things in Spanish. It

inglés provisionalmente esta dependencia se va a ocupar de ubicar en la universidad a estudiantes cubanos, de los que llegaron hace poco a E.U. Y como no hablan inglés contestan unas entrevistas escritas en español, mi trabajo sería pasarlas a máquina. Pagan a $4.50 la hora y se trabajan 8 horas diarias. Este es el trabajo que más me interesa.

2. Fábrica de radios de transistores pagan igual la hora de trabajo.

El primer trabajo es por medio de una amiga de este matrimonio que es la encargada de este trabajo. Ella se llama Yolanda Castillo.

Papá, Mamá, considero que es muy importante que tengan confianza en mí. Yo sé que como hice las cosas, pueden desconfiar, pero yo sabía que nunca me iban a dejar. ¡Me voy a portar muy bien! Voy a ir con mi tía Cuca y si ella me ofrece su casa me quedaré. Ya hablé con ella y sí me dijo que me fuera a su casa, tengo su dirección y número de teléfono. También tengo la dirección de mi tío Felipe por si la necesito.

Sólo quiero trabajar unos meses y regresar con ustedes a continuar en la escuela.

Hector me ha hablado por teléfono 2 veces, si algo se me llega a ofrecer hablaré con él o con Esther.

Quiero que estén tranquilos, el que yo esté ahora sola me va ayudar mucho para responsabilizarme un poco de mi misma.

Voy a escribir constantemente para platicarles como me está yendo.

Espero que ustedes también me escriban, aunque sea para jalarme las orejas. Hasta pronto.

Los quiere,
Patricia Zárate

Ahora fuimos a misa a un templo que se llama la Asunción de María; fue una misa bilingüe y con mariachi.

doesn't matter if I don't speak English for the time being, this department is going to be occupied with placing Cuban students in the university, some of the ones who recently arrived in the U.S. And as they don't speak English, they answer some written interview questions in Spanish, and my job would be transcribing them on the typewriter. They pay $4.50 an hour and you work 8 hours a day. This is the job that interests me most.

2. Transistor radio factory, they pay the same for an hour of work.

The first job is through a girlfriend of this couple, who is the person in charge of this job. Her name is Yolanda Castillo.

Papa, Mama, I consider it very important that you trust me. I know that with the way I did things you may distrust me, but I knew you were never going to let me do it. I'm going to behave myself very well! I'm going to go to my aunt Cuca and if she offers me her house I'll stay. I already spoke with her and she told me yes, to go to her house, I have her address and phone number. I also have the address of my uncle Felipe in case I need it.

I just want to work a few months and return to you to continue in school.

Hector has called me on the phone twice, if I need anything I will talk to him or Esther.

I want you to be calm, my being alone right now is going to help me a lot to start being responsible for myself.

I'm going to write constantly to tell you how it's going with me.

I hope you also write me, even if it is to box my ears. Until soon.

Loving you all,
Patricia Zárate

Just now we went to mass at a church called *la Asunción de María*, it was a bilingual mass with mariachi.

*S*andra Cisneros, a native of Chicago, is the daughter of a Mexican father and a Mexican-American mother. Internationally acclaimed for her poetry and fiction, and the recipient of numerous awards, Cisneros is the author of Loose Woman (1994), The House on Mango Street (1984), Woman Hollering Creek and Other Stories (1991), and My Wicked Wicked Ways (1987). Her work has been translated into eight languages. She lives in San Antonio, Texas, and is currently at work on a novel, Caramelo. The following essay tells the story of how her father came to terms with his only daughter's career as a writer, but only after her work was translated into Spanish.

ONLY DAUGHTER

Sandra Cisneros

Once, several years ago, when I was just starting out my writing career, I was asked to write my own contributor's note for an anthology I was part of. I wrote: "I am the only daughter in a family of six sons. *That* explains everything."

Well, I've thought about that ever since, and yes, it explains a lot to me, but for the reader's sake I should have written: "I am the only daughter in a *Mexican* family of six sons." Or even: "I am the only daughter of a Mexican father and a Mexican-American mother." Or: "I am the only daughter of a working-class family of nine." All of these had everything to do with who I am today.

I was/am the only daughter and *only* a daughter. Being an only daughter in a family of six sons forced me by circumstance to spend a lot of time by myself because my brothers felt it beneath them to play with a *girl* in public. But that aloneness, that loneliness, was good for a would-be writer—it allowed me time to think and think, to imagine, to read and prepare myself.

Being only a daughter for my father meant my destiny would lead me to become someone's wife. That's what he believed. But when I was in the fifth grade and shared my plans for college with him, I was sure he understood. I remember my father saying, "*Que bueno, mi'ja*, that's good." That meant a lot to me, especially since my brothers thought the idea hilarious. What I didn't realize was that my father thought college was good for girls—good for finding a husband. After four years in college and two more in graduate school, and still no husband, my father shakes his head even now and says I wasted all that education.

In retrospect, I'm lucky my father believed daughters were meant for husbands. It meant it didn't matter if I majored in something silly like English. After all, I'd find a nice professional eventually, right? This allowed me the liberty to putter about embroidering my little poems and stories without my father interrupting with so much as a "What's that you're writing?"

But the truth is, I wanted him to interrupt. I wanted my father to understand what it was I was scribbling, to introduce me as "My only daughter, the writer." Not as "This is only my daughter. She teaches." *Es maestra*—teacher. Not even *profesora*.

In a sense, everything I have ever written has been for him, to win his approval even though I know my father can't read English words, even though my father's only reading includes the brown-ink *Esto* sports magazines from Mexico City and the bloody *¡Alarma!* magazines that feature yet another sighting of *La Virgen de Guadalupe* on a tortilla or a wife's revenge on her philandering husband by bashing his skull in with a *molcajete* (a kitchen mortar made of volcanic rock). Or the *fotonovelas*, the little picture paperbacks with tragedy and trauma erupting from the characters' mouths in bubbles.

My father represents, then, the public majority. A public who is disinterested in reading, and yet one whom I am writing about and for, and privately trying to woo.

When we were growing up in Chicago, we moved a lot because of my father. He suffered bouts of nostalgia. Then we'd have to let go of our flat, store the furniture with mother's relatives, load the station wagon with baggage and bologna sandwiches and head south. To Mexico City.

We came back, of course. To yet another Chicago flat, another Chicago neighborhood, another Catholic school. Each time, my father would seek out the parish priest in order to get a tuition break, and complain or boast: "I have seven sons."

He meant *siete hijos*, seven children, but he translated it as "sons." "I have seven sons." To anyone who would listen. The Sears Roebuck employee who sold us the washing machine. The short-order cook where my father ate his ham-and-eggs breakfasts. "I have seven sons." As if he deserved a medal from the state.

My papa. He didn't mean anything by that mistranslation, I'm sure. But somehow I could feel myself being erased. I'd tug my father's sleeve and whisper: "Not seven sons. Six! and *one daughter.*"

When my oldest brother graduated from medical school, he fulfilled my father's dream that we study hard and use this— our heads, instead of this—our hands. Even now my father's hands are thick and yellow, stubbed by a history of hammer and nails and twine and coils and springs. "Use this," my father said, tapping his head, "and not this," showing us those hands. He always looked tired when he said it.

Wasn't college an investment? And hadn't I spent all those years in college? And if I didn't marry, what was it all for? Why would anyone go to college and then choose to be poor? Especially someone who had always been poor.

Last year, after ten years of writing professionally, the financial rewards started to trickle in. My second National Endowment for the Arts Fellowship. A guest professorship at the University of California, Berkeley. My book, which sold to a major New York publishing house.

At Christmas, I flew home to Chicago. The house was throbbing, same as always: hot tamales and sweet tamales hissing in my mother's pressure cooker, and everybody—my mother, six brothers, wives, babies, aunts, cousins—talking too loud and at the same time. Like in a Fellini film, because that's just how we are.

I went upstairs to my father's room. One of my stories had just been translated into Spanish and published in an anthology of Chicano writing and I wanted to show it to him. Ever since he recovered from a stroke two years ago, my father likes to spend his leisure hours horizontally. And that's how I found him, watching a Pedro Infante movie on Galavisión and eating rice pudding.

There was a glass filled with milk on the bedside table. There were several vials of pills and balled Kleenex. And on the floor, one black sock and a plastic urinal that I didn't want to look at but looked at anyway. Pedro Infante was about to burst into song, and my father was laughing.

I'm not sure if it was because my story was translated into Spanish, or because it was published in Mexico, or perhaps because the story dealt with Tepeyac, the *colonia* my father was raised in and the house he grew up in, but at any rate, my father punched the mute button on his remote control and read my story.

I sat on the bed next to my father and waited. He read it very slowly. As if he were reading each line over and over. He laughed at all the right places and read lines he liked out loud. He pointed and asked questions: "Is this So-and-so?" "Yes," I said. He kept reading.

When he was finally finished, after what seemed like hours, my father looked up and asked: "Where can we get more copies of this for the relatives?"

Of all the wonderful things that happened to me last year, that was the most wonderful.

*A*chy Obejas is a writer, poet, playwright, and teacher. Her first collection of short stories, We Came All the Way from Cuba So You Could Dress Like This *(1994), marks the first booklength publication by an openly lesbian Cuban. Her poetry and fiction have been published in several anthologies and literary magazines. Her journalism appears regularly in* The Nation, Chicago Reader, Windy City Times, *and* High Performance. *She writes a weekly column for the* Chicago Tribune. *She has also won numerous awards in journalism and creative writing at Columbia College in Chicago. This is a new version of a story that first appeared in* Third Woman *in 1986.*

POLAROIDS

Achy Obejas

The Polaroids stay.

Long hours later, their brilliant reds and milk-white faces are still fresh.

Here we have the frontal view, showing the nostrils relaxed, the shirt with the lace around the collar. In this one (careful, don't smudge it), the side view: The plaid skirt's zipper breaks the pattern.

Phyllis, whose desk is perpendicular to mine and carefully displays neat stacks of reporter's notebooks, says she's seen the Polaroids a thousand times.

"You can't let that stuff get to you," she tells me. It's not a cynical voice; it's soft and bored and tempered with the distant and wise affection of a woman in her fifties, but Phyllis is only thirty-one. "You'll see, by summer's end, you won't even blink."

I hope I blink, but I don't tell her. It would be a problem: She would have to defend her indifference and the discussion would bring us closer. I smile and blink, deliberately, and she nods and ignores me.

The police radio, its row of mystery lights racing from

one end to the other, sits on my desk, a constant fountain of pops, hiccups, and burps. On the other side of the newsroom, one of the stalwarts, a stiff-fingered night editor called Red (the name's a reminder of a rich and thick head of hair now as flat and dry as a parking lot) switches on the six o'clock newscast. In the background, the wire machines obliviously continue tapping. I take my coffee cup and walk to the break station.

"I hear they gave you a hard time at the sheriff's office today."

It's Rick Harmon, another reporter and a quietly handsome dark man with small, shy eyes like a mole. He was once Ricardo Hernandez.

"They weren't that bad," I tell him.

"They just pop the Polaroids on you?"

"Yeah . . ."

"They always do that to new people, sooner or later. It's supposed to be very funny, I guess. Were you disgusted?"

"No, scared, sort of."

"Scared?"

"Well, I mean, she didn't look very pretty."

"What did you expect?"

I want to say: I expected something more like the picture that ran on page 3, the one of the unknown girl with ordinary features and brown hair and brown eyes (I only know this from the text; in the doctored photograph her eyes are closed), but I don't say anything.

Minutes later, I cover my desk with the latest edition. But I don't read it. Now every photo is a Polaroid, glaring, void of details. In these, her eyes are only half closed and under the eyelids is a tiny line which separates the skin. Her mouth is limp, soft. Below, the skirt is pulled up slightly.

"You're not reading," says Phyllis, her voice a childish, singsong reprimand. "You've got to stop. Wanna go get a salad or something?"

"No, I'm not hungry."

"Honey, you're going to have to eat sometime, you know. Coffee is not in any one of the four basic food groups and that's all you've had today. I know you're a little queasy and all, but caffeine's only going to make it worse."

"I'm not queasy, really."

"Okay," she sings again.

The police radio crackles. A robbery. The address is on the far side of town, a Mexican area of small, dry yards and pink-and-lime houses.

"Well, we'll know the results of that in a few hours, when the cops get there," Phyllis says venomously. Rick shifts uncomfortably at his desk; the chair squeaks.

"God, there's nothing going on tonight," I say, to no one in particular. "I've been here six hours already and all I've written is a twenty-line short about a kid who got his stolen bicycle back."

"Ah, the life and hard times of the police reporter," mocks Phyllis. "One day a mass murder, the next a mere stolen bicycle returned. Look at it this way, your twenty-line short is probably the only good news in the whole edition."

"Oh, yeah, and it'll look great in my portfolio."

She turns around: "Rick, please call up some of the local gangs, see if you can stir up a rumble so Jimmy Olsenwoman here has something exciting to write about."

Rick looks up weakly.

"Hey," Phyllis continues—she's inspired now—"if you get really lucky, maybe Matilda will jump."

"Who's Matilda?" I ask.

"A crazy woman who usually goes up to the Woolworth Building about a half hour before deadline. Problem is, she never jumps."

"Great . . ."

"We haven't heard from her in a while. She's due. Why, maybe we could get somebody to push her off, then you'd have a really juicy story."

"That's not exactly what I want," I explain. "I just wish I could work on something else while listening to this stupid radio."

"When you were a kid couldn't you do your homework and watch TV at the same time?"

"Yeah, Phyllis, but this isn't exactly TV," I say, tapping the racing lights on the radio.

"You're right: It's more boring than TV."

"No, come on; I mean, everything's so extreme," I say. "Do you realize I've been on this beat two weeks and already I've seen more dead bodies than the average mortician."

"Look, you saw the map before you took the job. You knew we were next to the Mojave, evidence depository for the world's finest homicides. Maniacs kill in Texas and bring the bodies here to us because our guarantee is so good: In two hours the sun bakes it beyond recognition or the coyotes have it for lunch."

"I know, I know. It's scary."

"You'll get over it."

Red turns off the television and saunters back to his desk and the green screen of his computer terminal.

"Anything?" Rick asks.

Red shakes his head. "Just another Sunday night. We'll go with whatever's on the wire for the morning edition, unless we get something from the cops."

"Doesn't look that way," I say, "but then, it's still early."

"Not that early," says Phyllis, rising from her desk and pointing to the window. "Jesus, look at that sunset."

Indeed, the view is spectacular: There, outside our staid windows permanently closed, magenta washes the sky with the severity of distant thunder.

"That's a rare one," Phyllis says softly after a moment. In the reddish light that comes from outside she seems weary and alone, but she's too aware of her own reflection and catches herself, quickly lowering her sights to the streets below and the bulky, nervous figure that crosses the intersection. "Hey, Rick, guess who's making her way up the street?"

"Who?"

"Matilda."

I adjust my eyes to the ghostly grey of the street and the brown speck that moves like a bug across the window glass.

"Jesus, I think she's headed for the Woolworth Building," says Phyllis. "See kid? You might get your story after all."

Rick, embarrassed, turns away to his computer terminal.

"Okay, already," I say, "so what's the story on this Matilda?"

"She's a nut," explains Phyllis. "Every so often she gets the urge to jump off the Woolworth Building, so she crawls up there and makes a big to-do out of it, but she never jumps. Never."

"So what does she do?"

"Nothing, just stands there. Eventually she just climbs down again."

"How does she get up there?"

"Who knows? By now she's so familiar with the place, the security guards probably just let her in. It's a little tradition here in town: Matilda and her would-be jump off the Woolworth Building."

"Maybe she's just getting the courage up to really do it someday. I mean, maybe someday she'll really jump."

"Don't be so romantic, kid, that woman'll never jump. She'd ruin the tradition," Phyllis concludes on the way back to her desk.

In the distance, Matilda stands in front of the Woolworth Building, her microscopic shoulders bent.

"Is she Mexican?" I ask.

"Oh, they say she is, but I don't believe it," Phyllis declares.

"Why not?"

"Oh, come on, this kind of extravagant behavior isn't really a part of their culture," she explains as she sits down.

"What does that mean?" It's Rick.

"Hey, don't get touchy, *Ricardo.*"

"I'm not touchy, I was just wondering," he says, red from the sting.

"I mean that most Mexican women had really lousy, difficult lives and don't have the time and privilege to go nuts. My guess is that when they contemplate suicide it's quieter and more efficient than pretending to jump off the Woolworth Building a hundred times," she continues. "To be frank, I wouldn't doubt if Matilda's some great plot by a local bigot group to make Mexicans look crazy."

"Phyllis, do you realize what you're saying?" I ask, amazed.

"Jesus, I'm just kidding."

"I'm not talking about your conspiracy theory; that's even believable somehow," I say. "But you're saying only white people can be legitimately mentally ill."

"I didn't say that. I said I thought Mexican women wouldn't be so conspicuous about it."

"Phyllis!"

"Look, you're making me make it sound worse than what I really mean. It's just that they have this shame thing, you know, and how could she face her family and her neighbors if she kept trying to kill herself and failing? What's she going to do, huh? Pretend it didn't happen? Move out and change her name?"

Rick, like Matilda, bends his shoulders from the weight.

"Oh, Jesus, Rick, I'm sorry," Phyllis says, her hand over her face.

He nods, eyes downcast, and blinks a few times. When I look back to the streets, Matilda's vanished.

"Anybody got anything new?" Red asks, looking over the top of his computer terminal. Everyone shakes their heads no. "What about you?"

"No, nothing new," I tell him.

"Will you call the sheriff's one more time, see if they have an I.D. on that girl yet?"

"You mean the one they found last night in the desert?"

"Yeah, your Polaroid cover girl," snaps Phyllis, angry with herself.

"And see if they have a conclusion yet on the rape question," Red adds.

A conclusion? In the Polaroids, though the skirt covers most of her thighs, blood is caked to the knees, dirty.

"Red, I think you can safely say—"

"Get the official version. Please." His eyes are faded, pleading over the frame of his glasses.

I go to my phone and make the call. No, there's no new information on her identity. No, there's no new lead on the assailant, the one who strangled her with his naked hands. Yes, she was raped.

The police radio gurgles. An amused dispatcher calls a patrol car to the Woolworth Building. It's Matilda's turn.

"Right on schedule," mutters Phyllis.

"Shouldn't they be calling the fire department?" I ask out loud. "I mean, for suicide prevention . . ."

"What for?" snorts Phyllis. "She never jumps, I tell you. Never."

"I'm going to check it out," I say, grabbing my jacket from the back of my chair.

"Hey, wait a minute," Red calls to me. "We're a half hour from deadline and I need the update on that girl."

"I'll be back, Red. Anyway, Phyllis says Matilda never jumps. I just want to get a look at this little tradition."

"You can't go."

"I'll give you the update, Red," Rick volunteers. "All right, where's the info?"

"Notepad on my desk," I say, exiting. In the background I can still hear Phyllis: "Hell of a story if she did jump . . ."

The town is cool at night. It's the first thing I notice on

the quiet downtown streets. The coolness is underscored by its emptiness; unlike neighboring Los Angeles, this town is a desert. I can hear my footsteps sharp on the sidewalk.

Two blocks down Matilda stands perched like a bird on the Woolworth Building. Below, two officers in blue from the police station and two deputies in brown from the sheriff's office put in the obligatory appearance. One of the deputies looks up, hands on his waist, and shakes his head, spitting on the concrete. The other laughs, then smacks his gum.

"Come on, Matilda, come down," says an officer.

Matilda, with a sweater over a pale housedress and hair scattered on end like a pine bush, stands silently on the edge.

"Maybe we should call Rodriguez," says a deputy, "so he can talk to her in Spanish."

"What for?" says the other. "She's crazy; she doesn't understand any language."

"Matilda . . . ," an officer calls up.

Matilda looks down at the men and at me, the sole spectator on this breezy night; I expect her to laugh, but she doesn't. She remains quiet, fingering the buttons on her sweater.

Even from where I am, I can see Matilda's face, an unmistakably brown map of lines and planes, older than her years and shamelessly beautiful.

"Loco," says a deputy, signaling a rattled head with his finger at his temple.

"All right," announces an officer, "who's gonna go up there?"

"What for?"

"To talk her off of there, dummy."

"Don't worry, she'll come down by herself."

I think: One way or another, she'll come down—down the stairs and through the doors or head over heels in the air.

In a minute it's dark and Matilda is barely visible against the deep California sky. Stars wink about her.

One of the policemen steps to his squad car and turns on a spotlight, focused on Matilda. The light on her face should be blinding, but nothing moves in Matilda. From five floors down I swear she doesn't even blink.

A moment later, my own eyes are closed, wet and stinging. When I open them again, I'm blinded by the red-hot flash of the Polaroid and Matilda, milk white.

*L*inda Macías Feyder *was born in Los Angeles, California, to a Mexican mother and a French-German father. She is editor of* Shattering the Myth: Plays by Hispanic Women *(1992). A teacher and writer in New York City, she is currently working on a collection of stories. Her story "Marta del Angel" was the winner of* Hispanic Magazine's *1991 fiction contest. It is the story of a young woman whose husband leaves one day for a construction job in Arizona and never comes back.*

MARTA DEL ANGEL

Linda Macías Feyder

My name is Marta del Angel. It's a pretty name; I am named after my father's dead sister. In California they call me Marta with a tongue stuck to their top front teeth when they come to the *t*. It sounds different here, like they are going to spit.

I married an American man I met in a supermarket parking lot. He worked in construction, and when I met him he was sitting in his truck swallowing beer. I fell in love with his arms; they were golden from the sun and a thin film of dust glistened on his blond hairs. There are the things of love, my father once told me. "*Cuídese mi hija*. It only takes one thing."

We rented an apartment in Oxnard not far from the water. I could hear the bells from the dock and at times a foghorn. The home, I kept it spotless and my husband never had to wait for his dinner. These are the lessons of my mother. Her kitchen was my classroom and I learned something. I woke up with the roosters to make fresh cheese for my brothers. My mother tested the coffee before serving it to my father. These things are not uncommon for young women like me.

The second summer of the marriage, my husband said he had a construction job in Arizona and he never came back. I kept his dinner in the freezer, and on lonely nights I would go to the boats and stare out across the ocean where on a clear day I could see the dark outlines of the Channel Islands. I liked to think they were the shores of Mexico and the foghorns were her tired sounds, like an old aunt I listened to. My American girlfriend told me he was probably just working hard. He'll come home, she said. I wanted to say to her, "You gringas, you are too stupid about men." She took me to the movies. I made her *tortas* when she came to visit me on her lunch break. I liked her. She wore large, dangling earrings that looked like coins strung together and I never met a woman who could fix her hair in so many different shapes. We talked about many things, but mostly about men. She was dating a boy three years younger than she, and he kept telling her he didn't want to get married until he was "settled." *Mentiras*, the liar. She said, "You see how mature he is." She kept saying this like she was trying to convince me. *"Pobrecita,"* I thought, "you believe what the men tell you."

I sat up nights and embroidered anything I could get my hands on. I didn't embroider the pretty roses and curling leaves my mother taught me to embroider; I now had skeletons and dark-winged birds on my dish towels and bed sheets. I stitched and thought about why I had come here, why I was the one out of my mother's seven daughters to follow her five sons across the border because I didn't want to stay behind and embroider table covers for the next wedding. I wanted more than dry, sleepy afternoons preparing tamales with *las señoras*. Making cheese. Watching *novelas*. I didn't want to be like the other girls in Ramblas, waiting for Christmas or Mother's Day or the Day of the Dead when the boys returned home for a visit puffed with pride and American dollars. I fixed my hair for them, decided for weeks what to wear to the dances that would celebrate them after they had left me with *los niños* and our suffering mothers who longed for them.

I said to Carol, my American friend, "Have you ever had a Mexican man?"

We sat on the steps leading to my apartment and watched Mrs. Hidalgo's pantyhose swing on a clothesline.

"A Brazilian," she said, "but it wasn't all it's cracked up to be. I don't know, I think he intimidated me. You know, all that stuff you hear. I wasn't sure if I was up to it."

Carol bit into an orange slice and juice squirted from her mouth. Her hair was held off her face by a tie-dye scarf and she braided the rest into two big loops.

"Why," she asked, "are they worth it?"

"I don't know," I said. "I never slept with anyone before I married my husband."

In the mornings I looked into my husband's sock drawer or closet and counted the number of shirts and rolled knee-highs he left behind. I always woke up with renewed hope and thought maybe Carol was right. I counted these things because I thought he wouldn't leave so many behind. There were too many.

Sometimes I called my mother in Mexico and she was usually watching a *novela* with my little sister. I didn't tell her my husband left me. It was hard to keep her attention for very long. She'd start to weep on the phone and I'd say, "What happened, mama?" and she'd say, "Oh, *mi hija*, the lady on the television looks just like you."

Mi hija. My daughter. I called when I knew my father wasn't home. I thought about the deal I made with my papi after his last son finished school and left for the border. My father was standing beneath a tree, *un pino triste*, with his low moustache, his long gaze, and his cowboy hat lowered to cover the knot above his right eye. I knew I was his favorite daughter.

I said, "Papi, let me finish school." None of his daughters completed more than three grades. "I can still do my chores," I told him. "Pay for me to finish school."

He dug his boot into the dry earth, *la tierra de Guanajuato*, the state he never left in his entire life. But he was still the smartest man in Ramblas. He read books about Egypt and he knew how to handwrite, unlike my mother, who never had an education.

"Why do you want to return to school?" he said lowering his eyes on me. "So you can meet a man, marry, and quit? You want me to pay for that?"

"No, Papi," I said. "I won't marry in school and I promise I'll graduate."

The wind whistled through the tree. My father saw a fisherman with a pole bent over the ledge of *la presa*, his thin shoulders hunched as if the small anchor pulled them. I said urgently, "Papi," and I almost grabbed his thick, brown wrist. He would stop and talk to any stranger, my father, no matter what he was doing. On dusty back roads in the hills, or walking a dried riverbed, he would sense, like a dog smells a buried bone, a stranger to talk to. His eyes would look over the horizon, squinting in concentration, and never on the stranger's face. He would talk about the harvest, the weather, the latest family to lose sons to the border, but mostly he would listen.

He turned and stepped onto the stone dam, making his way to the lone fisherman. I followed behind him in open-toed sandals, carefully picking my steps. I knew I had lost his attention and I searched around me for something to fill the time I would spend waiting. But there was nothing and nobody. How often my brothers, sisters, and I wished he would meet strangers in town. If he met them in a crowded bus station or near the *zócalo* we could occupy ourselves easily. But he never did. In those places he walked as the stranger, with a stone face and rigid posture; he would say he had to get back to the ranch by noon.

"*Buenos días*," my father said to the fisherman.

I found a smooth stone jutting out of the dam and took my seat ten feet from them. I picked up a gray rock and threw it at a bird searching for something to eat between the stones. Father stood with his hands clasped on his hips, his dusty black leather jacket open and rising above his stomach. They stared across the lake. I could hear them talking about *la bruja de Aguascalientes.* The fisherman said he had a deaf friend and this witch, she made it so that he could hear again. Their voices droned on and blended with the wind until I wasn't aware of their talking and I daydreamed.

"*Marta, venga,*" my father called to me. The fisherman looked in my direction, his eyes crinkled in a smile but his mouth remained turned down.

I lifted myself from the stone and shuffled toward them.

"Marta," my father said, "I have asked Don Tomás what he thinks about your promise."

I stared at the fisherman, this stranger, with his empty fishnet and slack, orange pole and then back to my father with wide eyes.

"I told him about *tu promesa de quedarte soltera,* and he tells me, '*Déjala*—let her go.' "

The fisherman looked down at his worn canvas shoes. "If you want it," he said to the wet stone beneath his feet.

Carol took me to a pet shop to buy me a bird. We picked out a green one with yellow cheeks; the man behind the counter showed us three different types of birdseed. I said to him, "Will it talk?"

"Not unless you give him vocal cords," he said, laughing.

To Carol I said under my breath, "Too bad, I would teach it to say '*pendejos.*' "

Carol laughed out loud and her earrings jangled. She liked it when I cursed in Spanish.

At home I watched the bird eat its seed. I tried to see if it swallowed. This bird, I liked to watch him bathe. He would flutter into himself, burying his face into his feathers. And he had such courage, my bird. He flew headfirst into my window-panes without a second thought. The next day he would do the same thing. He sang clear and beautiful. It didn't matter that he was without vocal cords.

I thought about the fisherman with his pole and no fish. My father called him *"un testigo,"* the witness to my promise. I was father's only daughter to complete a high-school educa-tion, and the only one to leave *la casa de mi padre, soltera.* Un-married.

I remembered my father's face on the day of my gradua-tion. He came drunk after toasting my achievement in a *pul-quería* full of strangers. He sat straight and glassy-eyed in a small cluster of waving parents. I remembered thinking his strangers had been my teachers. If I hadn't had *un testigo* would I have finished school? I watched Papi remove his hat, some-thing he did only in churches and the few moments before lay-ing his crop-weary body to bed. The lump above his brow shone brightly against the old adobe walls.

"Carol," I said one afternoon, watching her pick the green peppers from her rice, "do you still think he'll come home?"

She looked up at me with a long face. She was sad and quiet on this day. Her young boyfriend left her for a girl with straight teeth, and I asked her this question to remind her that her problem was nothing.

She brought a pink fingernail to her temple and tapped it there. "You know," she said, "I didn't know how to say this to you, but I'm not so sure anymore."

She brought her legs up on the chair and wrapped her arms around her knees. I felt sad now, because I didn't expect her to finally tell me the truth. I looked at the bird in his cage. I had tied bows of red ribbon on the bars and the one he pecked rested loose on the floor. I watched him clean his feathers. His beak worked rapidly.

Carol said, "From now on I may sleep with younger men, but I'll never picture them at the altar, Martha, I swear it."

In the morning, I walked to the water and my steps made the wood dock creak. I read the names of the boats: *Treasure Chest, Whimsy, Dolores.* Who was Dolores? I passed two guys with skin like my own sitting with their legs dangling over the edge of the dock. One of them hissed, *"Chi, chi, chi,"* and I kept staring at the boats. I thought about Carol. I wondered about me. We needed *testigos*, she and I, a face off the street.

I passed an old woman with a paper sack, but she didn't see me. I remembered my father bought three fish, but the fisherman had no change so he kept the money and Papi chose two more. They were the only fish he caught all day. They were silver and yellow in the sunshine and they flopped around the stone dam. I stood next to my father and watched the fisherman take a buck knife and slit their stomachs while they still sucked for breath. I watched the red life drain out of them.

The fisherman took them down to the water and rinsed them off. My father said to him, "I think we will have rain tomorrow."

Marisella Veiga was born in Havana, Cuba. She was raised in both Saint Paul, Minnesota, and Miami, Florida. Her poetry, articles, and translations have appeared in numerous publications. She currently lives, writes, and teaches in Miami. In this story an older woman's wisdom is contrasted to that of a new generation of Latinas.

FRESH FRUIT

Marisella Veiga

I was up the first time about five, made coffee, and heated up some milk for it. When I turned on the kitchen light, the dog came and stood near the stove. He seemed cold. Right before lunch I usually boil some meat and bones for him, but it was not time for that feeding, so I gave him a little warm milk instead. I snapped the light off and went to sit on the porch, where I usually have my coffee and listen to the roosters and the occasional car traveling along the highway.

The young woman across the street, Susana, went to work earlier than usual today. The driveway gate clanked loudly when she closed it, as if it was meant as a shout to someone inside the house, "There, you have it!" I'd like to see someone actually walk away from his home that easily.

She started that old car with tremendous faith. It's as loud as a motorcycle. Sometimes, as the car warms up, she looks over to see if I am on the porch and waves. In the morning she is relaxed, friendlier. By late afternoon, she is tired and a bit arrogant, thinking that what she does all day is more important than what I do. I can tell by the excuses she makes when I call her to come over for a short visit.

"I just got home from work and have to shower," she yells from across the street, one hand busy with a set of keys, the other holding a briefcase. Other times, when she's tired, there's a longer litany: "I'm hungry. There's no food in the house. I have to go to the market, then make dinner." There's a plea in her voice on those days, yet I do not do anything to alleviate her exhaustion. What she means is that there's no time for an old lady on the schedule unless a hot meal is included.

She'll push her plate away at the end of the meal, thank me, smoke a cigarette, and five minutes later cross the street to her house without being any sort of company afterward. My husband, Wilfredo, is just like that.

Susana, of course, has the option to not make anyone anything. Every morning at the corner cafeteria she reads a newspaper while having breakfast. Someone cooks it and somebody else takes the dishes away when the meal is done. She does not even see the faces of the people performing these services. Throwing away money, that's all. I told her she could pay me less and have more delicious food, but I don't think she's interested in saving money either, or forming a home with a husband.

Why? For one, though I have advised her, she has not bothered to invest in a red dress. It's an attractive color that suits her, and would appeal to a man, and one never knows. A husband could help her along, and she, in turn, could help him. When I told her my idea, she said, "Red? I don't like that color at all."

When Wilfredo and I were first married, we rented a small apartment in this neighborhood, near the sea, and spent Sundays on the beach. Years later, he bought this house and a few years after that a farm in the mountains, so our home would not lack fresh fruit or vegetables. I haven't seen the farm in years; I don't leave the house, but he drives up there often and returns with the back of his jeep loaded with bunches of plantains. He hangs them on hooks to ripen in the garage.

I give them out to neighbors as a way of showing appreciation for their attentions to me. Whenever I tell Susana to take a couple, she hesitates. Oh, the diet she is currently on does not allow for much of anything fried, and that's how she likes them. A little prompting and she takes three thick ones home, hiding them in the briefcase. I know she eats them up fast, fried as *tostones*, not waiting for them to ripen for a sweeter tasting dish. No, she is an impatient sort who likes to take hard bites of hot salty starches.

She refuses things like custards, although I have seen her eyes widen when I've brought one out to the table and set it next to her coffee. No sweets. Give her salt, the sea, the beginning of the meal and she's happy. I know. Now, I want the sweet, the fruit that comes after the meal is done.

He's home. I heard the car horn sound, a warning so I am not frightened when someone begins jiggling the padlock on the porch door. When Wilfredo returns in the evening, he greets me with a kiss on the cheek, though he is coming from his mistress's house. We have lived in this house for twenty years now, and she has lived in another one, which he also owns, all along.

I tolerate his nightly visits with her. I have no choice. In a way, they are a relief because he does not look at me anymore to satisfy his longing. He thinks I think I'm too old for sex. He doesn't leave her, won't abandon me, and the neighbors know that in the end he sleeps in this house every night. One might say I am no longer acting completely as a wife.

He does not allow his mistress to cook for him. That is why I believe that, after all these years, he loves me most because he comes home twice a day to my table.

The young woman across the street, despite all her American ways, which she learned at school, does not know how to do this. Yes, she is free to wander beyond her gate, to walk into a restaurant any time of day, like any mall, and buy meals made by someone cooking anonymously in the kitchen. She has money, a way to ride around town. She speaks English and French and travels to the other islands. She drinks beer and sometimes stays out late, while I sit on my porch waiting for Wilfredo to arrive. I don't get bored.

Her house is empty all day until she walks into it. She can stroll along the shore of the sea anytime, but there, nobody gives a damn. There she goes, out to dinner alone again, taking a book along for company. I'll start frying up plaintains. Wilfredo will be home in an hour.

After the meal and some conversation, he will turn off the lights in the dining room. I'll wash the dishes and close up the kitchen, and finally bring the dog inside the house for the night. We will go through the rest of the rooms, turning off the lights in the entire house, before going our separate ways.

M ary Helen Ponce is the author of Hoyt Street (*1993*), Taking Control (*1987*), and The Wedding (*1989*). *Her work appears in several journals and anthologies published in the United States and in Mexico. She has taught literature and creative writing at universities in Santa Barbara and Northridge, California, and in New Mexico. This new story describes a dinner date that turns sour before the dessert arrives.*

JUST DESSERT

Mary Helen Ponce

"**S**he wasn't a good wife," he tells me, his dark eyes troubled. "Not at all.

"Yeah . . . ," he continues, warming to the subject—and hopefully to me—"gave her everything anyone could want: house, cars, charge accounts. Never asked what she did, either, where she went. She just . . ." His voice drifts off, his brown Latin eyes—as I call them—glitter dangerously in the soft candlelight.

It's our third date. We're beginning to feel comfortable with each other, to discuss freely the things we hold dear. I know I like him . . . and I can tell he, too, likes me. He hasn't said so. Not yet, anyway, but I can tell by the way he looks at my hair, my breasts, my moist lips.

The restaurant is classy; it reeks of Rodeo Drive. The waiters bustle around, their quick hands fluttering in between the tables set at strategic points. The food is good, the champagne cold. At center table a decorative basket holds a variety of breads, a regular feature of this eatery. Along one wall, green palmettos sway to the artificial breeze of the ceiling fans.

I remember to use the correct fork, dip my soup spoon away from me, avoid crumbling the soft bread, but he doesn't care. He moves back and forth between his salad and main course, switches dinner and salad forks, butters a roll with a spoon, and with a knife stirs the ice in his water glass.

It's been two years since I met a really nice (unattached), financially secure (solvent) man. He's the right age, color, height, and weight. A *perfect* ten!

I don't know him all that well. Not in the Biblical sense, that is, but I know I will. Still, I like what I know about him: he's Italian (like me), loves family, calls his mother once a week, follows the 49ers (I'm a Raider fan), and now and then goes to Sunday Mass. Lust is in the air!

"I gave her everything," he sighs, "more than she ever had. Worked two jobs from dawn to dusk." He looks past me at a pretty waitress going by, adjusts his tie, then sips wine from a crystal goblet. "She never wanted for anything." His muscular hand squeezes the glass, then falls slowly to his lap. "The girls went to Ramona Convent; the boys to Cathedral High. I shelled out bucks for my kids!"

Not knowing what to say, I say nothing. Mostly I stare at his mouth . . . the most delicious mouth I have ever seen on a man. Since Elvis Presley, that is. His face is wide, clean shaven; his forehead smooth and unwrinkled. Streaks of grey highlight his dark brown hair; his ears lie close to his head. Best of all, he's mine, mine. At least for tonight!

He drives a gorgeous car, a Lamborghini imported from Italy that's his pride and joy. It has a hand-tooled aluminum body, is upholstered in real leather, and goes from zero to sixty miles an hour in 4.3 seconds, he informed me early on. And it cost a mint. He doesn't drive it much, only for special occasions. Like tonight.

"I was gone a lot," he admits, his voice soft. "I hardly knew my older kids . . . had to get the business going. Construction is tough. I left home at five . . . had to make it to the site by six . . . make sure my guys were on the job, supplies delivered, you know." He spreads his hands for emphasis; the blunt finger lightly brushes my hand. I feel my skin tingle.

"All she did was stay home and watch TV." He digs into the steaming pasta with gusto.

"She"—the words "your wife" stick to my tongue—"watched TV all day long? With five kids?"

"Yeah. Took them to school—or got someone else to, you know. Got her a big station wagon, a nice four-door job with all the extras . . . room for my kids and their friends. Cost me a mint, too."

He pops a Greek olive in his pouty mouth, sips water, then spears the remains of my cannelloni into his mouth. In one giant swoop he stabs the cherry tomatoes in my salad; they disappear inside his lovely mouth. He gestures to our waitress for more wine. He smacks his soft, pink lips, then stares out the window at the ocean.

I like what I see. A handsome, robust man in his prime. A hardworking man who loves his family and wants nothing but the best for them. A responsible man, unlike some of the creeps I know who never call their mothers, rarely see their kids, think church is for sissies, and on dates like to go Dutch. I'm about to drool all over the linen tablecloth.

"She had no reason to leave," he says, cutting into a bloody steak. "I wouldn't have. Left, I mean . . ." He sneaks a look at the waitress, dribbles steak juice on the tablecloth. "I would never do anything to hurt my kids. I wasn't happy, I admit, but who is?" He dips his fingers into a tiny bowl, then wipes them on the napkin. "I fooled around some." He grins, toying with the steak knife. "After all, I'm a man. But I wanted my kids to have a home, even if she had to be in it. But they saw her for what she was." He sips the blood red wine, munches on bread, then looks across at me. "They're grown up now. Let's see . . ." He removes a leather wallet from inside his blazer and opens it to a series of snapshots: boys and girls of all ages, dark hair, dark eyes. Typical Italians. "Mario, here, is twenty-five, Louis twenty-four. This is Antoinette . . . I mean

Toni. Madonna's the one in pink, and this here is my baby, Carmina."

"How old are they?"

"Who?"

"The girls."

"I think Toni's twenty-two, Maddy's twenty, and my baby, uhhh, Mina, is still a kid. She was still in high school when her mother took off. The boys were on their own, you know, with their own place." He spears a chunk of asparagus, rolls it in cheese sauce, then continues. "She ruined Mina's last year. That's one thing I'll never forgive her for. Never." He looks hard at me, his eyes suddenly dark, the lush mouth set in a snarl. "I can't forgive a woman who leaves her children before they're old enough to . . ."

I feel threatened, my fingers twist the napkin to and fro. The food in my stomach weighs heavy; the wine is going to my head. I long to say there's *nothing wrong* with grown-up kids looking after themselves, but he's on a roll. He needs to talk, I rationalize, to confide in someone he trusts. And this is what I wanted, isn't it? To be an important part of someone's life.

He sips wine; his tongue flickers in and out. He empties the wineglass, then loosens his jacket. His hand comes to rest near my thigh; I feel the tiny hairs on the back of his fingers. I can feel his heat.

Should I tell him that I, too, left home when my kids were in high school? That *their* lives weren't ruined? They saw how things were—the power plays, fights over money, numerous separations—and in fact were relieved when their dad and I split up.

I'm beginning to feel terribly uncomfortable. It could be the wine, but it's *really* the things he's saying. All the talk about his ex and kids is giving me a headache. I wish he'd lean over and kiss me instead. Just a small, quick kiss.

I stare at the mouth shaped like a rosebud, moist and pink, the kind seldom seen on a man. I wonder how it would feel to run my thirsty tongue all over his neck, nibble on his . . .

"She was a lousy mother. A real bitch. Always finding fault with my kids. You could hear her a block away: make your beds, pick up your clothes. Nag, nag, nag." He stops to breathe—and to gulp wine. Around us, folks pretend not to hear. I want to say something, anything to stop the tirade, but he is in control.

He orders Amaretto, cracks open a walnut, and offers me the luscious, meaty pulp. With his wide fingers he scrapes the meat from the hull onto his hand. His sensuous lips slowly move up and down as he chews. I stare, mesmerized by the pink, succulent mouth.

"I warned her," he says, sipping cappuccino from a porcelain cup. "The kids are gonna hate you if you don't lay off 'em." He waits for my comment, then plunges ahead. "I never backed her up . . . had to protect my kids. They didn't deserve—"

"How can kids not deserve their mother?" The words are out before I can stop them. Startled, he looks at me, wipes his mouth. I'm saved by a pretty blonde waitress with the dessert cart. He flirts with her, wanting to know if the rum cake is really made with rum. He's torn between the cheesecake and Napoleon, so orders both. In an expansive mood, he compliments the young woman, who acts embarrassed (yet pleased). She blushes, stammers a reply, then in apparent relief swiftly rolls the cart away.

He splashes cream in his coffee, tastes it, then makes a face. "I hate cold coffee. My ex learned to keep a pot ready—or else." He signals to the harried waitress, who offers an apology, replenishes his cup, then makes a hasty retreat. From the corner of my eye I see the headwaiter make a note on a pad.

Dammit! I don't want the waitress to get sacked. Not over a cup of coffee! Determined to say something, I glare at him, at his perfect, rosy pink mouth. He dips a finger into the Napoleon, licks it, then looks away, his dark, dreamy eyes on the blonde now in a heated discussion with the headwaiter.

"I'm a man. My kids gotta obey me. *Me, me*, not her. Her job was to do what I said, not play the kids against me. After all,

I'm the guy that's bustin' his ass all day, while she . . ." He wipes his mouth, reaches across the table, and begins on the Thompson grapes.

"Kids are supposed to be afraid of a father. *My* old man scared the heck out of me, and I turned out okay." He smiles at me for confirmation; his dark eyes flicker over my bare arms and come to rest on my breasts. "But no, she wanted them to obey *her.* Can you believe that?"

"I don't see anything wrong with—"

"I don't mind the girls' obeying her." He interrupts himself as he wipes the chocolate stuck to his fingers on my napkin. "Men gotta learn from men. Who else is gonna show them to be tough? It's a hard world out there, let me tell you. Building is a rough trade. A man has to learn to give orders." He wipes his mouth with the damask napkin, brushes back a stray lock of hair. "My boys know about orders." He laughs, then leans close to whisper, "Actually, they kick ass."

I once liked the way he laughed. First with the eyes, then a small chuckle that accelerated into a loud chortle. Genuine, not too offensive. When something was really funny, he threw back his head and laughed until—as he put it—his belly was about to burst.

Once more I gaze at the gorgeous hunk sitting across from me. At the finely chiseled face, strong Roman nose, greying hair. Once more my eyes zero in on that luscious mouth, that slightly moist mouth I long to bite. I think I'm in lust.

"My boys are just like the old man here." He taps his chest, looking smug. "They give orders, keep their guys alert. Worked with me since they were kids. When Mario turned sixteen I made him foreman. When he made partner, I gave Louis his job."

"And the girls?"

He licks the last of the Napoleon, then digs into the cheesecake. "Toni works for the phone company, Maddy takes classes. Ceramics, I think. And my baby . . . Mina's still finding herself. She's got lots of time. So what if she's out half the night . . . sleeps most of the day? She's got nothing to worry about. The old man here's got bucks. One of these days she'll meet a nice Italian boy and . . ." He snaps his fingers, pleased with himself.

I toy with a spoon, staring all the while at his hands, at the strong fingers I long to feel in my mouth, on my breasts, between my thighs. With trembling hands I drop sugar in my already sweet coffee, then take a sip. What does he want? I wonder. To hear me say I approve? That he's doing the right thing by his daughter?

I feel terribly vulnerable, as if on trial. I, too, was a bad mother. I made my children pick up after themselves, forced them to eat their peas. When they turned three, each was assigned to empty wastebaskets. From there they graduated to clearing the table and loading the dishwasher. Later they folded laundry and—horror of horrors—ironed clothes, including my bras and slips. Have I scarred them for life?

"She drank . . ."

"Who?"

"My ex. She and her girlfriends boozed."

"Boozed?"

"Wine. I never said much, figured she needed a break. They sometimes killed a gallon of Dago red." He's angry, his face a deep red. "It got me when the kids came home from school and found her sleeping on the sofa . . . had to make their own sandwiches—ya know, cook. That really got my goat."

"The sandwiches?"

"No." He takes a bite of creamy cheesecake, brushes crumbs off the tablecloth. He seems impatient with the waitress, now refilling his coffee cup.

"What got me was . . ." He stops to sip the scalding coffee, as across the room the headwaiter makes a notation. "It was her job to look after my boys, but no, they had to make their food. Make your sisters do it," I told them. "That's what women are for!

"But by then the girls were full of ideas. Women's libbers! I threatened to cut them off . . . and I'm a generous man." Eyes blazing, he leans across the table, picks apart a cluster of grapes.

"Yeah, well they—Toni and Maddy—told me off. Me! Their father, the guy who busted his butt for years. They moved out, got jobs. It really gets me, ya know . . . my girls not needing me no more." Perspiration lines his fine brow; his eyes look haunted; his pink mouth is beginning to harden. Across from us, an elderly couple tries not to stare; the headwaiter avoids my eye.

"I'm their father! They're still my kids! Who else is gonna—"

"Their mother?"

He blinks, then leans over; his tie misses the water glass. "What do women know of hard work? All my ex ever did was stay home. She never had to work." Visibly irritated, he bites off a piece of hangnail. "She had it made; all women have it made . . . all they do is drink coffee and watch the soaps."

"Soaps?"

"Spend more time in front of the tube than cooking." His mouth—that lovely, perfect mouth—is compressed into a line; his brown eyes are blurred, unfocused. "She was a lousy house-keeper."

He's singing a familiar tune.

I, too, was a lousy housekeeper, more concerned with keeping my kids well fed and happy than with scrubbing walls. I swept dirt under the rug, mopped the kitchen floor without first sweeping, then sat to read for hours. In order not to miss a PBS special, I often left the supper dishes in the sink until morning. But unlike his poor wife, I never drank wine. I took pills.

The last year of my marriage was spent in a Valium-induced haze. At first the tiny pills (my family doctor pre-scribed the smallest dosage) were to help me cope. But I came to depend on them during those dark days—and nights when all I yearned to do was sleep. I never neglected the kids, though. Once they were off to school I slunk back to bed, pulled down the shades, and fell into a deep sleep.

I'm getting a headache. Was it the wine? The brandy? Could be I need coffee? I signal to the ever-attentive waitress, who immediately fills my cup.

We leave the restaurant late at night; the valet is long gone, but the Lamborghini is where we left it. Unlike at other times, he does not hold my hand as we walk toward the car. *I feel a growing tension between us and want to say something, but what?*

Always solicitous, he reaches over to open the door, then clicks it shut behind me. I stretch my legs, buckle up, then check my lipstick. Satisfied, I smooth my dress and wait. In the car he loosens his tie, leans close, and takes my hand in his.

"She hated sex." His voice, almost a hiss, catches me unawares.

I pull my hand away, fidget with the car radio, frantic for music, talk radio, a commercial, anything to keep from hearing about his ex-wife. Yet a part of me wants to know how he feels about sex—*what he likes.*

I fidget in my seat, shocked to the core at the mouth—that gorgeous mouth—now spewing intimate details of a past life, an ex-wife who was messy, frigid, puritanical. Slowly, deliberately, his callused hand reaches across the seat to caress my arm, then slides across my sheer dress and down to my thighs.

I am filled with longing. We're meant to be lovers. To give love, show love, make love. But, dammit, it's the wrong time of the month!

"She always had an excuse. Either a headache, or it was the wrong time of the month. It got to where I stopped asking and got myself a . . ."

Trapped in the elegant car, I pull away, lean against the plush leather, then press the window button; the cool Pacific air soothes my hot face. I feel sick. I'm going to throw up all over the plush Lamborghini and make a big mess. He'll never call me again!

He smiles—a condescending smirk, really, one I equate with slick car salesmen—then jabs the key into the ignition switch, checks the rearview mirror, straps on his seat belt, then pulls onto the 101 freeway. The car motor purrs; we hit top speed in zero seconds.

We glide past Malibu. I strain my eyes, trying to make out the boats bobbing in the water, but all that is visible is tiny lights. At a stoplight a car crammed with teenagers pulls alongside. They ogle the car, take in the sleek body, shiny chrome, custom rims, then move up for a better view. I picture how we must look to them: a nice-looking couple out on the town. A *married* couple whose grown-up kids are on their own.

"How do *you* feel about sex?" His voice has a new urgency; his eyes bore into mine. With practiced ease he takes a hand off the wheel, removes a gold cigarette holder from his breast pocket, lights a cigarette and inhales. Hot ashes float across my face to land on the carpet.

I don't want to say the wrong thing or appear too eager. It's been a while for me—and hopefully for him, too, but sex to me is terribly personal. I know it's good for the complexion— and does wonders for sleep—but what with AIDS and all, it pays to be choosy. I squirm in my seat, playing for time.

Earlier, when saturated with wine, I wondered how it would be to rip his clothes off, run my hands over his hairy chest, pinch his nipples, bite his ears. A slow, deep kiss. But now, nothing feels right. How could something so wonderful change so quickly?

"I'm not sure how I feel." Unable to hear me, he leans close. His hair brushes my cheek, sends a chill up my spine. I can smell his cologne—Polo, I think. I wish I could bite his mouth, put an end to all this talk.

"How do you feel about sex? About me?"

He's not about to let it go! I take a deep breath and turn to him. His lovely mouth glistens in the soft spring night. That pink, slightly curved mouth that won't quit. In the pale light, his greying hair shimmers like silver. His nose quivers with excitement; his blunt fingers grip tight the steering wheel.

"I'm not frigid, if that's what you're asking. I . . ." The words die in my mouth, my throat is beginning to constrict. "I like sex like any normal person, but I won't do anything a man wants."

"My ex was a prude," he grunts, yanking off his tie. He hums softly, fidgets with the car radio, stops at a jazz station. Billy Eckstine is singing "Fools Rush In." I hum along, keep time with the beat.

"My foreman Joe and his wife are swingers. Sometime back I threw a party—I think it was our anniversary—so I invited them and their friends. I picked a couple . . . a redhead with . . . a great body. *Her* old man was dancing with my wife, uhhhh, my *ex-wife*, kept saying she was pretty and had great legs. I figured it was okay."

"You never said she was pretty!" I sense the panic in my voice. From the photos—especially of the girls—I should have guessed their mother, too, was pretty. But did she have to have great legs?

". . . anyway, I got her in the bedroom, told her what we were gonna do, who her partner was. Ya know . . ."

"And?"

"She started crying. Acted like she'd never heard of swinging, ran out the door. Embarrassed me in front of my friends! But folks were staying over . . . she acted like nothing happened. Next day she made frittatas for everybody." He puffs on the cigarette; smoke fills the air. "Would you have done that?"

"I'm not sure I care for group sex." I pick the words with care. My tongue feels swollen; my throat aches for water. Still, I make the effort. "A man and woman who mean something to each other shouldn't want to . . ." I sound so dumb! I'll bet the teenagers who passed by us have better answers.

"I wouldn't want a man I'm committed to to even look at

another woman," I stammer. "I mean, what's the point?"

Thoroughly disgusted, he looks away. The gorgeous mouth, like that of a petulant child, is drawn.

I feel sick. This time I will throw up. I lean my head out the window, breathe deeply, then hold my hand over my mouth.

This isn't how I imagined the evening! I had hoped we would make plans for a quiet weekend (a sex weekend) at the Calabasas Inn or some such place. But it's not going to happen. Dammit, why couldn't he talk of something other than his ex-wife? Why did I let him dominate the conversation? The evening? Just what is he saying? That he likes kinky sex? What's wrong with plain sex? I don't mean the missionary position . . . I'm not that uptight, but . . .

He guides the Lamborghini out of traffic, turns right onto a promontory overlooking the Pacific, shuts the motor off, pushes back the leather seat, then reaches for me.

He kisses me, softly at first, then grinds his beautiful mouth against my hot, dry lips. I can taste the brandy; I can smell his lust. Slowly, cautiously, I press my mouth against his, against the perfectly shaped mouth that is stifling me.

"I can't breathe." The words are out before I can stop them. He sits up, gives me a piercing look, then moves away. Head swimming, I slump against the plush seat.

"Want to stop at the Bel Air? It's nearby."

Could he mean the Bel Air Hotel? The posh playground of movie stars? The pink bungalows where the rich and famous stay? I've never been there but hear it's fabulous. Celebrities like Warren Beatty and the sultan of Brunei keep rooms there. Even Christopher Plummer, of the fabulous thighs, stays there. I feel myself weakening.

He reaches into the glove compartment, removes a thick cigar and lights it. The stench makes me sick. I try not to breathe, so once more I open the window, then stare out at the dark, mysterious ocean.

"Want to spend the night at the Bel Air?"

"Uhhhh."

"You might never get the chance again."

He's threatening me! Damn Italian machismo. Who does he think I am, one of his kids? His ex-wife?

Always polite, he waits for my response. His blunt fingers—splayed across the steering wheel—mark time to Sarah Vaughan's "Broken-Hearted Melody." The vein in his throat pulsates. He's angry, and will dump me if . . .

"I'd rather go home."

"Was it the brandy?"

"No."

He gives my arm a gentle squeeze. I feel the strength in his fingers, sense the compact body under the silk shirt, cashmere blazer, Gucci tie. He looks deep in my eyes. "Somehow I'd hoped you'd be the one . . ."

The Lamborghini comes to life; the hand-tooled body hums. He shifts into reverse, checks for traffic, then guides the car back onto the deserted freeway. We leave the Valley and head north.

Swiftly, we approach my wooden house tucked away in the Angeles Forest. His eyes—those gorgeous Latin eyes—are glued to the empty road. I move close, glance his way, but he ignores me and instead fiddles with the luminous dials that all but cover the wide dashboard.

We reach a mountain road; the white car accelerates, takes the curves with ease. He turns into my tree-lined driveway. Engine running, he waits for me to get out. I open wide the car door, poke my leg out. Above me, the overhead light illuminates his face, the perfect symmetry of his nose. The lovely mouth.

It's over. The romance is clearly over. I will not kiss the beautiful mouth again. Nor will I feel his hand on my knee, my breasts, my . . .

I want to say something, but what? Suggest we start over? Can a relationship grow on lies?

I smile at him; he smiles back, fidgets with the key, anxious to have me out of his car, his life. His lovely, moist mouth smiles briefly, the dark eyes slide over my breasts. "It was nice," he murmurs, as he sneaks a glance at his Rolex.

He drives off. The Lamborghini takes the curve at top speed, then disappears around the corner.

I open the door, remove my shoes and coat, and turn on a lamp. Just then, Brutus bounds into the room, sniffs my feet, then plops onto the chintz sofa. From the window ledge Pinocchio licks his paws, arches his tail, then dives to the floor—and lands in a heap.

I bathe. The tepid water soothes my pulsating body. Once dry, I rub creamy lotion on my arms and legs, dust my breasts with Old Rose bath powder, pull on a thin nightgown, secure doors, yank back the cotton sheets, and crawl into my solitary bed.

Monica Palacios started her career by writing funny short stories; they soon turned into a slick comedy act in San Francisco. Today she is based in Los Angeles and is known as a writer/performer. Currently she is touring with her bold autobiographical piece Latin Lezbo Comic, which was featured on PBS. Her new spoken-word slide show is called Confessions. Her work has been published in several magazines and newspapers, as well as in Chicana Lesbians (1991), Lesbian Bedtime Stories, vol. 2 (1990), Consuming Passions: Lesbians Celebrate Food (1995), and Latinas on Stage (1995). She has written two one-acts, La Llorona Loca and Seagullita. She is cochair of VIVA, Lesbian and Gay Latino Artists, where she has produced performance and art shows. The following story is dedicated to her love, Dyan.

PERSONALITY FABULOSA

Monica Palacios

I fell asleep on the classifieds that were spread across my bed. I was naked. Kinky? I wish. No, I had passed out from eight hours of looking through every roommate ad in the Los Angeles area. It was already the fifteenth and I had to find a place by the end of the month. My adorable apartment was going to become someone's parking space—I hate progress. What knocked me out was the last ad I read: "2 holistic, vegetarian, nonsmoking, nonexisting lesbians are looking for a 3rd lesbian to share a communal, collective, clairvoyant household. Call Yin or Yang between sunrise and sunset. Cats OK—we have 57." No thanks, ladies. I'll go live on a Greyhound Bus.

The phone rang. As I dragged my butt out of bed, I noticed newsprint on my belly. Great. I'll probably get skin cancer and die in two years. If I was lucky, maybe my death would come sooner, solving my moving dilemma. I answered the phone on the fourth ring. "Hello," I said as if I cared.

"Hi, my name is Alicia." She pronounced her name in perfect Spanish—which I loved. She continued. "I came across your roommate ad at Santa Monica College. I think we should meet."

"You don't have cats, right?" I asked.

"Nope. No pets. Not even ants."

I prepared for the big bonus question, "You are a lesbian?"

Alicia paused for a second. "Well, the last time I checked, everything was one hundred percent lezbo. No penis envy here."

"Very funny, Alicia," I said, feeling a little self-conscious saying her name in Spanish. I mean, I had no choice. And anyway I can speak Spanish—not fluently, but I feel pretty damn proud when I order food at Taco Bell. I proceeded with my lesbian investigation as the theme song from *Dragnet* played in my head. "I don't mean to ask such a stupid question, but people are so desperate to find roommates—they'll lie! And then I have to send a man wearing a fedora and a trench coat after them." She laughed. I was pleased. "I hope I'm not sounding pushy."

"No, not at all. I enjoy women who don't beat around the bush."

The smoothness of her voice was like a bite of a San Franciscan mint—cool and sweet. "How about seven? Oh, and ah, I live in Santa Monica, two blocks away from the beach."

She gave me her address and I threw in that I was an aspiring writer, trying to create that million-dollar screenplay, play, grocery list—anything, really. But I assured her I had a steady paying gig, working for several catering companies. We said good-bye and I thought: strong woman, fresh voice, beach pad—cool.

The address led me to a quaint courtyard filled with luscious roses, with three cottage-type houses surrounding the garden. The center house had the number I was looking for, so I followed the round steps that made me walk funny to the door. Right before my middle finger made its way to the doorbell, the door opened. She was Rita Hayworth in *Gilda*. She was a gorgeous Latina. She took my breath away—I choked!

"Do you need water?" Her question ended with a soft smile—no, a smirk—and I loved it. Alicia placed her hand on my shoulder. *Ay caramba!* Oh god, she's making my loins hot and she's a potential roommate? Scary.

My glands calmed down; I straightened up, became the essence of cool, and casually wiped my mouth to make sure I wasn't drooling. "No water. I'm fine."

"I'm Alicia. Nice to meet you." She gave me a strong shake, looking at me with her beautiful, sparkling hazel eyes.

I sucked in some air and quickly looked around the room. "Great place. Do you have any dental floss?" I knew it sounded weird, but there was something stuck in between my back teeth and I was giving Alicia a chance to come to my aid. Oh, baby, take my temperature!

Alicia laughed. "You walk in here choking and now you need dental floss. Is this a test?" Again, flashing me that adorable smirk.

She led me into the bathroom and told me the dental floss was in the medicine cabinet. I noticed a picture on the wall to my left of Alicia kissing a woman on the cheek while wrapped in her arms. Friend—I thought. You can kiss and hug your friends. No big deal. What am I doing? Floss, girl!

Heading for the living room, I noticed two more pictures of the *other woman* in the hallway. I had to know. I have one of those sick curious minds. But there was a small part of me that didn't want to verbalize my tacky question, so I managed to be playful about it as I asked in a gangster sort of way, "Who's the babe?"

"That's my ex-wife." She looked down. It wasn't the best question to have asked. God, I'm a dope brain.

"I'm sorry. I didn't mean to get into your business. I'm a cat—forever curious. You could have had photos of you and a llama and I would have asked, 'Who's the llama?' " I managed to get that smirk. Her eyes sparkled at me for two seconds, and I flashed her the peace sign.

"Let me show you the rest of the house," she said. Alicia was the tour guide of the month, showing me the sites with her edible personality, her short black tank dress, her long wavy hair (you know, that wild Latin look), her healthy bronzed skin, and her face—I wanted to bite into it. She wasn't a roommate. She was trouble. I couldn't live with a sex goddess! I'd want to hump her at all times. As she gave me the grand tour, I floated behind her, inhaling her existence. Every now and then I'd throw in some funny line, but I was under her spell. Then I started to worry. Did she find me attractive? Is she considering me as a roommate? I hate when I get like this.

"Do you attend Santa Monica College, or do you hang out there to stare at young coeds?" She interrupted my insecure thoughts.

"Well, if you must know, I have enrolled to take a Spanish class—conversational of course. I am not a beginner at my ancestral tongue. *¿Dónde está Pepe?—fajitas—*for here or to go?" Alicia cracked up. "Okay, I can't speak the language fluently and I'm pretty embarrassed about it, so I'm taking a class. But you still think I'm cool, right?"

This time she let out a good laugh. "Don't worry about it. Many Latinos don't speak Spanish. And yes, I still think you're cool."

I hoped she was going to continue to say: "I think you're cute too . . . I think you're beautiful . . . I think you're probably great in the sack . . ." I think I'm full of shit!

Then I did a silly thing. I asked her to have dinner with me the next evening. We could find out more about each other and I could see if she would let me pick off her plate. She suggested a vegetarian Indian restaurant. (I wasn't surprised.) I told her I was a vegetarian too. She laughed, and said, "How very lesbian of us." But I was thinking more like, how very lesbian of me to disguise a dinner date as a casual business meeting.

I left her house feeling very mischievous and—oh, what's the word—horny! So I headed for the Santa Monica Pier, which was within walking distance, to escape into the arcades. A couple of rounds of skee ball was better than a cold shower any day.

• • •

I arrived at the restaurant fifteen minutes early to freshen up. The restroom felt like a freezer as I removed my sweaty T-shirt to put on the white cotton shirt from the Gap—lesbian central. I looked at myself in the mirror and promised I was going to be on my best behavior.

After I hosed down, I sat and waited for Alicia by the entrance. I looked up to check the time, and she walked in looking as radiant as a brown angel should. We smiled. I could already smell her perfume, her hair, her skin—I stood up in a flash to break the trance. "You must have ice cubes in your underwear because you look pretty cool. As cool as a cucumber." Yeah, I had a way with words that drove the women crazy.

She blushed and softly said, "I don't wear underwear."

"Well maybe you have the cubes stashed somewhere else." I flashed her a smile and placed my hand on her bare shoulder. I refrained from having an orgasm because it wasn't the time or place. Alicia was wearing an off-white strapless summer dress that truly highlighted her Latina beauty. The dress was simple, but she was so elegant in it. "Let's go get a table."

We sat down. I wanted to have an out-of-body experience so I could see how charming we looked. She let out that her day had been hectic and a glass of chardonnay was in order. Yeah, baby, loosen up. She was going on about work, not noticing I was metaphysically licking her face.

"So who gave you those beautiful eyes?"

"My father." Alicia took a small sip of wine.

"I'm assuming you're a Chicana." She nodded. "Me too. Well, Mexican-American—Chicana—same thing. I like saying 'Chicana' because it's political and it pisses people off." Alicia gave me her smirk as if to say, I'd like to discuss this with you some other time.

I quickly changed the subject. "So, what about those Dodgers?" Her smirk grew a little as she shook her head, stirred her wine with her index finger, then placed it in her mouth and sucked the wine off. I was surprised at her Ann-Margret behavior, but I thoroughly enjoyed it.

Alicia looked at the floor and then slowly leaned into the table, resting her weight on her elbows, giving me her eyes. Wow. Her eyes were seductive pools of sweet lust. Were we making love? It sure felt like it.

"Ramona, I have something to tell you." Her voice gave me a chill and made my nipples erect. Good thing I was wearing my extra-strength bra—absolutely pokeproof.

After all that flirty stuff, was she going to deliver some bad news? No way. Oh, god, was she going to tell me she was really a man trying to become a woman, trying to become a lesbian, trying to get a credit card and she needed a cosigner?! I mean, people have their rights but I wasn't about to be a cosigner! Here I was getting ready for her to lean over and give me a kiss—wait a minute. Her face was almost serious, but the corners of her mouth were starting to curl.

"Alicia, are you messing with my head?"

"Yeah." She giggled. Very adorable. "You make me feel comfortable enough to play." Her hand covered mine.

"Do I make you feel comfortable enough so that you want to live with me?"

Her twinkling eyes looked away as her mouth tried to produce words, but she ended up smiling at me. "Ramona, I don't know." She pulled her hand away and transformed it into a resting spot for her chin.

"You don't know if you feel comfortable, or you don't know if you want to live with me?"

"Both."

Did she say both? My plan had failed. What's going on here? She's supposed to want me as a roommate. Our living situation turns into this great romance. I win the lottery and we travel in comfortable cotton clothing that always looks neatly pressed! My head went on, but I had to respond. "So you're not—I mean—you're not attracted to—not that a roommate should be—" I stopped talking because I didn't know how.

"Ramona, we need to walk over to Ben and Jerry's and share a big ol' ice cream sundae. This way we can figure out our roommate situation."

Okay, I get what's happening here. She was attracted to me, but she was doing that young-girl, I-want-to-be-in-control thing. She was only a year younger, but that's all it takes. But I knew how to handle this filly: let her roam, continue to charm her, and she will happily trot into my corral.

The waiter delivered the check. Of course she insisted on paying, but I picked up the tab. "Don't insult me," I smiled.

"You're a tough cookie." She applied lipstick and stared at me the whole time. I was pleased.

We packed up our things: I zipped up my small black backpack, and she slipped her lipstick back in a black snakeskin case. I was practical and charming. She was stylish and so damn sexy. I couldn't believe I was still pursuing this roommate thing.

As we walked the two blocks I realized how much attention she attracted. She was a genuine goddess. As we passed people they stared, admiring her pretty brown skin glowing off her white dress.

We looked through the windows of art galleries and agreed these artists were related to the owners, because most of the work was crap. I really was getting off on the fact that we agreed on many things: sharing food with certain people, that Black funk music is great with sex, that we loved our solitude and we could get moody—*I'm hot—I'm cold—love me—get away from me!* I was enjoying the evening way too much to depart without a goodnight kiss. I had promised myself, but the tension was making me want to rip my head off my shoulders. The thought of pressing my lips against her luscious Latina mouth was making my shorts feel tight and my underarms sweat. I needed a release and pronto, so I gently scooted her into the alley.

"Alicia . . . as far as I'm concerned . . . I can't be your roommate because I'm too attracted to you and I want to see you again." The words sprang out of my mouth like a Jill-in-the-box. Damn. As my fingers combed back my hair, I wished I had delivered my statement more gracefully. Oh well. If she found this scene uncomfortable, she would have left my ass ages ago.

She grabbed my hand. "I'm attracted to you too."

I felt a wave of electrical charge slither around my body. I closed my eyes and I could see myself pushing her up against the wall, pressing my soul against hers as I deeply massaged her back all the way down to her ass. I wanted all of her inside my mouth.

When I landed, Alicia was still standing in front of me with a beautiful smile. I slightly opened my mouth as if to make room for her bottom lip or her face. She stepped toward me, placed her fingers on my lips, and we inhaled simultaneously.

Roommates—yeah, right.

PART III

Nuestra Política

C herríe Moraga is a poet, playwright, and essayist. Her books include Loving in the War Years *(1983)*, This Bridge Called My Back: Writings by Radical Women of Color *(1981)*, and The Last Generation *(1993)*. Her plays include Giving Up the Ghost, Shadow of a Man, *and* Heroes and Saints. *She has won numerous awards for her plays and poetry. She lives in San Francisco and is currently an artist in residence at BRAVA! where she is director of a bisexual/gay/lesbian youth* teatro *group. Her unique blend of politics and literature is showcased in the following essay.*

ART IN AMERICA CON ACENTO

Cherríe Moraga

I write this on the one-week anniversary of the death of the Nicaraguan Revolution.*
We are told not to think of it as a death, but I am in mourning. It is an unmistakable feeling. A week ago, the name "Daniel" had poured from *nicaragüense* lips with a warm liquid familiarity. In private, doubts gripped their bellies and those doubts they took finally to the ballot box. Doubts seeded by bullets and bread: the U.S.–financed Contra War and the economic embargo. Once again an emerging sovereign nation is brought to its knees. A nation on the brink of declaring to the entire world that revolution is the people's choice betrays its own dead. Imperialism makes traitors of us all, makes us weak and tired and hungry.

I don't blame the people of Nicaragua. I blame the U.S. government. I blame my complicity as a citizen in a country

---

* An earlier version of this essay first appeared in *Frontiers: A Journal of Women Studies*, vol. 12, no. 3 (University of Colorado, 1992). It was originally presented as a talk given through the Mexican-American Studies Department at the California State University of Long Beach on March 7, 1990.

that, short of an invasion, stole the Nicaraguan revolution that *el pueblo* forged with their own blood and bones. After hearing the outcome of the elections, I wanted to flee the United States in shame and despair.

I am Latina, born and raised in the United States. I am a writer. What is my responsibility in this?

Days later, George Bush comes to San Francisco. He arrives at the St. Francis Hotel for a $1,000-a-plate fund-raising dinner for Pete Wilson's gubernatorial campaign. There is a protest. We, my *camarada* and I, get off the subway. I can already hear the voices chanting from a distance. We can't make out what they're saying, but they are Latinos and my heart races, seeing so many brown faces. They hold up a banner. The words are still unclear but as I come closer closer to the circle of my people, I am stunned. "*¡Viva la paz en Nicaragua!*" it states. "*¡Viva George Bush! ¡Viva UNO!*" And my heart drops. Across the street, the "resistance" has congregated—less organized, white, young, middle-class students. *¿Dónde 'stá mi pueblo?*

A few months earlier, I was in another country, San Cristóbal, Chiapas, México. The United States had just invaded Panamá. This time, I could stand outside the United States, read the Mexican newspapers for a perspective on the United States that was not monolithic. In the Na Bolom Center Library I wait for a tour of the grounds. The room is filled with *norteamericanos*. They are huge people, the men slouching in couches. Their thick legs spread across the floor, their women lean into them. They converse. "When we invaded Panama . . . " I grow rigid at the sound of the word "we." They are progressives (I know this from their conversation). They oppose the invasion, but identify with the invaders.

How can I, as a Latina, identify with those who invade Latin American land? George Bush is not my leader. I did not elect him, although my tax dollars pay for the Salvadoran Army's guns. We are a living, breathing contradiction, we who live *en las entrañas del monstruo*, but I refuse to be forced to identify. I am the product of invasion. My father is Anglo; my mother, Mexican. I am the result of the dissolution of bloodlines and the theft of language; and yet, I am a testimony to the failure of the United States to wholly anglicize its mestizo citizens.

I wrote in México, *"Los Estados Unidos es mi país, pero no es mi patria."* I cannot flee the United States, my land resides beneath its borders. We stand on land that was once the country of México. And before any conquistadors staked out political boundaries, this was Indian land and in the deepest sense remains just that: a land *sin fronteras*. Chicanos with memory like our Indian counterparts recognize that we are a nation within a nation. An internal nation whose existence defies borders or language, geography, race. Chicanos are a multiracial, multilingual people, who since 1848 have been displaced from our ancestral lands or remain upon them as indentured servants to Anglo-American invaders.

Today, nearly a century and a half later, the Anglo invasion of Latin America has extended well beyond the Mexican/American border. When U.S. capital invades a country, its military machinery is quick to follow to protect its interests. This is Panamá, Puerto Rico, Grenada, Guatemala . . . Ironically, the United States' gradual consumption of Latin America and the Caribbean is bringing the people of the Americas together. What was once largely a Chicano/*mexicano* population in California is now *guatemalteco, salvadoreño, nicaragüense.* What was largely a Puerto Rican and Dominican "Spanish Harlem" of New York is now populated with *mexicanos* playing *rancheras* and drinking *cerveza*. This mass emigration is evident throughout the Third World. Every place the United States has been involved militarily has brought its offspring, its orphans, its homeless, and its casualties to this country: Viet Nam, Guatemala, Cambodia, the Philippines . . .

Third World populations are changing the face of North

America. The new face has got that delicate fold in the corner of the eye and that wide-bridged nose. The mouth speaks in double negatives and likes to eat a lot of chile. By the twenty-first century our whole concept of "America" will be dramatically altered; most significantly by a growing Latino population whose strong cultural ties, economic disenfranchisement, racial visibility, and geographical proximity to Latin America discourages any facile assimilation into Anglo-American society.

Latinos in the United States do not represent a homogeneous group. Some of us are native born, whose ancestors precede the arrival not only of the Anglo-American but also of the Spaniard. Most of us are immigrants, economic refugees coming to the United States in search of work. Some of us are political refugees, fleeing death squads and imprisonment; others come fleeing revolution and the loss of wealth. Finally, some have simply landed here very tired of war. And in all cases, our children had no choice in the matter. U.S. Latinos represent the whole spectrum of color and class and political position, including those who firmly believe they can integrate into the mainstream of North American life. The more European the heritage and the higher the class status, the more closely Latinos identify with the powers that be. They vote Republican. They stand under the U.S. flag and applaud George Bush for bringing "peace" to Nicaragua. They hope one day he'll do the same for Cuba, so they can return to their *patria* and live a "North American style" consumer life. Because they know in the United States they will never have it all, they will always remain "spics," "greasers," "beaners," and "foreigners" in Anglo-America.

As a Latina artist I can choose to contribute to the development of a docile generation of would-be Republican "Hispanics" loyal to the United States, or to the creation of a force of "disloyal" *americanos* who subscribe to a multicultural, multilingual, radical restructuring of América. Revolution is won not only by numbers, but by visionaries, and if artists aren't visionaries, then we have no business doing what we do.

I call myself a Chicana writer. Not a Mexican-American writer, not a Hispanic writer, not a half-breed writer. To be a Chicana is not merely to name one's racial/cultural identity, but also to name a politic, a politic that refuses assimilation into the U.S. mainstream. It acknowledges our *mestizaje*—Indian, Spanish, and *africano*. After a decade of "hispanicization" (a term superimposed upon us by Reagan-era bureaucrats), the term "Chicano" assumes even greater radicalism. With the misnomer "Hispanic," Anglo America proffers to the Spanish surnamed the illusion of blending into the "melting pot" like any other white immigrant group. But the Latino is neither wholly immigrant nor wholly white; and here in this country, "Indian" and "dark" don't melt. (Puerto Ricans on the East Coast have been called "Spanish" for decades and it's done little to alter their status on the streets of New York City.)

The generation of Chicano literature being read today sprang forth from a grassroots social and political movement of the sixties and seventies that was definitely anti-assimilationist. It responded to a stated mandate: *art is political.* The proliferation of *poesía, cuentos,* and *teatro* that grew out of *El Movimiento* was supported by Chicano cultural centers and publishing projects throughout the Southwest and in every major urban area where a substantial Chicano population resided. The *Flor y Canto* poetry festivals of the seventies and a *teatro* that spilled off flatbed trucks into lettuce fields in the sixties are hallmarks in the history of the Chicano cultural movement. Chicano literature was a literature in dialogue with its community. And as some of us became involved in feminist, gay, and lesbian concerns in the late seventies and early eighties, our literature was forced to expand to reflect the multifaceted nature of the Chicano experience.

The majority of published Chicano writers today are products of that era of activism, but as the Movement grew older and more established, it became neutralized by middle-aged and middle-class concerns, as well as by a growing conservative trend in government. Most of the gains made for farm workers in California were dismantled by a succession of reactionary governors and Reagan/Bush economics. Cultural centers lost funding. Most small-press Chicano publishers disappeared as suddenly as they had appeared. What was once a radical and working-class Latino student base on university campuses has become increasingly conservative. A generation of tokenistic affirmative-action policies and bourgeois flight from Central America and the Caribbean has spawned a tiny Latino elite who often turn to their racial/cultural identities as a source not of political empowerment, but of personal employment as tokens in an Anglo-dominated business world.

And the writers . . . ? Today more and more of us insist we are "American" writers (in the North American sense of the word). The body of our literary criticism grows (seemingly at a faster rate than the literature itself), we assume tenured positions in the university, secure New York publishers, and our work moves further and further away from a community-based and national political movement.

A writer will write. With or without a movement.
Fundamentally, I started writing to save my life. Yes, my own life first. I see the same impulse in my students—the dark, the queer, the mixed-blood, the violated—turning to the written page with a relentless passion, a drive to avenge their own silence, invisibility, and erasure as living, innately expressive human beings.

A writer will write with or without a movement; but at the

same time, for Chicana, lesbian, gay, and feminist writers—
anybody writing against the grain of Anglo misogynist culture—political movements are what have allowed our writing
to surface from the secret places in our notebooks into the
public sphere. In 1990, Chicanos, gay men, and women are not
better off than we were in 1970. We have an ever-expanding
list of physical and social diseases affecting us: AIDS, breast
cancer, police brutality. Censorship is becoming increasingly
institutionalized, not only through government programs, but
through transnational corporate ownership of publishing
houses, record companies, etc. Without a movement to foster
and sustain our writing, we risk being swallowed up into the
"Decade of the Hispanic" that never happened. The fact that a
few of us have "made it" and are doing better than we imagined
has not altered the nature of the beast. He remains blue-eyed
and male and prefers profit over people.

Like most artists, we Chicano artists would like our work
to be seen as "universal" in scope and meaning and reach as
large an audience as possible. Ironically, the most "universal"
work—writing capable of reaching the greatest number of
people—is the most culturally specific. The European-American writer understands this because it is his version of cultural
specificity that is deemed "universal" by the literary establishment. In the same manner, universality in the *Chicana* writer
requires the most Mexican and the most female images we are
capable of producing. Our task is to write what no one is prepared to hear, for what has been said so far in barely a decade of
consistent production is a mere *bocadito*. Chicana writers are
still learning the art of transcription, but what we will be capable of producing in the decades to come, if we have the cul-
tural/political movements to support us, could make a
profound contribution to the social transformation of these
Américas. The *reto*, however, is to remain as culturally specific
and culturally complex as possible, even in the face of mainstream seduction to do otherwise.

Let's not fool ourselves, the European-American middle-class writer is the cultural mirror through which the literary and theatre establishment sees itself reflected, so it will continue to reproduce itself through new generations of writers. On occasion New York publishes our work, as it perceives a growing market for the material, allowing Chicanos access to national distribution on a scale that small independent presses could never accomplish. (Every writer longs for such distribution, particularly since it more effectively reaches communities of color.) But I fear that my generation and the generation of young writers that follows will look solely to the Northeast for recognition. I fear that we may become accustomed to this very distorted reflection, and that we will find ourselves writing more and more in translation through the filter of Anglo-American censors. Wherever Chicanos may live, in the richest and most inspired junctures of our writing, our writer-souls are turned away from Washington, the U.S. capital, and toward a *México Antiguo*. That is not to say that contemporary Chicano literature does not wrestle with current social concerns, but without the memory of our once-freedom, how do we imagine a future?

I still believe in a Chicano literature that is hungry for change, that has the courage to name the sources of our discontent both from within our *raza* and without, that challenges us to envision a world where poverty, crack, and pesticide poisoning are not endemic to people with dark skin or Spanish surnames. It is a literature that knows that god is neither white nor male nor reason to rape anyone. If such ideas are "naive" (as some critics would have us believe), then let us remain naive, naively and passionately committed to an art of "resistance," resistance to domination by Anglo-America, resistance to assimilation, resistance to economic and sexual exploitation. *An art that subscribes to integration into mainstream America is not Chicano art.*

•   •   •

All writing is confession. Confession masked and revealed in the voices and faces of our characters. All is hunger. The longing to be known fully and still loved. The admission of our own inherent vulnerability, our weakness, our tenderness of skin, fragility of heart, our overwhelming desire to be relieved of the burden of ourselves in the body of another, to be forgiven of our ultimate aloneness in the mystical body of a god or the common work of a revolution. These are human considerations that the best of writers presses her finger upon. The wound ruptures and . . . heals.

One of the deepest wounds Chicanos suffer is separation from our Southern relatives. Gloria Anzaldúa calls it a "1,950-mile-long open wound," dividing México from the United States, "dividing a *pueblo*, a culture." This *"llaga"* ruptures over and over again in our writing, Chicanos in search of a México that never wholly embraces us. "Mexico gags," poet Lorna Dee Cervantes writes, "on this bland *pocha* seed." This separation was never our choice. In 1990, we witnessed a fractured and disintegrating América, where the Northern half functions as the absentee landlord of the Southern half and the economic disparity between the First and Third Worlds drives a bitter wedge between a people.

I hold a vision requiring a radical transformation of consciousness in this country, that as the people-of-color population increases, we will not be just another brown faceless mass hungrily awaiting integration into white Amerika, but that we will emerge as a mass movement of people to redefine what an "American" is. Our entire concept of this nation's identity must change, possibly be obliterated. We must learn to see ourselves less as U.S. citizens and more as members of a larger world community composed of many nations of people and no longer give credence to the geopolitical borders that have divided us, Chicano from *mexicano*, Filipino-American from Pacific Islander, African-American from Haitian. Call it racial memory. Call it shared economic discrimination. Chicanos call it *"Raza"*—be it *Quichua, Cubano,* or *Colombiano*—an identity that dissolves borders. As a Chicana writer that's the context in which I want to create.

I am an American writer in the original sense of the word, an Américan *con acento.*

M argarita Engle was born in Los Angeles, California, to a
Cuban mother and American father. She writes a column that
has been syndicated on a regular basis since 1982 to over two hundred
newspapers. She currently lives in Fallbrook, California. The following excerpt from her first novel, Singing to Cuba (1993), describes
a return visit to her homeland.

FROM *SINGING TO CUBA*

Margarita Engle

When I dressed like a foreigner and stayed inside the tourist zone, official guides watched my movements closely. Hotel maids, waitresses, and taxi drivers made incessant inquiries about my solitary activities. Yet I found that if I dressed like a Cuban and spoke like a Cuban, remaining stoically silent most of the time, speaking to strangers only when necessary, and addressing them as comrade when I did, then I would be watched even more carefully, by the ubiquitous men in *guayaberas* who stood on every street corner, flanked every ration line, and rode every *guagua*, monitoring the sporadic whispered conversations.

I decided I was best off dressing like a tourist when alone and like a Cuban when accompanied by relatives. Although officially I was prohibited from visiting relatives, and officially my cousins were denied the right to speak to foreigners, I found that every cousin I visited expressed a strong desire to behave like ordinary families in ordinary places, going out in public together, walking and talking together as if the absurd array of small deranged laws did not exist.

Miguelito, more than any of the others, loved to walk up

and down the streets of Old Havana with me, pointing out historical sites and discussing our lives just as if we were not taking any risk by being seen together. When he wanted to go out, Aurora made him carry my wedding picture in his pocket, with the letter *Abuelita* Amparo had written when she sent it, to prove we were really cousins and not just a heretofore quiet dissident, finally bursting, speaking openly to a foreigner.

Miguelito sometimes sang as we walked. He sang about a marble house which crumbled while its residents were asleep. Both ceiling and floor caved in, and a woman, still reclining on her bed, told the neighbors that at first she thought it was just a dream but when she woke up, her leg was broken, and she could see the sky. Aurora had assured me that all of Miguelito's songs were true, taken from the seemingly impossible things which, in Cuba, she laughed, happen every day.

He sang about a poet who lived alone in a house by the sea. A storm carried away one half of his house, taking with it his typewriter and his entire library, leaving him to dwell in the other half, still writing about the sunset and the sea, while waves came swirling about his feet, coming in through the gap where once there had been a wall.

Sometimes, before going out, Miguelito would hang a big antique silver crucifix around his neck. It was the kind of jewelry Cubans were not supposed to have kept after the revolution. Soon after the Maximum Leader took control of the island, its inhabitants had been ordered to turn in all their guns, money, jewelry, and other valuables, so that everyone could start over with nothing. Nearly everyone gave up their firearms, but even the most dedicated communist bureaucrats buried their valuables rather than turn them over. Now, with the economy collapsing, the government was luring the heirlooms and jewelry out of hiding by allowing Cubans to sell hoarded valuables in exchange for shopping privileges in otherwise prohibited dollar stores.

When Miguelito wore his big silver crucifix, he looked like a foreigner, like a lean moustached cowboy from nineteenth-century Texas or Mexico. He left the top button of his shirt open to make sure the crucifix showed and he walked with pride, relieved to be taking a step so bold and defiant. He told me that as a Cuban, wearing a crucifix in public could brand him as a second-class citizen, faithful in a land still officially atheistic. Within his own neighborhood, he was taking a risk. In the tourist zone, he felt anonymous and spoke freely of the elation he felt when disregarding the usual elaborate code of conduct.

When Miguelito, with his crucifix, and I, with my foreign clothes and camera bag, walked through Old Havana together, we both felt safe. When we rode the beet-and-mustard-striped *guagua*, we knew we were, like all Cubans, vulnerable. Few tourists braved the crowds and heat of the Cuban *guagua*. Most confined themselves to Tourist-Taxis and air-conditioned tour buses. In the *guagua* Miguelito and I stood out as the only people daring to converse. My cousin was so tired of silence that even on a crowded *guagua* he would lean his head down toward the window and say without lowering his voice, "This is all I have ever known. In my entire life, this is all I have ever seen." People would look away, pretending they hadn't heard.

With a sweep of his hand he would indicate everything beyond the window, decaying marble houses, winged statues, hordes of young men on bicycles, the sea wall, the harbor, El Morro Castle. When the *guagua* passed La Cabaña Fortress, I was relieved to see my cousin remain quiet. No matter how much he wanted to point out the dungeons, such overt defiance would be foolish.

I looked out at the tourists snapping photographs of each other standing next to the cannons. I couldn't help thinking of all the names I read each month, when my human rights bulletins arrived, of men arrested for joining a movement of artists seeking freedom of expression, and human rights monitors arrested by State Security, held without charge.

On the *guagua*, surrounded by silent Cubans, Miguelito went on asking questions about the U.S., my family, my friends, my life. He asked about my schooling, my wedding, about jobs, vacations, grocery shopping. He asked about child-birth and books, movies and music. He asked about rhythm-and-blues singers, and about the irrigated orchards near my arid northern home, and about the coyotes which roamed the orchards hunting jackrabbits, roadrunners and ground squir-rels. We rode many different *guaguas* along many different routes, past Revolution Square with its tanks and armed guards, past a colonial cemetery with its magnificent variety of carved angels, past an enormous white monument to José Martí, and the towering Soviet Embassy, a skyscraper which pierces the Cuban sky with its listening apparatus for spying on U.S. communications systems. Miguelito named the land-marks as we passed them. I didn't want my cousin to keep tak-ing chances, so I asked if we could get out and walk.

The streets of Havana were filling with tourists as Cuba prepared to host the Pan American Games. Tourists from Eu-rope and Latin America were flooding the hotel zone and the secret police could hardly keep up with their massive efforts to monitor the movements of Cubans and ensure that they didn't violate the rule against speaking to foreigners. The Neighbor-hood Committees were being trained as riot squads. In every crowd of Cubans, police informers were planted to disrupt any incipient protest through Acts of Repudiation, by mobilizing groups of citizens to surround and beat anyone who openly voiced discontent.

Descriptions of Acts of Repudiation came in the monthly human rights bulletins. Committee members surround the house of a dissident or they surround him on the streets. They chant slogans and create the appearance of a spontaneous pro-government demonstration. The Act of Repudiation can go on for hours or it might end abruptly with the arrest of its target. Sometimes the dissident's house is ransacked. Family members and visitors may be held captive inside the house. Acts of Re-pudiation are effective because they instill in the dissident a fear of isolation, creating the illusion that only he and his fam-

ily are unhappy with a system loved by multitudes. The Act of
Repudiation is designed to stimulate a wave of self-doubt and
to terrify bystanders who swear they will never speak out and
place their own families in such a precarious position.

Miguelito and I had just emerged from a *guagua*. The afternoon sky had suddenly clouded over and a light rain was beginning to fall. As we walked, we found ourselves surrounded
by blue-uniformed civil police. Miguelito kept right on talking
and gradually the blue uniforms drifted away. Soldiers replaced
them. Again we were surrounded. Still, my cousin kept talking.
The cluster of soldiers walked beside us, behind us, and in
front. I counted fourteen of them.

Looking beyond them, at the crumbling walls, I noticed a
small red cross and a child's handprint, the only graffiti I had
seen since arriving in Havana. I felt like someone discovering
pictographs in a prehistoric cave. They reminded me of a story
by Reinaldo Arenas called "Singing from the Well," about a
child who starts scribbling on tree trunks, sending his stern
family into a flurry of accusations when they decide he is crazy.

I thought of Anacaona, the ten sisters who emerged as
Cuba's first all-female singing group after three years of hiding
inside their Havana house during the anarchy of Machado's
overthrow in the early 1930s.

How many artists must now be waiting behind closed
doors, practicing secretly, waiting for the day when they could
come out of their houses singing and dancing!

I withdrew the camera from my bag and began fussing
with the lens as I walked. Then I started snapping photographs
of the soldiers. One of them waved his semiautomatic weapon
at me in a threatening gesture that meant stop. I smiled and
turned the camera toward the broken walls of the houses
around me. I pointed the lens up toward the roofless apex and
disintegrating columns of a once-elegant building that looked
like the ruined remains of some ancient Greek temple.

Beside me, Miguelito was smiling, looking as fearless and
confident as any newly arrived foreigner still unaware of the

vast network of vigilant guides, secret police, and informers. The soldiers glanced at each of us, then at each other. They shrugged, grinning, and moved away, pursuing some young Cuban women who had begun to flirt with them. Soon they were walking far ahead of us, surrounding the girls, who were laughing and conversing with them in loud fast voices, still sounding as I remembered from 1960, raucous and musical, like wild parrots joined by small song birds as they all fed from the same fruit tree.

*I*nés Hernández-Avila is a professor, scholar, and poet who is Chicana and Nez Perce. She is on the faculty of the University of California at Davis Native American Studies Department. "Enedina's Story" takes place entirely in a kitchen. Ingredients include politics, food, lemongrass tea, and candid thoughts on men-women relationships. This story is dedicated to Beatríz Pesquera.

ENEDINA'S STORY

Inés Hernández-Avila

All day Friday Enedina and Marina were at Enedina's place cooking some of the *comida* for the *Brigadistas* fund-raiser. They had offered a commitment of one hundred plates of mole, rice, beans, and potato salad, and now they had to come through.

The beans were easy to take care of. The women had put them on in the morning, two big ollas full, *con mucho ajo*. On her way to Enedina's, Marina had gone over to *la señora* Ramírez's house to borrow the other ollas they would need. Since she was nearby, she had stopped at Gil's Bakery on Seventh Street to bring them some *pan dulce*; she got there early enough to get some of the fresh *empanadas de camote* straight from the oven, as well as some *pan de huevo* and some *corazones*. She knew people had a habit of dropping in at her friend's house often. Enedina had made the two of them some simple tacos—*papas con huevo* with a little cheese, a little salsa (her own recipe the way her father had taught her; the secret was in the roasting of the ingredients)—and some *café con canela y piloncillo* to get them going. The coffee made this way was especially good on crisp, reclusive mornings such as this one.

The weather had been a little *caprichoso* for April. There had been more April showers than usual, and that day was no different. There was a steady if gentle rain waking up the earth and caressing Enedina's roses and the herb garden she was so proud of. As she looked out the kitchen window she noticed the lemon tree's leaves and branches reaching out eagerly for the touch of rain. She herself had made a quick run across town to pick up her guitar from a friend who had checked it over for her. Before she left her house, she and Marina had cleaned the chickens and put them to boil. By the time she returned, Marina had taken them out to cool, so the two sat down to begin the deboning. The brisk walk over to her friend Victor's had been good for her. She loved the smell of the wet inviting earth and the strong fragrance of the thirsty flowers. Maybe later she would make some *té de limón* for them.

Marina made a real good mole sauce from scratch, and Enedina was going to pay careful attention to every detail. She had laughingly admitted to Marina that her own mole sauce usually came from the Tía María jars, which wasn't bad (she had impressed many a houseful of people with it!). Marina's sauce, which she had called the Sabrosa Native American Hemispheric Sovereignty Mole Sauce, had won first prize, however, at one of their group's other fund-raising ventures— the First Annual Mouthwatering Movimiento-Style Traditional Recipes Cookoff they had held on the previous Labor Day weekend. Enedina was excited to be in the presence of her friend who knew the secrets of mole.

They had decided to debone the chickens because of the numbers they were feeding and so that everyone who paid for the meals would feel that they got a fair share of the meat from the *pollo*. Also, since they all had to clean up afterward, they wouldn't have to deal with bones. As they sat working, they talked about the next day's cultural events. Enedina was going to be one of the performers after the dinner, and she wanted to go over with Marina the new poems she would read.

The conversation reminded Marina: "*Oyes, Enedina, se me*

olvidó decirte. When you went to pick up your guitar from Victor, Lucha called to say that Pedro came back from his New York trip early, so he wants to read poetry at the Quetzalli this weekend *también, todos ustedes*. She said he asked if he could be last in the lineup. She wanted to know what you think, since right now you're scheduled to be last. She says Deborah and Santiago still want their *teatro* piece in the middle, and Miguel still wants to follow the *teatro*. Tony's scheduled to go on first, but he doesn't mind going second if Pedro is willing to go first. Pedro says he wants to read a poem for Nicaragua, one for Big Mountain, and one for the women warriors. *Qué suave, ¿no?*"

Enedina didn't answer immediately. She had just finished filling a bowl with deboned chicken and covering it with a clean *toalla*. As she placed it on the counter, she said, "*Sí, suave*, except that Pedro insisted all along that he wasn't going to be around, and he knows that we work collectively on our presentations, so that everyone's in agreement. This isn't the first time he's done this."

She stood at the counter thinking, listening to the *lluvia sonando*. "No, Tony should stay in the first slot. His songs are for Cuba and for the Americas. Who comes after Tony? Wait, it's Luciana, her poems are about *mujeres en lucha*; Pedro can go between the two of them. *Déjame llamarle pa' trás a Lucha pa' decirle*."

Enedina's feet suddenly felt heavy as she crossed the room to dial. After she finished her conversation with Lucha, she went to her bedroom for her abalone shell. She lit a smudge mix of cedar and copal and brought it into the kitchen. Marina happily took in the incense and waved it about her face and body. Enedina passed the shell over the food they were preparing, then set the shell down near them on the counter. She put some water on for tea and began to rummage through her tapes until she found one she liked, Atahualpa Yupanqui— the old man's music soothed her. Just hearing the first strokes of his guitar calmed her.

She returned to the table with another bowl to fill with

pollo. The smudge had made her feel better. "Good news from Lucha," she told Marina. "Lalo and Gabriel just came back from *el Valle.* They're going to sing with us at the end, when we do the songs with the *comunidad.* But you know something, Mari, I don't know if I can stomach *aquel* Pedro. The guy's beginning to give me the creeps."

"*Pero ¿cómo?!*" Enedina's comment was so unexpected, Marina was propelled out of her reverie about the next day's events. She had been fantasizing about her new love interest, the graduate student in history who was coming around to the cultural activities now that he had discovered them. He was a Chicano from Dallas, but he hadn't really been involved in anything before. Marina intended to get him much more involved! As she pulled herself from her vision of the two of them dancing together, she said, "I thought you liked Pedro. You were excited about him coming to Austin to live. You were one of the ones who said he'd done good work in the Indian community and all that. *¿Qué pasó? ¿Porqué te cambiaste de opinión?*"

"I don't know. I've been watching him just this little bit that he's been here—how long has it been, a couple of months? It's true, *al principio lo veía con respeto.* I was excited that he was coming to town . . . There's just something about him *que no me cae.*" Enedina kept pulling the chicken from the bones, making sure not to waste any. She felt the raindrops grow stronger as they comforted the house. She turned to look out the window and thought of the ancestor spirits coming to visit in each drop. She was glad they could listen to Atahualpa. She was glad they could smell the smudge and the food. She got up to put lemongrass into the boiling water. She covered the pot and turned the flame off. "*Te acuerdas que cuando llegó aquí,* I was one of the ones who spent a lot of time with him?" she asked Marina.

"*Pués sí,* you were one of the people he said he'd heard of. He'd read your work, and he knew people you knew. *¿Quiénes* *eran?* One was that Sun Dancer guy, *¿qué no? ¿Cómo se llamaba?*"

"Bill. *Se llama Bill Fast Horses.* Yeah, Bill's *buena gente.* He is a Sun Dancer, and as far as I know, he's a good man. I've never heard anything bad about him, you know, from women or from men."

"Well, then, doesn't that say something? If this guy, this Bill, if he's a friend of Pedro's, doesn't that mean that Pedro's okay?" Marina had stopped working to contemplate this new turn of events. "Doesn't it?"

Enedina stopped what she was doing, too, and looked at her friend. "I hadn't told you, but I called Bill a couple of weeks ago. Pedro made it seem like they were good friends, but Bill says they've just met at big gatherings, you know, where you don't get to spend time with everyone. I told him about the pipe Pedro has, and he laughed and said, 'You know, Enedina, there's so many pipes floating around now, you'd think that they were premiums that you get when you sign up for a new credit account!' I laughed, too, and said maybe someone should close Pedro's account. He said, 'Maybe so!'"

As Enedina got up to pour them the tea, she noticed that the one song by Atahualpa that she had doubts about was playing. The one where the speaker of the song asks a metalworker to make him an *"hombre firme"* and the metalworker replies, "A man is a 'firm man' because he's a man." Then the speaker of the song asks for the man to make him a woman of silver who is not false. The metalworker replies, "Of the firm women, the mold has been lost." She remembered how when she had brought up the song to her good friend Gabriel, he had studied her quizzically and said, "That's your problem, isn't it, Enedina? You hate men!" *Ahh, qué raza, raza . . . estos hombres, cuando aprenderán,* she thought. She put sugar in her cup and stirred. She usually liked her tea with no sugar or honey, but for some reason she enjoyed lemongrass tea sweetened, probably because it reminded her of ceremonias *en México.* She turned to Marina, who had a frown on her forehead from concentrating. "*¿Te pongo azúcar?*"

"*Sí, pero bueno, entonces, dime,* why does Pedro give you the creeps?"

Enedina blew on her tea a little before she sipped it. Her body immediately responded to the goodness of the lemongrass. "I talked to him a lot when he first got here. *Como dices, me buscó.* I guess I noticed how he's a little too smug about himself, like he's sure that he's the most politically sophisticated person around, because he's been on the West Coast, *me imagino,* because he's traveled a lot with the Treaty Council and he carries that sacred pipe, or because he's been in prison, or all of the above! I thought he took a little too much delight in telling me about the 'old days,' you know, when he was supposedly a *chingón* drug dealer, about how everyone feared and respected him. It's like he almost bragged about it."

Marina was startled. "He bragged about it? But how can he? He says he's on this spiritual path now. I mean, look at all he says about how drugs are bad, and how the *juventud* shouldn't be caught up in the drug scene, how they should walk the red road and get in touch with their indigenous roots. Geez, he's got that job now with the teenage counseling program; I've never heard him brag about what he did before. Anyway, was that what he got busted for, for drugs? I guess I've never even wondered about that."

"He got busted for dealing heroin to kids, and then in prison he supposedly saw the '*Movimiento* light.' I'm not saying he's still dealing drugs or that he hasn't changed. All I know is that he made a point of telling me that he was still dealing inside for a while, I guess so I would know just how 'bad' he was before, or something. But it is ironic that he's counseling now and talking spirituality, because he's still smoking *mota* big time, *y se pone bien ansioso* if he doesn't have any, and he never passes up a beer."

"But look at how many of us still do the same!"

"I know, I know, but the rest of us aren't coming across as

some spiritual leader the way he is. I mean, with me, he wanted me to know that he's got this pipe, *por ejemplo*, and eagle feathers, and corn pollen, and cedar, *y todo!* Anyway, we're all supposed to be trying to clean up our acts, because the old-timers and the sharper young people in the *comunidad* who know better can see right through us when we start talking *movimiento y la causa* through clouds of marijuana smoke or when the liquor won't even let us stand up straight, much less be coherent. You know how we've all talked about that before."

"You're right," Marina conceded, remembering the long sessions that their group had held, criticizing themselves and the entire Chicano-movement community for acting sometimes as if you weren't Chicano or Chicana if you didn't smoke pot and drink. They had talked about the necessity of not blowing it in front of either the young people or the ones their parents' age, for the most part *gente obrera*, many of whom had been disciplined enough not to let alcohol or drugs drag them down, while many others were themselves battling alcoholism or other addictions. Marina's face flushed as she remembered one evening in particular, at a community gathering, when she herself had been feeling *bien sentida*. She had begun drinking everything in sight to dull the pain of her love affair with Jorge having gone wrong. That night, as she swayed from table to table, falsely displaying her party enthusiasm, Lalo had suddenly appeared before her, offering her his cup. She grabbed it and took a big swig, when, to her shock, she discovered his cup contained plain water. His face said everything he needed to say to her that night. She would never forget that moment.

"What are you thinking about?" Enedina asked.

"No, you're right. We can't expect people to take us seriously when we can't even stay sober. I was just remembering when Lalo tricked me with his cup of water, *¿te acuerdas que te lo platiqué?*" Marina asked sheepishly.

"Hey, I have my own stories, too, don't forget," Enedina said quickly, noticing her friend's embarrassment. "For one, we all know only too well how tequila can have me weeping in public in no time . . . and then there's the time I woke up one morning in Miguel's bed with not one single memory of how I got there. Mind you, Miguel, who I considered a brother! I'll never forget the grin on his face as he stood in the doorway of his bedroom, and I lay wide-eyed watching him from his bed . . . *Híjole, que pena.*"

Marina burst into laughter at the scene Enedina had described for her. The famous *mujeriego* Miguel and her friend Enedina, who had always claimed a platonic relationship with him, in bed together. "You're kidding! *No me habías dicho! Oyes, si me permites la pregunta,*" she said, striking a reportorial pose, "How was he?"

"Damn, Mari, *te digo que no me acuerdo!* All I know is, Luciana told me the next day, after I got home, that the night before, she and I had gone to the Que Pasa for a beer, Miguel had walked in, he had his guitar, and we started singing for the *gente*. I do remember that they wanted love songs, *sabes,* *'Amaneci en tus brazos' y 'Yo quiero tenerte muy cerca de mí'* kind of stuff! People started buying us one beer after another. I would hardly start one before I had another one in front of me. So anyway . . . Luci said that she went to the restroom before she left the club. When she came out to the car, she found us standing on the sidewalk locked in this passionate embrace. When she got our attention, Miguel said he would take me home. He took me home, all right, to his home! *¡Qué pasión, ni qué pasión, no me acuerdo de nada!*" she said, as Marina covered her chuckle with her hand.

Enedina laughed with Marina, but she hurt inside, too. She didn't like knowing that she'd blacked out that night, and she was ruefully thankful that if she had to end up with someone, at least it was Miguel, who probably didn't remember too much of the night himself (she had never asked him; she hoped instead that he had blacked out, too, before anything actually happened, if she was lucky) and who, for all his *mujeriego* ways, was not known to be violent to women, at least not in the sense that he had ever been known to beat a woman or to force himself on her, although she wondered about that night she had spent with him. If women held anything against him, it was that he could not be faithful, but he had never tried to pretend that he was, although now that she thought about it, that also meant that he merely used women for his own gratification, which was a violation. Women's feelings before or beyond the sexual act meant nothing to him, but she had known that, and for that reason had preferred having him as a friend, a *compañero de lucha* rather than a lover. She felt sorry for all of the women who thought they might be the one to change him.

Enedina sighed and thought to herself how much the generous *lluvia* was helping her through this day. She stood up to stretch and shake out of her body all the *recuerdos* that had been brought up. She had known Miguel a long time and had considered him a younger brother. She had always wondered whether his increased womanizing had anything to do with his having been left by the one woman Enedina thought he had actually loved. That one had not only left him; she had left the state to be rid of him, and none of them had heard from her again, which was too bad, because many of them had cared about her. *Sonia se llamaba, nicaragüense ella con dos hijas muy preciosas.* He had not been faithful to her, either, but Sonia had refused to stick around and stand in line for his attentions. Enedina had admired her for her decisiveness, even though she had felt bad for Miguel.

Pero ¿quién lo mandaba? Y ¿quién me manda a mí? she thought. That blackout was one of the experiences responsible for her staying off liquor in recent months. She had taken to drinking a mixture of sage and cedar tea. An elder in the California Indian community whom she had met on her travels told her that sage and cedar tea were good to detox the body from alcohol, that if a person drank enough of the tea, after a while they would not be attracted to alcohol anymore. It had been working for her so far. Maybe she would suggest to Marina, *como un consejo cariñoso,* that she should drink some, too.

"Now what are you thinking about?" Marina asked her

friend. They were done with the deboning and she was beginning to prepare the ingredients for the mole sauce. She had also put the potatoes to boil for the potato salad. The rain had softened its fall, and there was even a tiny bit of sunlight coming through the clouds. "Don't get gloomy on me, Niña! We are strong women, ¿me oíste? That's what you're always telling me, ¿que no? Lo de Miguel ya pasó, and we learn from every mistake. Diosa mía, do we learn. Besides, we have to stay in a good mood or the food will suffer, remember! ¡Hay que cocinar con amor, con cariño, con alegría, y con valor! And you, amiga, you still have to make your wonderful arroz, y pónle mucho ajo y comino!" She went over to switch the music to Esteban Jordán and began singing with him. "You've lost that lovin' feelin', ohh-ohh," sounded throughout the house in polka rhythm, accompanied by Esteban's earthy and powerful accordion. "Let's dance!" She grabbed Enedina, and the two of them polkaed around the kitchen, laughing. "Gracias, Mari, but . . ."

"I need your lo-ove!" Mari sang into Enedina's ears.

"But, Miguel . . ."

"I need your lo-ove! What about Miguel?" Mari swung Enedina around to the music.

"I should talk to him, no?"

"I need your lo-ove! Why?"

"Because . . . he hurts women, a lot of women; because he hurts himself most; because we work together, we sing together, we're compañeros!" She finished as the song ended.

Marina threw herself onto the sofa and grabbed a pillow to hug to her middle. "Yes, amiga, you should talk to Miguel if you think it'll help. Just don't forget that he has to want to change and that his transformation is not your responsibility, ¿entiendes?" Marina stood up again and headed towards the kitchen. "And who knows," she said, "maybe you'll be able to reach him because you're not interested in him as a lover." She paused, put her hand on her hip and looked back with a mischievous authority in her eyes. "Especially since your affair with him was hardly memorable, shall we say?!"

"*¡Cabrona!*" Enedina laughed as she threw the pillow at her. "Oh, man, but am I trying to be the one to change him in a different way?! *Porque sabes*, it's not just him, *¿verdad?* And you're right, it's not my responsibility!"

Enedina, more lighthearted than she had been all day, went back into the kitchen, led by the aromas of chocolate *molido*, crushed almonds and peanuts, garlic, *comino*, chiles. "Uummm, I smell mole! Wait for me, Mari, *me tienes que enseñar!* And I need to get the rice started!"

*L*ucha Corpi was born in Jáltipan, Veracruz, Mexico. In 1964 she moved to the San Francisco Bay Area. She is a writer, poet, educator, translator, and arts administrator. Corpi's novels include the Latina mystery Eulogy for a Brown Angel *(1992) and* Delia's Song *(1989). She is also the author of two bilingual collections of poetry,* Variations on a Storm/Variaciones sobre una tempestad *(1990) and* Noon Words/Palabras de mediodía *(1980). Her poems and stories have appeared in numerous works in the United States and Mexico. She currently lives and teaches in Oakland, California. This piece is one of a planned collection of autobiographical essays.*

EPIPHANY: THE THIRD GIFT

Lucha Corpi

Ever since I was four years old, women insisted on giving me dolls. By age seven I had an assortment of them, made of papier-mâché, clay, and cloth. Using my older cousin's torn silky stockings, my grandmother had also made a few of them for me. And one of my mother's friends had brought me a porcelain "little lady" from Mexico City, which was kept in my mother's wardrobe so I wouldn't break or damage it.

As a child I didn't understand why everyone around me insisted on giving me dolls, especially since I had made it clear that I really didn't like to play with them.

I much more enjoyed climbing trees and running around with the boys—my older brother, a cousin, and their friends. I loved playing marbles, spinning tops until they hummed. Playing walk-the-high-wire on a narrow brick fence or, in Tarzan-like fashion, swinging on long vines from the rubber tree to the fence thrilled me no end. But most of all I preferred reading.

During recess and after school, I would go into the area in the principal's office that doubled as the school library. There I would look at the illustrations and read over and over the few natural sciences and biology books on the table. At home, after doing my homework, I would avidly consume any text lying around.

At the time, my father, who worked for the Mexican National Telegraph Company, had undergone a cornea transplant and had to wear a patch over one of his eyes for a while. Straining his other eye, he slowly read the daily reports coming into his office, but by the time he went home, that eye burned inside its lid.

Since I could read well, he asked me to read selections to him after supper from *La Opinión*, the region's daily newspaper. I was happy to do something for my father, whom I loved very much, but reading to him also gave me an opportunity to learn new words, for my father would patiently explain anything I didn't understand.

Although I didn't fully grasp the issues reported in the news articles, my world nonetheless expanded, for I also began to learn about international, national, and regional politics, geography, and literature.

Naturally, reading and looking at my small tropical world from high above the tallest trees became more exciting activities for me than playing with those cute celluloid creatures that could do nothing but stare into empty space. Every so often I'd rub my face against the silky surface of the cloth dolls, feel the warm terseness of the papier-mâché under my fingers or the smooth coolness of the porcelain whenever my mother allowed me to hold the doll in her wardrobe. But most of the time, to my mother's chagrin, the dolls rested one upon the other like fallen dominoes alongside a wall in my room.

For a few months after my seventh birthday, no one—including my mother—had given me any dolls, and I thought the adults around me had finally gotten over their need to do so. But I was wrong, for the sixth of January neared.

Like millions of children in Mexico, at home we received presents on the Twelfth Night after the birth of Jesus Christ—Epiphany—a time to commemorate the revealing of baby Jesus to the Magi and their offering to him of myrrh, incense, and gold.

On that January 6, 1952, my parents gave me three gifts: a doll (no great surprise!), a doll's house, and a book—a children's version of *The Arabian Nights*, which came wrapped in red tissue paper.

I used the wrapping tissue as a book cover and was just getting ready to read when my mother walked into my room.

"Isn't your doll just beautiful?" my mother asked. I looked at the doll—I'll have to call her "She" because I never gave her a name. *She* was a fair celluloid creature with light brown hair and blue eyes that matched the color of her ruffled dress. Her apron and socks were white.

I puckered my lips and raised my eyebrows, not really knowing how to let my mother down easily.

"But this one is different," my mother explained, trying to talk me into playing with the toy. "Look," my mother emphasized, "this doll talks; she says, 'Mommy.'"

Then my mother turned the doll over, raised her tiny dress, and pulled on a chain to wind the doll's voice mechanism.

Something must have been wrong with the mechanism, because the noises *She* made sounded more like a cat's cries than a baby's babbles. My grandmother had often told me that our neighbor's cat cried like that because it needed love.

"*Anda buscando amor*—it's looking for love," my grandmother would explain, purposely neglecting to elaborate on the kind of love a cat in heat desires.

Interpreting my grandmother's comment literally, on several occasions I had tried to hug the cat to give it love, but it had scratched me and run away. Sure, nonetheless, that the doll needed love, I hugged her tightly for a long time. Useless, I said to myself finally, for the doll kept making the cat-looking-for-love noises. I decided to play instead with the doll's house, which my father had set down on the front porch, where it was cool in the afternoon. I went out to play with it. But since inspecting and rearranging the tiny furniture seemed to be the only activity possible, I quickly lost interest.

I could hear my friends in the yard talking and egging each other on to walk the high wire. Bending over or squatting to play with the doll's house had left my body and spirit in need of physical activity. So I went into my room to put on my shoes to join my friends in the yard. I was tying my shoelaces when I saw again the third of my gifts—*The Arabian Nights*—wrapped in the red tissue paper, and I began to read it. From that moment on, the doll and the doll's house began to collect dust, and *Scheherazada* became my constant companion.

Every day, after doing my homework, I climbed the guava tree my father had planted a few years before. Nestled among its branches, during the next three weeks, I read and reread the stories in *The Arabian Nights* to my heart's content. But I was unaware that my mother had become concerned as she noticed that I wasn't playing with either the doll or the little house.

My parents had always encouraged us to read. My mother wouldn't have dreamed of asking me to give up my reading session, but she began to insist that I take the doll up the tree with me.

Trying to read on a branch fifteen feet off the ground while holding on to the silly doll was not an easy feat. Not even for an *artist of the high wire and the flying trapeze*. After nearly falling off the branch twice, I finally had to devise a way to please my mother and keep my neck intact. Cutting two thin vines off a tree, I removed their skin and tied them together into one long rope; then I tied one end around the doll's neck and the opposite one around the branch. This way I could just let the doll hang in midair while I read.

I was always looking out for my mother, though. I sensed that my playing with the doll was of great importance to her. So every time I heard my mother coming, I lifted the doll up and hugged her. The smile in my mother's eyes told me my plan worked. Before suppertime, I entered the house through the kitchen so my mother could see me holding the doll.

During the next few days, my mother, the doll, and I were quite happy. But the inevitable happened one afternoon. Totally absorbed in the reading, I did not hear my mother calling me until she was right under the tree. When I looked down, I saw my mother, her mouth open in disbelief, staring at the dangling doll. Fearing the worst of scoldings, I climbed down in a flash, reaching the ground just as my mother was untying the doll.

"What is *this?*" she asked as she smoothed out the doll's dress.

My mother always asked me that or a similar rhetorical question when she wanted me to admit to some wrongdoing. From that point on, we would both follow an unwritten script. After my giving the appropriate answer for the particular situation we faced—"It's a doll, hanging," in this case—my mother would then ask me a second question. In this case, she would have asked, "And why is this doll hanging from the tree?"

To my surprise, on this occasion my mother wasn't following the script. Dumbfounded, she kept on staring at the doll, then she glanced at me. I swallowed hard. At that moment, I realized I had just accomplished the impossible: *I had rendered my mother speechless!*

I also sensed for the first time in my seven years that I had done something *terribly, terribly* wrong—perhaps even unforgivable.

Making me carry the doll in my arms, my mother led me back to the house, still without a reprimand. But I was sure that I would be paying for my transgression by nightfall when my father came home. By suppertime, I feared, the storm would hover right above my head. But my father came home, and supper came and went, and I went to bed at my usual time with my ears, hands, and butt untouched.

The day after the hanging-doll incident, my father came home early and suggested that he and I play with the doll's house. He had stopped by my grandmother's house a block away and had picked up some tiny clay bowls, glasses, and pots she had bought for me. Among the kitchenware there was even a tiny metate, in case we wanted to grind *masa* to make tortillas, he said.

Already dust had collected on the little house's roof and on the tiny furniture, and it took us fifteen minutes to wipe everything clean before we could begin to put the kitchenware and the furniture back in the rooms.

A short while later I realized that playing with the doll's house this second time was just as boring as the first time. But my father seemed to be having so much fun I didn't have the heart to inform him I wasn't in the least interested. So quietly I slipped out of the room and picked up *Scheherazada* on my way to the yard. Absorbed as he was in arranging and rearranging the tiny furniture, he didn't even take notice of my quick exit.

At suppertime, again, I expected a good *jalón de orejas*. Instead, waving a finger but laughing, my father said, "Ah, *mi chaparrita traviesa* (my naughty little woman)."

"Miguel Angel, you're spoiling this child," my mother mildly objected.

My father's only reply was a chuckle.

Almost twenty years passed before I found out from both my parents why the hanging-doll episode had been so significant for them. By then I had already moved to California, my father had been diagnosed with terminal cancer, and I was a parent myself.

After recounting the episode of the hanging doll amid my father's and my laughter, my mother, teary eyed and sentimental, confessed that all those years she had been afraid I would turn out to be an unnatural mother because, as a child, I had hung the doll from the branch. She was delighted I had turned out to be a most loving and understanding mother to my three-year-old son Arturo.

During my nineteen years at home, neither my father nor my mother ever gave up trying to socialize me—"civilize" me, my mother would often say.

Throughout those years, they inculcated in me that intellectually and artistically I was as capable as my brothers. So they provided me with the best education they could afford. They made clear to me, nonetheless, that all this was being done not just to satisfy my own needs as an individual; above all, I was being educated to serve the needs of the family I would one day have.

"When you educate a man," my father would often tell my younger sister and me, "you educate an individual. But when you educate a woman, you educate the whole family." Then he would caress my sister's cheek and mine as he added, "I don't remember who said that a child's education begins twenty years before he's born. But whoever said it was surely right. My grandchildren's education begins with yours, *mis chaparritas.*"

It wasn't unusual for Mexican fathers—almost regardless of class—to deny their daughters the advantages of formal schooling on the false premise that as women they would always be supported and protected by their husbands. The important thing was, then, my uncles perfunctorily stated, to get as successful a husband as could be found for the girls in the family. Problem solved.

My father was not quite the typical Mexican father in this respect. But even this atypical man, who has been and will continue to be one of the most influential people in my life, was subject to the social norms and pressures that made the education of a woman a separate (if equal) experience.

Consistently throughout my life I was convinced by both my father and my mother that what I truly wanted—a career as either a medical doctor or an astronomer—was not what was best for me.

"As a medical doctor you will have to care for and examine male patients; you will be subject to men's low designs," my father warned every time I brought up the subject.

"You will suffer," my mother added, waving her finger admonishingly, to emphasize what she really wanted to say: "*Conform.*"

With impeccable logic my father would state the advantages for a woman of a career in dentistry: independence (not working for a man), flexibility of schedule (time to take care of the children as well), and great financial rewards.

Relentlessly I would plead for a second wish, a career in astronomy. My father would caress my cheek gently and say, "But, my little woman, an astronomer has to work at night. When would you spend time with your children? And your husband? Surely, he would find someone else to keep him company at night."

"And you will suffer," my mother would interject in her usual manner. "Your children will grow up having a zombie for a mother, and you'll die young," she would state to strengthen her argument, with a stern and sad face, as if I were already the victim of an ancient curse.

Because I wanted to pursue a career, I eventually agreed to attend the school of dentistry in San Luis. I was happy the first two years, since my classmates and I carried the same subjects as first-year medical students, in addition to dental labs. But when I stared into a real open mouth for the first time, I began to suspect that I was not cut out to be a good dentist. The first time I sweated out the extraction of a molar, my suspicions were confirmed. After the first ten tooth fillings, I knew I would surely go insane one day.

For a couple of years I had been going steady with Guillermo, who was preparing to move to Berkeley, where he hoped to attend the University of California. As painful as it was to leave my family and my country, I had no qualms in quitting dentistry school, marrying him, and moving to California.

Through my relationship with my husband I rediscovered the pleasure of reading for my own enjoyment. Although I would not start writing poetry for another five years after my arrival in Berkeley, I knew I wanted to make the study of literature my life's pursuit.

By the time I began to write poetry, I was already undergoing a painful separation from my husband, feeling cut off from the cultural and emotional support of family and friends, working as a bilingual secretary to support my son and put myself through college at Berkeley, grieving for my late father and expressing my daily thoughts and experiences in a language not yet my own.

For the next few years, in an almost manic manner, I wrote at least one poem a day, possessed by the terrifying notion that if I stopped writing I would stop breathing as well.

Every so often, when I visit my mother in Mexico, she recalls the incident of the hanging doll and thanks God aloud for making me a good parent. Then she sighs as she inventories my vicissitudes in life, pointing out that I would be a rich dentist and a happily married woman now, living still in Mexico, instead of being a divorced woman, a poor schoolteacher, and a Chicana poet in California.

I look back at that same childhood incident, recall my third gift, the book I wrapped in red tissue paper, and for a fleeting instant I, too, take inventory of the experiences that have made me who and what I am. I pause to marvel at life's wondrous ironies.

*G*loria Anzaldúa is a Chicana tejana *lesbian-feminist poet and fiction writer.* She is editor of Making Faces, Making Soul/Haciendo Caras: Creative and Critical Perspectives by Women of Color *(1990), and coeditor of* This Bridge Called My Back: Writings by Radical Women of Color *(1981). She has taught Chicana studies, feminist studies, and creative writing in various universities and has conducted writing workshops around the country. Her work has appeared in many journals. The following two excerpts from her groundbreaking work* Borderlands/La Frontera: The New Mestiza *(1987) are examples of her forthright and courageous writing. She writes of discrimination against Chicanos as well as the discrimination of one Chicana against another.*

FROM *BORDERLANDS/LA FRONTERA: THE NEW MESTIZA*

Gloria Anzaldúa

Linguistic Terrorism

Deslenguadas. Somos los del español deficiente. We are your linguistic nightmare, your linguistic aberration, your linguistic *mestizaje*, the subject of your *burla*. Because we speak with tongues of fire we are culturally crucified. Racially, culturally, and linguistically *somos huérfanos*—we speak an orphan tongue.

Chicanas who grew up speaking Chicano Spanish have internalized the belief that we speak poor Spanish. It is illegitimate, a bastard language. And because we internalize how our language has been used against us by the dominant culture, we use our language differences against each other.

Chicana feminists often skirt around each other with suspicion and hesitation. For the longest time I couldn't figure it out. Then it dawned on me. To be close to another Chicana is like looking into the mirror. We are afraid of what we'll see there. *Pena.* Shame. Low estimation of self. In childhood we are told that our language is wrong. Repeated attacks on our native tongue diminish our sense of self. The attacks continue throughout our lives.

Chicanas feel uncomfortable talking in Spanish to Latinas, afraid of their censure. Their language was not outlawed in their countries. They had a whole lifetime of being immersed in their native tongue; generations, centuries in which Spanish was a first language, taught in school, heard on radio and TV, and read in the newspaper.

If a person, Chicana or Latina, has a low estimation of my native tongue, she also has a low estimation of me. Often with *mexicanas y latinas* we'll speak English as a neutral language. Even among Chicanas we tend to speak English at parties or conferences. Yet, at the same time, we're afraid the other will think we are *agringadas* because we don't speak Chicano Spanish. We oppress each other trying to out-Chicano each other, vying to be the "real" Chicanas, to speak like Chicanos. There is no one Chicano language just as there is no one Chicano experience. A monolingual Chicana whose first language is English or Spanish is just as much a Chicana as one who speaks several varieties of Spanish. A Chicana from Michigan or Chicago or Detroit is just as much a Chicana as one from the Southwest. Chicano Spanish is as diverse linguistically as it is regionally.

By the end of this century, Spanish speakers will comprise the biggest minority group in the U.S., a country where students in high schools and colleges are encouraged to take French classes because French is considered more "cultured." But for a language to remain alive it must be used.* By the end of this century English, and not Spanish, will be the mother tongue of most Chicanos and Latinos.

• • •

* Irena Klepfisz, "*Di rayze aheym*/The Journey Home," in *The Tribe of Dina: A Jewish Women's Anthology*, Melanie Kaye/Kantrowitz and Irena Klepfisz, eds. (Montpelier, VT: Sinister Wisdom Books, 1986), 49.

So, if you want to really hurt me, talk badly about my language. Ethnic identity is twin skin to linguistic identity—I am my language. Until I can take pride in my language, I cannot take pride in myself. Until I can accept as legitimate Chicano Texas Spanish, Tex-Mex, and all the other languages I speak, I cannot accept the legitimacy of myself. Until I am free to write bilingually and to switch codes without having always to translate, while I still have to speak English or Spanish when I would rather speak Spanglish, and as long as I have to accommodate the English speakers rather than having them accommodate me, my tongue will be illegitimate.

I will no longer be made to feel ashamed of existing. I will have my voice. Indian, Spanish, white. I will have my serpent's tongue—my woman's voice, my sexual voice, my poet's voice. I will overcome the tradition of silence.

> *My fingers*
> *move sly against your palm*
> *Like women everywhere, we speak in code. . . .*

> —MELANIE KAYE/KANTROWITZ*

SI LE PREGUNTAS A MI MAMA, "¿QUE ERES?"

Identity is the essential core of who we are as individuals, the conscious experience of the self inside.

> —KAUFMAN**

Nosotros los Chicanos straddle the borderlands. On one side of us, we are constantly exposed to the Spanish of the

* Melanie Kaye/Kantrowitz, "Sign," in *We Speak in Code: Poems and Other Writings* (Pittsburgh, Pa.: Motheroot Publications, Inc., 1980), 85.
** Gershen Kaufman, *Shame: The Power of Caring* (Cambridge, Mass.: Schenkman Books, Inc., 1980), 68.

Mexicans, on the other side we hear the Anglos' incessant clamoring so that we forget our language. Among ourselves we don't say *nosotros los americanos, o nosotros los españoles, o nosotros los hispanos*. We say *nosotros los mexicanos* (by *mexicanos* we do not mean citizens of Mexico; we do not mean a national identity, but a racial one). We distinguish between *mexicanos del otro lado* and *mexicanos de este lado*. Deep in our hearts we believe that being Mexican has nothing to do with which country one lives in. Being Mexican is a state of soul—not one of mind, not one of citizenship. Neither eagle nor serpent, but both. And like the ocean, neither animal respects borders.

> *Dime con quien andas y te diré quien eres.*
> (Tell me who your friends are and I'll tell you who you are.)
>
> —MEXICAN SAYING

Si le preguntas a mi mamá, "¿Qué eres?" te dirá, "Soy mexicana." My brothers and sister say the same. I sometimes will answer *"soy mexicana"* and at others will say *"soy Chicana"* or *"soy tejana."* But I identified as *"Raza"* before I ever identified as *"mexicana"* or "Chicana."

As a culture, we call ourselves Spanish when referring to ourselves as a linguistic group and when copping out. It is then that we forget our predominant Indian genes. We are 70–80 percent Indian.* We call ourselves Hispanic** or Spanish-American or Latin American or Latin when linking ourselves to other Spanish-speaking peoples of the Western hemisphere and when copping out. We call ourselves Mexican-American***

---

* John R. Chávez, *The Lost Land: The Chicano Image of the Southwest* (Albuquerque, N.M.: University of New Mexico Press, 1984), 88–90.

** "Hispanic" is derived from *Hispania* (*España*, a name given to the Iberian Peninsula in ancient times when it was part of the Roman Empire) and is a term designated by the U.S. government to make it easier to handle us on paper.

*** The Treaty of Guadalupe-Hidalgo created the Mexican-American in 1848.

to signify we are neither Mexican nor American, but more the noun "American" than the adjective "Mexican" (and when copping out).

Chicanos and other people of color suffer economically for not acculturating. This voluntary (yet forced) alienation makes for psychological conflict, a kind of dual identity—we don't identify with the Anglo-American cultural values and we don't totally identify with the Mexican cultural values. We are a synergy of two cultures with various degrees of Mexicanness or Angloness. I have so internalized the borderland conflict that sometimes I feel like one cancels out the other and we are zero, nothing, no one. *A veces no soy nada ni nadie. Pero hasta cuando no lo soy, lo soy.*

When not copping out, when we know we are more than nothing, we call ourselves Mexican, referring to race and ancestry; *mestizo* when affirming both our Indian and Spanish (but we hardly ever own our Black ancestry); Chicano when referring to a politically aware people born and/or raised in the U.S.; *Raza* when referring to Chicanos; *tejanos* when we are Chicanos from Texas.

Chicanos did not know we were a people until 1965 when César Chávez and the farmworkers united and *I Am Joaquín* was published and *la Raza Unida* party was formed in Texas. With that recognition, we became a distinct people. Something momentous happened to the Chicano soul—we became aware of our reality and acquired a name and a language (Chicano Spanish) that reflected that reality. Now that we had a name, some of the fragmented pieces began to fall together—who we were, what we were, how we had evolved. We began to get glimpses of what we might eventually become.

Yet the struggle of identities continues, the struggle of borders is our reality still. One day the inner struggle will cease and a true integration take place. In the meantime, *tenemos que hacer la lucha. ¿Quién está protegiendo los ranchos de mi gente? ¿Quién está tratando de cerrar la fisura entre la india y el blanco en nuestra sangre? El Chicano, sí, el Chicano que anda como un ladrón en su propia casa.*

Los Chicanos, how patient we seem, how very patient. There is the quiet of the Indian about us.* We know how to survive. When other races have given up their tongue, we've kept ours. We know what it is to live under the hammer blow of the dominant *norteamericano* culture. But more than we count the blows, we count the days the weeks the years the centuries the eons until the white laws and commerce and customs will rot in the deserts they've created, lie bleached. *Humildes* yet proud, *quietos* yet wild, *nosotros los mexicanos-Chicanos* will walk by the crumbling ashes as we go about our business. Stubborn, persevering, impenetrable as stone, yet possessing a malleability that renders us unbreakable, we, the *mestizas* and *mestizos*, will remain.

* Anglos, in order to alleviate their guilt for dispossessing the Chicano, stressed the Spanish part of us and perpetrated the myth of the Spanish Southwest. We have accepted the fiction that we are Hispanic, that is Spanish, in order to accommodate ourselves to the dominant culture and its abhorrence of Indians. (Chávez, 88–91.)

E *smeralda Santiago has been published in the* New York Times, *the* Boston Globe, *the* Christian Science Monitor, *and* Vista *magazine. The following is an excerpt from her memoir,* When I Was Puerto Rican *(1993). It illustrates through the eyes and ears of a child the complex relationship between Puerto Ricans and the United States.*

FROM *WHEN I WAS PUERTO RICAN*

Esmeralda Santiago

"Today," Miss Jiménez said, "you will be vaccinated by the school nurse."

There had never been a school nurse at Macún Elementary School, but lately a woman dressed in white, with a tall, stiff cap atop her short cropped hair, had set up an infirmary in a corner of the lunchroom. Forms had been sent home, and Mami had told me and Delsa that we would be receiving polio vaccines.

"What's polio?" I asked, imagining another parasite in my belly.

"It's a very bad disease that makes you crippled," she said.

"Is it like meningitis?" Delsa asked. A brother of one of her friends had that disease; his arms and hands were twisted into his body, his legs splayed out at the knees, so that he walked as if he were about to kneel.

"No," Mami said, "it's worse. If you get polio, you die, or you spend the rest of your life in a wheelchair or inside an iron lung."

"An iron lung!?!?" It was impossible. There could not be such a thing.

"It's not like a real lung, silly," Mami laughed. "It's a machine that breathes for you."

"*¡Ay Dios mío!*" Polio was worse than *solitaria*.

"But how can it do that?" Delsa's eyes opened and shut as if she were testing to see whether she was asleep or awake.

"I don't know how it works," Mami said. "Ask your father."

Delsa and I puzzled over how you could have an iron lung, and that night, when Papi came home from work, we made him draw one for us and show us how a machine could do what people couldn't. He drew a long tube and at one end made a stick figure face.

"It looks like a can," Delsa said, and Papi laughed.

"Yes," he said, "it does. Just like a can."

Miss Jiménez sent us out to see the nurse two at a time, in alphabetical order. By the time she got to the *S*'s, I was shaky, because every one of the children who had gone before me had come back crying, pressing a wad of cotton against their arm. Ignacio Sepúlveda walked next to me, and even though he was as scared as I was, he pretended he wasn't.

"What crybabies!" he said. "I've had shots before and they don't hurt that much."

"When?"

"Last year. They gave us shots for tuberculosis." We were nearing the lunchroom, and Ignacio slowed down, tugged on my arm, and whispered, "It's all because of politics."

"What are you talking about? Politics isn't a disease like polio. It's something men talk about at the bus stop." I'd heard Papi tell Mami when he was late that he'd missed the bus because he'd been discussing politics.

Ignacio kept his voice to a whisper, as if he were telling

me something no one else knew. "My Papa says the government's doing all this stuff for us because it's an election year."

"What does that have to do with it?"

"They give kids shots and free breakfast, stuff like that, so that our dads will vote for them."

"So?"

"Don't you know anything?"

"I know a lot of things."

"You don't know anything about politics."

"Do so."

"Do not."

"Do so."

"Who's the governor of Puerto Rico, then?"

"Oh, you could have asked something really hard! . . . Everyone knows it's Don Luis Muñoz Marín."

"Yeah, well, who's *el presidente* of the Jun-ited Estates?"

"Ay-sen-hou-err."

"I bet you don't know his first name."

I knew then I had him. I scanned Papi's newspaper daily, and I had seen pictures of *el presidente* on the golf course, and of his wife's funny hairdo.

"His first name is Eekeh," I said, puffed with knowledge. "And his wife's name is Mami."

"Well, he's an imperialist, just like all the other gringos!" Ignacio said, and I was speechless because Mami and Papi never let us say things like that about grown-ups, even if they were true.

When we came into the lunchroom, Ignacio presented his arm to the nurse as if instead of a shot he were getting a medal. He winced as the nurse stuck the needle into him and blinked a few times to push back tears. But he didn't cry, and I didn't either, though I wanted to. There was no way I'd have Ignacio Sepúlveda calling me a crybaby.

• • •

"Papi, what's an imperialist?"

He stopped the hammer in midstrike and looked at me. "Where did you hear that word?"

"Ignacio Sepúlveda said Eekeh Aysenhouerr is an imperialist. He said all gringos are."

Papi looked around as if someone were hiding behind a bush and listening in. "I don't want you repeating those words to anybody . . ."

"I know that, Papi. . . . I just want to know what it means. Are gringos the same as *americanos?*"

"You should never call an *americano* a gringo. It's a very bad insult."

"But why?"

"It just is." It wasn't like Papi not to give a real answer to my questions. "Besides, *el presidente*'s name is pronounced Ayk, not Eekeh." He went back to his hammering.

I handed him a nail from the can at his feet. "How come it's a bad insult?"

He stopped banging the wall and looked at me. I stared back, and he put his hammer down, took off his hat, brushed his hand across his forehead, wiped it on his pants, sat on the stoop, and leaned his elbows back, stretching his legs out in front of him. This was the response I expected. Now I would hear all about gringos and imperialists.

"Puerto Rico was a colony of Spain after Columbus landed here," he began, like a schoolteacher.

"I know that."

"Don't interrupt."

"Sorry."

"In 1898, *los Estados Unidos* invaded Puerto Rico, and we became their colony. A lot of Puerto Ricans don't think that's right. They call *americanos* imperialists, which means they want to change our country and our culture to be like theirs."

"Is that why they teach us English in school, so we can speak like them?"

"Yes."

"Well, I'm not going to learn English so I don't become American."

He chuckled. "Being American is not just a language, *negrita*, it's a lot of other things."

"Like what?"

He scratched his head. "Like the food you eat . . . the music you listen to . . . the things you believe in."

"Do they believe in God?"

"Some of them do."

"Do they believe in phantasms and witches?"

"Yes, some Americans believe in that."

"Mami doesn't believe any of that stuff."

"I know. I don't either."

"Why not?"

"I just . . . I believe in things I can see."

"Why do people call *americanos* gringos?"

"We call them gringos, they call us spiks."

"What does that mean?"

"Well," he sat up, leaned his elbows on his knees and looked at the ground, as if he were embarrassed. "There are many Puerto Ricans in New York, and when someone asks them a question they say, 'I don spik inglish' instead of 'I don't speak English.' They make fun of our accent."

"*Americanos* talk funny when they speak Spanish."

"Yes, they do. The ones who don't take the trouble to learn it well." He pushed his hat back, and the sun burned into his already brown face, making him squint. "That's part of being an imperialist. They expect us to do things their way, even in our country."

"That's not fair."

"No, it isn't." He stood up and picked up his hammer. "Well, I'd better get back to work, *negrita*. Do you want to help?"

"Okay." I followed him, holding the can of nails up so he wouldn't have to bend over to pick them up. "Papi?"

"Yes."

"If we eat all that American food they give us at the *centro comunal*, will we become *americanos?*"

He banged a nail hard into the wall, then turned to me and, with a broad smile on his face, said, "Only if you like it better than our Puerto Rican food."

*G*raciela Limón is a native of Los Angeles. In 1990 she went to El Salvador as part of a delegation that was formed to investigate the assassination of Jesuit priests there. She is a professor in the Department of Modern Languages at Loyola Marymount University in Los Angeles. In this excerpt from her first novel, In Search of Bernabé (1993), a Salvadoran woman's search for her "disappeared" son leads her to cross the U.S.–Mexican border illegally with the help of a coyota.

FROM *IN SEARCH OF BERNABE*

Graciela Limón

L uz and Arturo arrived at the Tijuana bus terminal forty hours later, exhausted and bloated from sitting in their cramped seat. As soon as they stepped out of the bus, they were approached by a woman who asked them if they wanted to cross the border that night. Without waiting for an answer, she told them she could be their guide. The price was five hundred American dollars apiece.

Luz stared at the woman for a few moments, caught off guard by the suddenness of what was happening. More than her words, it was the woman's appearance that held Luz's attention. She was about thirty-five. Old enough, Luz figured, to have experience in her business. The woman was tall and slender, yet her body conveyed muscular strength that gave Luz the impression that she would be able to lead them across the border.

The *coyota* returned Luz's gaze, evidently allowing time for the older woman to make up her mind. She took a step closer to Luz, who squinted as she concentrated on the woman's face. Luz regarded her dark skin and high forehead, and the deeply set eyes that steadily returned her questioning stare. With a glance, she took in the *coyota*'s faded Levi's and plaid shirt under a shabby sweatshirt, and her eyes widened when she saw the woman's scratched, muddy cowboy boots. She had seen only men wear such shoes.

Luz again looked into the woman's eyes. She was tough, and Luz knew that she had to drive a hard bargain. She began to cry. "*¡Señora, por favor!* Have a heart! How can you charge so much? We're poor people who have come a long way. Where do you think we can find so many *dólares?* All we have is one hundred dollars to cover the two of us. Please! For the love of your mamacita!"

The woman crossed her arms over her chest and laughed out loud as she looked into Luz's eyes. She spoke firmly. "Señora, I'm not in the habit of eating fairy tales for dinner. You've been in Mexico City for a long time. I have eyes, don't I? I can tell that you're not starving. Both of you have eaten a lot of enchiladas and tacos. Just look at those *nalgas!*"

She gave Luz a quick, hard smack on her behind. Then, ignoring the older woman's look of outrage, the *coyota* continued to speak rapidly. "Look, Señora. Just to show you that I have feelings, I'll consider guiding the both of you at the reduced rate of seven hundred dollars. Half now; the rest when I get you to Los Angeles. Take it or leave it!"

Luz knew that she was facing her match. She answered with one word. "*Bueno.*"

The *coyota* led them to a man who was standing nearby. He was wearing a long overcoat, inappropriate for the sultry weather in Tijuana. The coat had a purpose, though, for it concealed deep inner pockets which were filled with money. The *coyota* pulled Luz nearer to the man, then whispered into her ear. "This man will change your pesos into American dollars. A good rate, I guarantee."

When Arturo began to move closer, the *coyota* turned on him. "You stay over there!"

Arturo obeyed.

Even though she felt distrust, Luz decided that she and

Arturo had no alternative. However, she needed to speak with him, so she pulled him to the side. "*Hijo*, we're taking a big chance. We can be robbed, even killed. Remember the stories we've been hearing since we left home. But what can we do? We need someone to help us get across, so what does it matter if it's this one, or someone else? What do you say?"

Arturo agreed with her. "Let's try to make it to the other side. The sooner the better. I think you made a good bargain. We have the money, don't we?"

"With a little left over for when we get to Los Angeles."

Before they returned to where the others were waiting, she turned to a wall. She didn't want anyone to see what she was doing. Luz withdrew the amount of pesos she estimated she could exchange for a little more than seven hundred American dollars. She walked over to the money vendor, and no sooner had the man placed the green bills on her palm than she heard the *coyota*'s sharp voice. "Three hundred and fifty dollars, *por favor!*"

She signaled Luz and Arturo to follow her to a waiting car. They went as far as Mesa Otay, the last stretch of land between Mexico and California. There, the *coyota* instructed them to wait until it got dark. Finally, when Luz could barely see her hand in front of her, the woman gave the signal. "*¡Vámonos!*"

They walked together under the cover of darkness. As Luz and Arturo trekked behind the woman, they sensed that they were not alone, that other people were also following. Suddenly someone issued a warning, "*¡La Migra! ¡Cuidado!*" The *coyota* turned with unexpected speed, and murmured one word, "*¡Abajo!*"

All three fell to the ground, clinging to it, melting into it, hoping that it would split open so that they could crawl into its safety. Unexpectedly a light flashed on. Like a giant eye, it seemed to be coming from somewhere in the sky, slowly scanning the terrain. No one moved. All that could be heard were the crickets and the dry grass rasping in the mild breeze. The light had not detected the bodies crouched behind bushes and rocks. It flashed out as suddenly as it had gone on.

"*¡Vámonos!*" The *coyota* was again on her feet and moving. They continued in the dark for hours over rough, rocky terrain. The *coyota* was sure-footed but Luz and Arturo bumped into rocks and tripped over gopher holes. Luz had not rested or eaten since she had gotten off the bus. She was fatigued but she pushed herself fearing she would be left behind if she stopped. Arturo was exhausted too, but he knew that he still had reserves of energy, enough for himself and for Luz.

Dawn was breaking as they ascended a hill. Upon reaching the summit, they were struck with awe at the sight that spread beneath their feet. Their heavy breathing stopped abruptly as their eyes glowed in disbelief. Below, even though diffused by dawn's advancing light, was an illuminated sea of streets and buildings. A blur of neon formed a mass of light and color, edged by a highway that was a ribbon of liquid silver. Luz and Arturo wondered if fatigue had caused their eyes to trick them because as far as they could see there was brilliance, limited only in the distance by a vast ocean. To their left, they saw the lights of San Diego unfolding beneath them, and their heart stopped when they realized that farther north, where their eyes could not see, was their destination.

Without thinking, Luz and Arturo threw their arms around one another and wept.

The lights of San Diego receded behind them. The *coyota* had guided Luz and Arturo over an inland trail, taking them past the U.S. Immigration station at San Onofre, and then down to connect with the highway. A man in a car was waiting for them a few yards beyond Las Pulgas Road on California Interstate 5.

The driver got out of the car as they approached, extending a rough hand first to Luz, and then to Arturo. "*Me llamo Ordaz.*"

Ordaz turned to the *coyota* and spoke in English. His

words were casual, as if he had seen her only hours before. "You're late. I was beginning to worry."

"The old bag slowed me down."

The *coyota* spoke to the man in English, knowing that her clients were unable to understand her. Then, she switched to Spanish to introduce herself to Luz and Arturo. *"Me llamo Petra Traslaviña.* I was born back in San Ysidro on a dairy farm. I speak English and Spanish."

There was little talk among them beyond this first encounter. The four piled into a battered Pontiac station wagon, and with Ordaz at the wheel, they headed north. The woman pulled out a pack of Mexican cigarettes, smoking one after the other, until Ordaz started to cough. He opened the window complaining, *"Por favor,* Petra, you wanna choke us to death?"

"Shut up!" she retorted rapidly, slurring the English *sh.*

The phrase engraved itself in Luz's memory. She liked the sound of it. She liked its effect even more, since she noticed that Ordaz was silenced by the magical phrase. Inwardly, Luz practiced her first English words, repeating them over and again under her breath.

Luz and Arturo were quiet during the trip mainly because they were frightened by the speed at which Ordaz was driving. As she looked out over the *coyota's* shoulder, Luz knew that she didn't like what she was feeling and hearing. She even disliked the smell of the air, and she felt especially threatened by the early morning fog. When the headlights of oncoming cars broke the grayness, her eyes squinted with pain.

The hours seemed endless, and they were relieved when Ordaz finally steered the Pontiac off the freeway and onto the streets of Los Angeles. Like children, Luz and Arturo looked around craning their necks, curiously peering through the windows and seeing that people waited for their turn to step onto the street. Luz thought it was silly the way those people moved in groups. No one ran out onto the street, leaping, jumping, dodging cars as happened in Mexico City and back home. Right away, she missed the vendors peddling wares, and the stands with food and drink.

Suddenly, Luz was struck by the thought that she didn't know where the *coyota* was taking them. As if reading Luz's mind, the woman asked, "Do you have a place you want me to take you to?"

Rattled by the question, Luz responded timidly. "No. We didn't have time to think."

"I thought so. It's the same with all of you."

The *coyota* was quiet for a while before she whispered to Ordaz, who shook his head in response. They engaged in a heated exchange of words in English, the driver obviously disagreeing with what the *coyota* was proposing. Finally, seeming to have nothing more to say, Ordaz shrugged his shoulders, apparently accepting defeat. The *coyota* turned to her passengers.

"*Vieja*, I know of a place where you two can find a roof and a meal until you find work. But . . ." She was hesitating. "*¡Mierda!* . . . just don't tell them I brought you. They don't like me because I charge you people money."

What she said next was muttered and garbled. Luz and Arturo did not understand her so they kept quiet, feeling slightly uneasy and confused. By this time Ordaz was on Cahuenga Boulevard in Hollywood. He turned up a short street, and pulled into the parking lot of Saint Turibius Church, where the battered wagon spurted, then came to a stand-still.

"*Hasta aquí.* You've arrived."

The *coyota* was looking directly at Luz, who thought she detected a warning sign in the woman's eyes. "It was easy this time, Señora. Remember, don't get caught by *la Migra*, because it might not be so good the next time around. But if that happens, you know that you can find me at the station in Tijuana."

Again, the *coyota* seemed to be fumbling for words. Then she said, "Just don't get any funny ideas hanging around these people. I mean, they love to call themselves *voluntarios*, and they'll do anything for nothing. *Yo no soy así.* I'll charge you money all over again, believe me!"

The *coyota* seemed embarrassed. Stiffly, she shifted in her seat, pointing at a two-story, Spanish-style house next to the church.

"See that house?"

Luz nodded.

"*Bueno.* Just walk up to the front door, knock, and tell them who you are, and where you're from. They'll be good to you. But, as I already told you, don't mention me."

She turned to Arturo. "Take care of yourself, *muchacho.* I've known a few like you who have gotten themselves killed out there."

With her chin, she pointed toward the street. When Arturo opened his mouth to speak, the *coyota* cut him off curtly. "My three hundred and fifty dollars, *por favor.*"

She stretched out her hand in Luz's direction without realizing that her words about other young men who resembled Arturo had had an impact on Luz. "Petra, have you by any chance met my son? His name is Bernabé and he looks like this young man."

The *coyota* looked into Luz's eyes. When she spoke her voice was almost soft. "They all look like Arturo, Madre. They all have the same fever in their eyes. How could I possibly know your son from all the rest?"

Luz's heart shuddered when the *coyota* called her madre. Something told her that the woman did know Bernabé. This thought filled her with new hope, and she gladly reached into her purse. She put the money into the *coyota*'s hand, saying, "*Hasta pronto.* I hope, Petra, that our paths will cross again sooner or later."

Luz and Arturo were handed the small bundles they had brought with them from Mexico City. As they stepped out of the car, the engine cranked on, backfiring loudly. When it disappeared into the flow of traffic, both realized that even though only three days had passed since they had left Mexico, they had crossed over into a world unknown to them. They were aware that they were facing days and months, perhaps even years, filled with dangers neither of them could imagine.

Feeling apprehensive, they were silent as they approached the large house that their guide had pointed out. They didn't know that the building had been a convent and that it was now a refuge run by priests and other volunteers. Neither realized that they were entering a sanctuary for the displaced and for those without documents or jobs. When they were shown in, Luz and Arturo were surprised at how warmly they were received. No one asked any questions. Afterwards, they were given food to eat and a place to sleep.

*D*emetria Martínez *lives in Tucson, Arizona, where she works as a columnist for the* National Catholic Reporter. *She was born and raised in Albuquerque, New Mexico, and received a B.A. from Princeton University. In 1987 she was indicted on charges related to smuggling Central American refugees into the United States. A jury later acquitted her on First Amendment grounds. She is also the author of a collection of poetry, "Turning," included in the book* Three Times a Woman. *A loving portrait of a strong and politically committed woman emerges from this excerpt from her first novel,* MotherTongue, *which won the 1994 Western States Book Award.*

FROM *MOTHERTONGUE*
Demetria Martínez

September 14, 1982

Mija—

Of course I'll teach you about the old *remedios*. You can start by going to the co-op and buying what I've listed below, *remedios* from my childhood and from my guidebook. How times change. The gringos don't laugh at us anymore when we boil up our little plants. They're reading "the studies" about how good all this is for you. For once science is on our side. And now I can thank God you're interested, if not in politics, then at least in the old ways. (My godmothering has not been in vain.) To start your medicine cabinet, go get:

Garlic and onions (eat them all the time, you should also
place sliced onions on windowsills to kill cold germs)
Ajenjibre (for hangovers)
Albacar (for cramps)
Cascara Sagrada (for regularity)

Damiana (to raise your spirits) (it also acts as a stimulant
  in another way, but we won't talk about that)

Jojoba oil (for beautiful skin)

Manzanilla (for insomnia)

Oshá (tastes like strong celery, causes you to break into a
  sweat when you chew it which gets cold and flu poisons
  out of you) (also said to ward off evil, in the old, super-
  stitious days, they used to sew it into hems of skirts to
  scare away rattlesnakes)

Yerba buena (for all of the above)

Good supply of Laredo, Texas, miracle candles, not to
  practice magic but to concentrate the mind on the
  healing powers of Our Lord

This will be a good start. Now remember, food is the best
medicine. All this depression going around—it's because we've
gotten too far away from the foods of our ancestors. And our
cells never forget. Beans, rice, avocado, cilantro, etc. We must
make every effort to eat what our elders ate, eat with the sea-
sons, and eat what is grown nearby. All these newfangled drugs
aggravate illness but hide the symptoms. No wonder we're all
crazy.

Now I know you wear that crystal around your neck. If
you ask me, some of that New Age Santa Fe stuff can be as bad
as drugs. People start out trying to cure a cold and next thing
you know, instead of taking garlic and lemon water, they've
hired someone to "channel" the voice of a Visigoth. Before you
go knocking on heaven's door, it's best to look for cures a little
closer to home. Roots, seeds, bark, oils, flowers, etc. It says
somewhere in the Bible that the earth is our cure, or something like that.

I confess I believe in reincarnation (purgatory isn't a place
but a coming back again and again until we learn all our lessons).
But just because you believe in past lives doesn't mean you

should dabble in them. Your ancestors were Jews (before the Inquisition) in the Old World and Christians and medicine men in this one. I guess that covers your bases as good as anything. Respect your current "incarnation." I'm off on this tangent because even here in Arizona, of all places, people are getting into "channeling." Only here it doesn't cost so much. If you want my opinion, I don't see much difference between all that and what my grandma did, praying in tongues at the Spanish Assemblies of God. Except it was free and anyone could do it.

I tell you all this because you can't study herbs without a sense of the ins and outs of the spiritual life. It all works together. You can see why I hate doctors (except our Socialist friend who helps refugees for free). And since I am your godmother, I want to keep you on the straight and narrow, what with all that New Age out there. Beware of fundamentalists, even the ones with crystals, hippie sandals, and trust funds. Now that's not to disrespect true spiritual seekers. After all, some of those Santa Feans have Free Tibet bumper stickers on their vans. So if turning inward helps them turn outward to do something useful in this vale of tears, then maybe God works even in the New Age. But I know you're not into politics (yet, ha ha).

Now be good. Or at least be careful.

Love & Prayers
Soledad

One day—was it late September or early October?—Soledad returned. And she knew by the play of shadow and light on my face and in my voice that it was done: José Luis and I were lovers. She was my godmother, my mentor. She knew better than to quell the Spirit, the spirit of light that is love and the spirit of recklessness that is something else altogether. In her life, with her husbands, divorces, her breaking the rules of the church, in all these experiences and more, Soledad had seen the two faces of God. So she was not about to tell me not to live dangerously. She might offer advice to ease the blows, but she would never say, do not love him. She was a healer precisely because she had suffered and savored the faces of God, the dark and the light. And every *remedio*, she said, has elements of both, of the sickness and its cure. I am thirty-nine now, eleven years younger than Soledad was the summer José Luis and I were lovers, and I am just beginning to fathom what she meant.

"*Mijita*, be careful, when I was your age I gave my heart away, and it took me years to find it again. *Mijita*, my Carlos was a good man but the war made him loco sometimes, and he would leave home for days. No, no, the only way to take the war out of a man is to end the war, all wars. What do you mean, the power of positive thought? You've been reading too many of those Eastern mystical books. You can't even hear yourself think in El Salvador. I know, I've been there, it's spooky as all get out. You know, the best thing you can do is to be his friend. Now I sound exactly like my mother. And you know what? I never did a damn thing she said until I was over forty. . . ."

I wish I had written down whatever it was that Soledad told me. All I can do now is imagine her words, but it's not hard because I can see her: tobacco-colored hair, old jeans, and a "Boycott General Electric" T-shirt, light brown skin prematurely creased because she loved life too much to care about the latest creams for peeling away wrinkles. In my memory, she is always chopping cilantro or heating corn tortillas on the blue flame of her gas stove. Before she quit smoking, her evening ritual consisted of holding a cigarette to the flame, sucking in a deep breath, then turning on the radio. She kept a shortwave on her windowsill next to a bottle of green dish soap. After a smoke she washed dishes, then listened to news of El Salvador tearing apart like bread. She never spoke much about the man she had married, then divorced, to keep him from being deported. At first even I was fooled; I thought she had married for love. And in a sense, she had. Having no children of her own, she adopted El Salvador. She knew its provinces, its disappearances. Every day she scanned Mexican and U.S. newspapers for news of deaths, crops, army movements, culling moments in history as carefully as she picked pebbles from beans before putting them to soak. One day she had me proofread a letter she was about to take to the post office. Dear Senator Marciando, My friends and relatives are being killed, she wrote, words short and fiery as fuses. By nature, Soledad tended away from anger. But she could pull it out and wave it like a knife when she heard of yet another death threat to the country she'd come to love.

Here is a recipe Soledad wrote out on a three-by-five card and taped to her refrigerator.

—POSOLE—

12:45   Wash corn several times
 1:15   Put corn to boil (8 lbs.)
 1:30   Corn begins to boil. Cook two hours. In separate pan put cut-up pork (7 lbs.) to boil plus ¾ whole onion plus 1 or 2 cloves garlic.
 3:30   Put meat in with corn. If corn water is getting low, add some pork broth. Add salt & oregano. Cook about ½ to 1 hour more.
Have fun!

"*Mijita*, your mother was right, you need to have some hobbies or sure enough, you'll develop *melancolía*. You'd be amazed at how learning to cook takes your mind off men—if you do it for your own pleasure. Why do you think I'm such a good cook? I was your age once, don't forget that. I know how it feels, to feel so in love that the sun and the moon trade places, it's so crazy. But be careful. No, no, I'm not saying I don't want it to work out, I do. But every woman should have a special place inside where she can think, where no man is allowed, a place that will, you know, endure. Why do you think I took up letter writing? No man is worth falling apart over. Take it from me. Now come on, let's go take a walk."

One day, Soledad's heart gave out. She had given so much to everyone but herself. When I went to the mortuary to view her body, I started to grieve all over again. Someone had cleaned her hands, wiped away the film of newsprint that had always marked them. That night at San Rafael Church, I said goodbye to her one last time before the open coffin. And pretending to touch her hand in a gesture of grief, I slipped the first few paragraphs of an Associated Press article under her palm. Two days before her death, Salvadoran guerrillas and government leaders signed an accord, shook hands all around, and proclaimed "cautious optimism" to a disbelieving world. I had cut out the article and taped it to my refrigerator next to a prayer for peace. Maybe Soledad was ready to go. Maybe she knew she had succeeded in teaching me to love a broken world.

*A*lma Luz Villanueva is a poet and fiction writer. She has authored two novels, The Ultraviolet Sky *(1988) and* Naked Ladies *(1994). She currently lives in Santa Cruz and teaches fiction and poetry at the University of California, Santa Cruz. The following story appeared in her* Weeping Woman: La Llorona and Other Stories *(1994). The time is any time and the place is any place. The story testifies to the strength of the bond between daughters and mothers.*

280

PLACE OF THE DEAD
Alma Luz Villanueva

Occasionally bodies washed up, but she'd gotten used to it, almost as though it were the most natural thing on Earth that bodies should wash up to shore like seashells. She only glanced at them; they'd ceased to horrify her like they had in the beginning—their missing eyes, disfigured faces, open abdomens, everything dissolving, shredding, bloating, soundlessly, so peacefully, as they rocked in the waves.

The people from her village would come, periodically, and bury them, especially when a child's body washed up on the shore. The people would take the small body to their own cemetery, burying it in the name of innocence, in the name of the Virgin. She would comfort the little one, they knew. Then they'd go home, silently, and light the candles on their altars, praying to the Virgin to keep their own children safe from the Insane Ones. They prayed with all their hearts that the Insane Ones would never, ever return to their village: killing, raping, killing. Just for its own sake, their eyes hard, glassy, insane, laughing at the sounds of sheer, naked suffering, grief.

They'd left, the last time, leaving half the village dead,

raping even many of the little ones and killing them for their final, ultimate pleasure. And then, two or three of the Insane Ones, not able to restrain themselves, had violated the small dead bodies. Only death could satisfy the Insane Ones. Only death itself.

They'd buried these little ones with particular care, handling them gently. The mothers the Insane Ones had left behind had swallowed their souls, so their grief was terrible and mute. The dead mothers joined their castrated and murdered husbands, their dead children, and were safely beyond human grief. And some of the young mothers, and the young childless women, had been taken.

The child didn't know her mother, for she'd been one of the women taken. She and her grandmother had hidden in the corner behind the harvested corn. When one of the Insane Ones came to find the food, he saw them; the old woman crouched down holding a sleeping baby of a few months.

The old woman held her granddaughter tighter to her bony chest and moved her lips, imploring the Virgin. She stared at the Insane One, waiting to die.

"Kill us both," the old woman whispered.

This one was very young, maybe sixteen. He picked up the bulky sack of corn and a small sack of beans. His rifle banged her knees as he bent forward to lift the sacks.

"Kill us both," the old woman repeated, her eyes fixed on his for movement.

He placed the sacks down beside him and unshouldered his rifle. He looked at the old woman's tired eyes and the baby's quick, soft breath as she slept. The baby shuddered. He shouldered his rifle, angrily, picked up the sacks and said, "Light me a candle, *abuela*," and for an instant his eyes looked like a boy's.

"*Sí, hijo.* May the Virgin watch over you." Her eyes had been grateful, but only for the child. And how would she keep this child now, with no milk? she asked herself. If only they don't find the goats, she begged the Virgin silently.

She heard the women screaming outside, the brutal male

voices, and she wondered how the child could sleep. She must be blessed to be so quiet. But your mother, *niña*, is not blessed.

The old woman shut her eyes and listened to the screaming turn to moans and cries of grief. She knew the Insane Ones were gone. "May the Virgin watch over you, *hija*," she whispered to her beautiful, her only, daughter. She would never see her alive again, she knew.

The child had found a lot of useful things this morning. She was sure her grandmother could use an umbrella, a shiny spoon, a rusty knife, the tennis shoes from the dead woman's feet. Her grandmother would be angry she had come to the shore again without her permission, but she also knew her anger would be brief seeing the shoes. Even the other children wouldn't come with her. They were afraid. So she came alone. Sometimes the older boys would beat her to the treasures, but she always seemed to find something.

A tin box was wedged into the sand tightly, so she squatted down and dug it out. Finally, when she opened it she was disappointed. A bunch of old, useless seashells were piled inside. She almost threw the shells away to keep the tin box—That's useful, she said to herself—but then she decided to keep them for her grandmother. "Maybe for her altar," she said out loud.

The old woman lit a candle every week for her daughter and for the boy who'd spared their lives. She'd adopted him, calling him *hijo*, the one who was sane among the Insane Ones. "Just a boy," she'd say as she lit his candle. When she lit her daughter's candle she was silent, like when she lit the one candle for all her dead babies. The one for her mother and father, silent, as the one for her husband. Silent. But for theirs, her own and her granddaughter's, she'd whisper, "Keep us close to your heart, *mi Virgen*."

The child sifted through the box of shells and pulled out an intact, delicately hued, pink shell. It was tightly clamped and closed against all eyes. She was tempted to pry it open; instead she shook it. A fine sand leaked out. She held it up to the morning sun, but the shell revealed nothing. She picked up the others, and though they were beautiful and whole and hardly chipped at all, only this pink shell was closed against her, with its secret safe inside.

She put this one in the hem of her dress and tied it into a tight little knot. Then she picked up the other treasures, tying the shoelaces together, and placed the large, wet tennis shoes around her neck. The rest she juggled in her hands and arms. She'd walk her secret way back to the village so the older boys wouldn't take anything from her. She began to imagine her grandmother's face after she was through being angry with her for coming to the shore. To the Place of the Dead. She saw her grandmother begin to smile as she untied the knot in the laces. And she'll love the knife too, the child smiled to herself. We'll sharpen it and take away the rust.

"I love the Place of the Dead," the little girl said out loud. And then she began to hum, to keep herself company, feeling her mother's gift—small and secret, perfect and whole, delicately pink and closed against her—bump gently against her leg as she walked, quickly, home.

About the Editor

••••••••••••••••••

L illian Castillo-Speed was born in East Los Angeles, as was her mother. She is the Director of the Chicano Studies Library at the University of California at Berkeley. She is also the head of the three Ethnic Studies Libraries on that campus. She has compiled several bibliographies on Chicanas, including the reference book The Chicana Studies Index. She is the database manager of the Chicano Database on CD-ROM as well as the series editor of the Chicano Studies Library Publications Unit.